THE INHERITANCE

THE INHERITANCE

HILDA STAHL

THOMAS NELSON PUBLISHERS
NASHVILLE

Published in Nashville, Tennessee, by Thomas
Nelson, Inc., and distributed in Canada by Lawson
Falle, Ltd., Cambridge, Ontario.

Library of Congress Cataloging-in-Publication Data

Stahl, Hilda.
The inheritance / Hilda Stahl.
p. cm. — (The White pine chronicles ;
bk. 2)
ISBN 0-8407-3216-3
I. Title. II. Series: Stahl, Hilda. White pine
chronicles ; bk. 2.
PS3569.T312I54 1992
813′.54—dc20 91-37476
CIP

Printed in the United States of America

1 2 3 4 5 6 7—96 95 94 93 92 91

With love

to a man of his word

JOSHUA JAY STAHL

(number seven of seven)

◊ With special thanks to ◊

The Freeport Public Library
Joanne Hesselink
Keith Kirkwood
Jeff Stahl
Norman Stahl

CHAPTER 1

♦ Trembling with sudden unexplained fear, Lark Baritt stopped short on the trail in the middle of the Havlicks' priceless white pine forest. A cool breeze flipped her taffy brown hair. She'd brushed it back into a smooth tail and tied it with a narrow blue ribbon at the nape of her slender neck. Her limp blue calico dress hung down over her leggings to the tops of her heavy boots. Her hand trembled as she touched the revolver in the pouch hooked to the leather belt at her narrow waist. She'd promised Jig, the old guard and her very best friend, she'd never set foot in the woods without the gun he'd given her for protection. There were people who would kill for the trees standing in the only virgin white pine forest left in lower Michigan. She lifted the cudgel Jig had carved from a branch of an American hornbeam. He had left a knot on one end the size of his fist. In his thick Swedish accent Jig had said, "This'll be of help to you when you're walking the line with me. You can bop a rattlesnake or a man. It'll work for both."

Lark blinked back tears as she thought of Jig. Twenty-five years ago Freeman and Jennet Havlick had hired the old woodsman to guard the 6000 plus acre forest they had inherited from Free's grandfather. Jig was eighty-three years old and growing weaker daily. He'd lived all his days as a woodsman since he'd come from Sweden in 1825. This year, 1890, when he'd grown so weak, the Havlicks had asked him to retire, but he'd refused. Lark had offered to walk the line for him until he was on his feet again, and he'd agreed because he knew he could trust her.

On alert, Lark glanced around. Had she heard the ring of an ax or the rasp of a crosscut against a tree? Or maybe it was the lack of sounds in the clearing that drew her attention. It was quiet, too quiet, unnaturally quiet. Was someone lurking on the trail ahead of her, waiting to pounce and kill her so he could steal some of the trees she was guarding? "I can't let my imagination run away with me," she muttered, trying to calm herself.

Many times in the twenty-two years she'd spent at the orphan asylum her imagination had run away with her. The worst time had been when she was six and Matron had locked her in a dark, damp room in the cellar for wetting the bed. Rats had squeaked around her and even had run across her bare feet. She'd pictured them eating her alive. She was sure that they would. They hadn't, of course, but the thought of it was as frightening to a six-year-old child as the reality would've been. The times after that when Matron had locked her in the cellar had been almost as bad, even when she was much older. Going to bed without supper or standing in the front hall for hours without moving or speaking while the other orphans teased her or tried to get her to talk had been horrible, but those times had been nothing like the dark cellar and the rats. The cellar room was Matron's favorite punishment and she used it liberally on all the orphans, but she had seemed to be especially fond of using it on Lark. Matron had never liked her. Lark was certain of that, but she didn't know why. She had always tried to stay out of trouble, but Matron seemed to find excuses to punish her on a regular basis.

Forcing away the agonizing memories, she lifted her chin and cocked her head slightly in order to hear better as she silently prayed for help. There were no unusual sounds to make her think there was someone waiting to leap out at her. Maybe she was nervous just knowing danger was possible.

Her eyes moving quickly from side to side, she studied the area around her. Mist rose from the bog to her left and marsh grass swayed in the breeze. Just beyond her in the pines birds twittered, ready to greet the day with song. Lark shivered and moved carefully in the tall grasses. After a deep, steadying breath, she started off again, walking the line she'd walked many times with Jig in the past fifteen years.

At first Matron had forbidden Lark to go, but Jig had talked to her and she had changed her mind. Lark had learned later that Jig had paid Matron to let her go. Just about everyone knew Matron hoarded money like squirrels do nuts. Apparently a little something to add to her stash could get Matron to agree to most anything. Lark was glad she'd had the freedom to walk these woods and be with Jig. Even if it had cost him several dollars it had meant everything in the world to her. He'd been the closest thing to a parent she'd known and he was her friend. She knew he loved her.

Lark stopped at the crest of a hill and brushed away a tear, then continued on. She must not let her thoughts keep her from being alert. She knew the west and north boundaries of the pines were hilly and inaccessible, but the east and south sides had to be guarded from dishonest lumbermen and tree robbers. The Blue River ambled along the east side of the pines, making it very easy for robbers to cut the trees and float the logs down the river before they were caught.

Lark paused briefly and surveyed the calm river at the bottom of the hill and the farms beyond. Then she headed south again through briars that made the trail barely visible. Suddenly birds filled the morning sky and insects buzzed around bright flowers at the edge of the woods. A blue racer a good five feet long slithered across the trail in front of her. She stopped to let it pass, and then walked on her way. At the swamp she looked closely for signs of water snakes before she waded through, the muck sucking at her heavy boots. In the heat of summer the swamp would be dry, sending the creatures living in it deeper into the woods. But now it was filled with wet muck and Lark knew to be careful. Jig had taught her that. She heard a bull frog croak a deep bass and several peepers answer with their high pitched peeps. The forest was alive with creatures. It felt like home to Lark, almost like an old house with familiar, friendly nooks and crannies. Still, there was danger in the forest and Lark could feel it.

The sun had turned hot and perspiration dotted Lark's face and dampened her dress as she walked up the long hill and then down. Her stomach growled with hunger. She'd been too tense about Jig to eat much breakfast at the asylum, but she'd packed a biscuit in her pouch. She dug it out and ate it, then drank water from the small canteen that hung from her belt. As she glanced ahead, her nerves tightened and her scalp prickled. She could sense danger, real danger, not something from her imagination.

Just then a tall man with a small brimmed hat covering most of his black hair stepped around the huge dry roots of a fallen tree and onto the path in front of Lark. He smiled at her, but his eyes looked as hard as steel.

Lark gripped her cudgel tightly, but she smiled as if she hadn't a care in the world the way Jig had taught her to put a thief off guard. Her feet felt like chunks of ice inside her heavy high-top boots. Her thin calico dress suddenly felt too hot. This was the very spot where Jig had been waylaid several times in the past. The huge tree root and the steep hill down to the river made it a perfect place for an ambush. "It's a surprise to see someone other than myself here," Lark said brightly, wondering if he could hear the wild beat of her heart.

"I'm Bruce Oliver and I seem to be lost," said the stranger, tipping his hat.

"Where is it you want to be, Mr. Oliver?" Lark forced her voice to stay calm.

"The little town of Blue Creek."

Lark saw the quick look the man shot past her and her nerves tightened. She noticed his clothes were dry and knew he hadn't forded the river on foot. "You'll have to cross back over the river and take the corduroy south and then west to find Blue Creek."

"Thank you. I guess I shouldn't have crossed the river in the first place." He licked his dry lips as he looked at her canteen. "I see you have a canteen." He motioned to it and said, "Would it be possible to have a drink?" He rubbed his damp forehead and dropped his hat back in place.

Lark unhooked her canteen while she listened for the slightest sound behind her. She watched the man's eyes and twice he flicked looks over her shoulder as if he were expecting someone. Her nerves tightened as she held the canteen out to him, and just as he took it she heard a footfall behind her. With lightning speed she turned, swinging the cudgel. A thickset bearded man lunged for her. The cudgel struck him on the side of the head and he dropped like a dead man at her feet. She turned back in time to see Oliver pull a gun from the belt under his jacket. She sprang forward and swung the cudgel again, striking Oliver's arm. The gun fell to the pine needle covered path as Oliver cried out in pain. Quickly she scooped up her canteen and Oliver's gun. Her legs trembled, and she locked her knees to keep from sinking to the ground. "Pick up your friend and let's go," she snapped.

"You broke my arm!" Oliver cried in shock.

"I'll crack your skull if you don't do as I say!" Lark kept the gun aimed at Oliver as he flung the unconscious man over his shoulder. He sagged under the weight. She longed to drop to the ground and burst into hysterical tears, but she snapped, "Now, walk!"

"Where?" asked Oliver with a groan.

Lark glanced around for sight of a wagon, then looked down at the river. She spotted a raft floating toward them. She'd get the men on board to help her. "Down to the river," she ordered. "You won't be stealing any trees today."

Oliver groaned again. "Page here said Jig was dead and the Havlicks didn't hire another guard."

Lark stiffened. "He's wrong! Jig's not dead! And *I'm* here to keep the trees safe." Lark followed Oliver down to the river, the gun held steadily in one hand, her cudgel in the other. She watched the raft float toward them, then when it drew close enough, she hailed it. She knew the two men in the raft were cooks who were following men searching for logs in the swamps.

"What's the problem, lady?" asked a huge man, leaning against the pole he used to guide the raft down the river.

"I'm Lark Baritt. This is Havlick property," said Lark, waving up behind her. "These men were trying to steal timber. I want them taken to the sheriff in Blue Creek. Could you take them for me?"

"Sure can, Missy," said the other man. "I cooked for Free Havlick some years back. He's a fair man and don't deserve to have his trees pirated."

"You got no proof we was trying to steal trees," said Oliver gruffly. The other man moaned and moved on Oliver's shoulder.

"Free Havlick will thank you for helping me," said Lark. "Take these men on in to Blue Creek with you and leave them with the sheriff. Tell him Freeman Havlick will be in to press charges."

"Get on board," ordered the cook as they poled close to the river's edge.

Oliver glared at Lark, and she smiled sweetly at him. He swore under his breath, and then stepped on the raft and dropped his partner in a heap.

Lark turned and on trembling legs walked back up the steep hill to the trail. She knew word would spread about what she'd done. Thieves would think twice before they tried to steal trees just because Jig was under the weather.

Suddenly Lark stopped and the short hairs on the back of her neck stood on end. Had she heard the rattle of a wagon and the jangle of harness? She ducked behind a massive white pine that could easily hide her as well as three of the little kids in the asylum. She rubbed her damp palms down her limp dress and touched the pouch where she carried the revolver. Was she hearing things or were thieves out in number because Jig was laid up? Maybe Oliver and his partner had a driver and a wagon across the river and she was hearing that, but she couldn't see any sign of a wagon.

A fly buzzed around Lark's head and she swatted it away. She pushed damp tendrils of brown hair off her face and patted her flushed cheeks. Everyone for miles around knew the ten sections of priceless trees were off limits. Still poachers tried to steal them. Through narrowed eyes Lark studied the tree trunks and underbrush. She wished Jig was with her. She couldn't afford another waylay or she'd be late getting back to Blue Creek Orphan Asylum where she worked as well as lived. She looked past the thick patch of violets and deep into the woods, but couldn't spot an intruder.

She leaned against a tree and looked up. The pine was about four feet across and stood arrow straight about a hundred and fifty feet tall. Its long, sweeping green branches began about a hundred feet above the ground. Its needles were over four inches long with five in each blue-green bundle. The gray bark was thick and deeply furrowed into narrow scaly ridges. The tree was worth a fortune with lumber being so dear. Lark couldn't imagine the value of the whole ten sections.

After lumbering the pines and the hardwoods of lower Michigan, the lumbermen had moved to the upper peninsula to rape the land of the giant white pines and uproot habitat for birds, animals, and insects, and ruin the rivers. Lark knew lumber was necessary to the growth of America, but she hated the waste the lumbermen left behind. Some replanted, but most left ugly stumps, deep ruts in the ground, and a spoiled countryside.

Freeman Havlick had given up lumbering to stay on his homestead near the white pines. He'd invested the money he'd made lumbering in real estate and businesses. Then he had turned to farming and buggy making. Lark was acquainted with the Havlicks because the community was small and Jennet was on the board of the asylum, but she'd never been close with them. But she was close to Jig, and she had to hurry and check on him before reporting to Matron. Lark needed to hurry, but she couldn't get her legs to move.

Birds sang and small animals scurried under the thick carpet of pine needles. From deep in the woods a bear growled, probably to protect its cub. Golden notes flowed from orioles flying at the edge of the forest. A flash of red caught Lark's attention and she watched a grosbeak land on a branch. It had a black back and cap and a red and white vest. Its gay song gave Lark the strength to step away from the tree and walk to the path that led to Jig's cabin at the south edge of the pines. Freeman Havlick had built the cabin for Jig and had finally convinced him to live in it instead of in the woods that had been his home all the years he'd lived in Michigan.

Once again Lark looked down the hill to the river. The raft was almost out of sight. She spotted a small boat tied to a tree root. *It probably belongs to Oliver and Page,* she thought, although she couldn't be sure, just as she wasn't certain they hadn't brought other thieves with them who were still hiding in the woods. She pushed back her fear, squared her shoulders, and walked quickly down the path.

The sweeping pine branches filtered out the hot June sunshine and mosquitoes buzzed around Lark's head, but she ignored them. Frogs croaked near the swampy bog that Jig had warned her against years ago when he'd taught her to walk the woods in safety.

She'd made friends with Jig when he'd visited the asylum. At first she'd been afraid of him, but after a few visits, she'd grown to care for him. Now he was father, brother, and best friend to her. She couldn't survive without him.

Finally Lark reached the hill that led down to the edge of the woods and the valley where Jig's small one room cabin stood. The pines in the valley made a wall behind the cabin and the pine covered hills behind it made the wall even higher. In front and to the sides of the cabin stretched a field where a few pines, oaks, maples, and hickory nut trees spread out to the edge of Freeman Havlick's farm. Two miles from there was the growing town of Blue Creek and about ten miles further on was Big Pine, the largest town in the area north of Grand Rapids.

Lark walked along the path flanked with yellow, white, and blue wild flowers to the cabin. She glanced at the bench near the covered well where she'd sat many times listening to Jig tell of his years with old Clay Havlick, the fur trader, and later with his grandson, Free Havlick, the lumberman. They'd talked of young Clay who would inherit the white pines on his twenty-fifth birthday. Even though Jig told her many things, he wouldn't talk about his life in Sweden before he came to America, leaving Lark to wonder about his early life. She knew his real name was Dag Bjoerling, but that was all she knew.

At the cabin Lark saw the stick at the side of the door, telling passing Indians they were free to stop in for food. The stick propped against the door meant "pass on by." The stick was an old Indian custom Jig still practiced to let the Indians know if they could stop in or not.

"Jig?" Lark called in a tight voice.

"Lark," answered Jig weakly, his voice muffled by the thick door.

Lark pushed the door open, then gasped at the closed-in smell. The fire in the cast iron cookstove, used both to heat the cabin and for cooking, was out. Light filtered through the dirty windows at either end of the cabin. Lark looked past the small round table to the low, narrow bunk built onto the wall. Jig lay on it, his muzzleloader on the floor beside him.

"I knew you'd come soon," he said, weakly lifting his shaggy gray head. His narrow face was grooved with wrinkles and his skin was dark and leathery from years of outdoor living. He wore the leather shirt and breeches he'd stitched together with rawhide.

With a strangled cry, Lark ran to him and dropped to her knees beside the bunk. She gripped one of his dirt encrusted, gnarled hands and whispered, "How are you, Jig?"

Awkwardly he patted her arm with his free hand. "Don't fret. I'm fine. Take me to the woods. I asked God to give me strength to see you and talk to you before I die. . . . He answered."

"Oh, Jig!" Tears burned Lark's brown eyes as she helped Jig sit on the edge of the bunk. He smelled as if he hadn't had a bath in weeks and Lark knew he hadn't. "Please, Jig, let me get Freeman or Jennet Havlick!"

Jig shook his head. "I said my goodbyes to them."

"What about Clay? I'll get him."

"Young Clay is in Detroit on business," said Jig as tears brimmed in his eyes. "I wanted to say goodbye to the great-grandson of my good friend Clay Havlick, but I won't get to." Jig reached for his boots and almost toppled over.

"Let me," said Lark as she helped Jig slip on his heavy walking boots over dirty, gray woolen socks. Then she helped him stand. His bones creaked and he moaned. Suddenly she realized how frail he'd become. She forced back a cry of agony.

She walked him across the puncheon floor and outdoors into the bright sunlight. He leaned heavily on her as she walked him to the bench and eased him down to rest before they made the last leg of the journey into the woods. She heard his labored breathing and she bit back a cry of alarm.

"I want your word that you will do what I ask of you, Lark Baritt," Jig said weakly.

Without hesitation she said firmly, "You have it, Jig." There was nothing he could ask of her that she wouldn't do. He was the only person she'd ever trusted. He'd taught her how to track, how to walk the woods without falling prey to the many dangers, how to shoot, but most importantly, he'd taught her about God.

Jig looked at the woods. "These woods belong to young Clay Havlick now that he's twenty-five."

Lark frowned. She hadn't realized Clay was already twenty-five. She didn't like to think of age. She was twenty-two and unmarried, and had no hope of being married. She'd probably spend the rest of her days at the orphan asylum. Maybe she'd become the matron, but she'd never marry, and she would never escape.

Jig held Lark's hand tighter. "I must tell you more of Willie Thorne."

"You said he's bad, that he almost killed Jennet and Free years back when Free was in the lumber business."

Jig nodded. "He's still trying to harm them. He bought a home on the outskirts of Blue Creek. He's come up with a new plan to destroy the Havlicks and those trees." Jig leaned back, struggling to continue.

"Don't talk," said Lark with a worried frown. She looked across the field toward the Havlicks' farm. Should she ring the bell at the corner of the cabin? It was there to call for help.

"I must tell you," said Jig barely above a whisper. "Willie Thorne wants his daughter to marry Clay, then have him give her the pines as a wedding gift. Once the pines belong to her, she'll let Willie Thorne lumber them."

"Clay would never marry Willie Thorne's daughter!"

"She is beautiful and she knows how to capture a man's heart," said Jig. "Clay has been working too hard and hasn't had time to look for a wife. If a woman sought him out, he might lose his heart to her."

Lark looked down at Jig's hand holding hers. She didn't want to admit it, but she was afraid Jig had slipped over the edge. No Havlick would have any dealings with a Thorne.

"You must believe me, Lark," said Jig hoarsely. "I speak the truth. I heard Willie Thorne and his daughter making plans. They didn't see me."

"Just how is she going to make Clay be interested in her?"

"Her first plan is to ride the train with him when he returns from Detroit. She will sit with him and engage him in conversation. She will use her wiles on him. He is too much of a gentleman to turn her away." Jig gripped Lark's hand tighter. "We must save Clay and we must save the trees. They're the only virgin stand left."

"Tell the Havlicks what Willie Thorne said!" cried Lark.

"I did, but they didn't think I heard right. They said they heard Willie forbid his daughter to even speak to a Havlick." Jig's voice broke. "But that was part of his plan. They are deceitful folks!"

Lark trembled. She hated to think her dear friend was imagining things, but she was afraid he was.

"Promise me you will stop young Clay from marrying Veda Thorne," said Jig urgently as he gripped her hand.

"How can *I* stop him?"

"You can do anything with God's help, Lark Baritt."

"Not this, Jig."

"Even this. I would do it, but it's too late for me." Jig lifted Lark's hand to his cracked lips and gently kissed the back of it. "My precious Lark. You have been a friend and a daughter to me for over fifteen years. It hurts me to lay such a task on you, but there is no other way. Back in '35 I promised my friend Clay Havlick I would look out for his people. I will not break that promise even in death. I will pass it on to you."

Lark bit her lip to hold back a cry.

"Young Clay would be hurt beyond all help if he marries Veda Thorne and she lumbers the pines the Havlicks have worked to save." Jig touched Lark's soft cheek. "Lark, *you* must marry young Clay."

"Me!" she cried. He'd never look at her. She was as plain as a post. She wasn't good enough for him or for any man of means. Matron had told her that for as long as she could remember. She wanted to argue with Jig, but she saw the pallor of his skin, and bit back the sharp words.

Jig frowned and his shaggy gray eyebrows almost met over his large nose. "Promise me, Lark. Promise that no matter what it takes you'll keep Clay from marrying Veda Thorne."

Lark's heart turned over. She didn't think the occasion would arise, but she nodded. She loved Jig too much to deny him anything. "I promise," she said around the lump in her throat. Sudden tears filled her eyes and slipped down her ashen cheeks. "I love you, Jig! I would do anything for you!"

"Thank you." Jig closed his eyes for a minute, then opened them. "I want to go home, Lark. I want to have strong legs again to run all over heaven. I want to see Jesus face to face. Be glad for me."

Lark's throat closed shut and for a while she couldn't speak. "I'm glad for you, Jig, but sad for me. I know I'm being selfish, but I want you with me."

Weakly Jig pushed himself up. "Help me to the woods so I can die in the shade of the pines I have enjoyed and loved and guarded all these years."

Lark pulled his arm over her shoulder and he leaned heavily on her. The smell of old leather and sweat burned her nose. Slowly they walked past the cabin and the covered well and into the woods to the narrow creek. She lowered him to a thick carpet of needles under a massive white pine. Overhead birds sang and beside them the creek rushed over rocks. A frog splashed into the clear, sparkling water. Lark sank down and laid Jig's head in her lap.

"Sing 'Blessed Assurance,' Lark," whispered Jig.

She lifted her chin and sang the hymn in a clear, melodious low soprano voice. At first her voice quivered with tears, then she sang in triumph the way she knew Jig wanted her to sing.

At Jig's cabin Clay Havlick looped the reins of his sorrel mare around the low branch of a bush, then lifted his head and listened to the joyous song that drifted out from the pines. He knew it was the orphan Lark Baritt singing. Clay had heard her sing at the asylum and in church. He knew she was singing for Jig. Clay pulled off his hat and stabbed his fingers through his thick, dark hair. He was tall with broad shoulders and lean hips and was well muscled from hard work. He wore the black traveling suit that he'd worn to Detroit. A muscle jumped in his suntanned cheek. Was he too late? Pa had said in his telegram last night that Jig might not make it through another day.

Clay frowned. Only Jig or his family could make him put aside his business to hurry home. But he had been able to find a bank to loan him the money he needed. He closed his eyes momentarily and groaned. Ma and Pa would have a fit when they learned what he'd done. "But I had to do it," he muttered, once again trying to convince himself he'd had no other choice. No one would loan him money to start his wagon business unless Pa co-signed or he had collateral. He glanced back toward the Havlick farm. He was twenty-five years old! Why should he have to have his pa sign for him? He looked toward the giant pines. The pines belonged to him. He'd used them for collateral and he'd borrowed the money to start his wagon business. His stomach knotted. Using the pines for collateral put them in danger and he knew it, but he'd done it anyway. "I'll keep up the payments no matter what it takes," he vowed firmly. "I won't lose the pines!"

Abruptly he pushed aside his thoughts of business and strode toward Lark's song, his steps quiet on the path. He tugged at the starched high collar of his white shirt as he stopped several feet from Lark and Jig to watch them. Lark had a glow about her that made her face almost beautiful. She finished the song, bent down, and kissed Jig's forehead. He touched her pale cheek with a trembling, gnarled hand. A lump rose in Clay's throat at the love he saw between them.

"Tell Clay goodbye for me," Jig said weakly.

"Tell me yourself," said Clay hoarsely as he walked to Jig and knelt beside him. Clay smiled at Lark.

Lark's heart jerked strangely the way it always did when he was nearby. She saw the pain in his dark brown eyes before he masked it.

Clay took Jig's hand and held it firmly. "Pa wired me to come and I came on the first train this morning." Tears filled Clay's dark eyes. "I'll miss you, my friend."

"I love you, young Clay."

"I love you, Jig." Adventurous times in the woods with Jig flashed through Clay's mind. Jig had been a grandpa, teacher, and friend to him. "Thank you for all the things you taught me down through the years."

Lark moved slightly. Should she give them time alone?

Weakly Jig pulled his hand from Clay's and reached for Lark's. He brought her hand to Clay's. As her hand touched Clay's, she tensed but didn't pull away. Shivers of awareness ran over her.

Clay looked down at the strong sun-browned hand that Jig had placed over his. Lark had always been around, but he'd never given much thought to her.

Jig whispered, "I pray God's best for both of you. Watch out for each other."

"We will," said Clay softly, willing to promise Jig anything, but not knowing why Jig would ask him of all people to watch over Lark. What could he do for her?

"I promise," whispered Lark, but she couldn't look at Clay because she knew what the promise really meant to her and Jig.

"Look in my special box when I'm gone," Jig whispered.

"We will," Clay answered.

Lark knew the special box Jig meant. She'd seen it in the corner of his cabin, but he'd never offered to let her look in it. At times her curiosity had almost overcome her, but she'd never looked no matter how badly she'd wanted to.

"Sing 'Safe in the Arms of Jesus,'" Jig said, his voice growing weaker and a faint smile on his face.

Tears burning her eyes, Lark lifted her head and began to sing. Clay joined with her and their voices blended in a harmony that sent a shaft of pure pleasure through Lark.

Before the song ended Jig's spirit left his body and soared to heaven to be with Jesus. Now Jig could run around heaven just as he'd once run in the woods.

Tears soaked Lark's cheeks and dripped down on her calico dress. She struggled to control her sobs, but couldn't.

Clay looked at her compassionately and started to reach out to comfort her, then drew his hand back. Finally he stood and brushed the tears from his eyes. "I'll carry him to the cabin and prepare him for burial. You go and tell my family."

Lark nodded. She sat still until Clay lifted Jig in his arms, struggling with the weight. She leaned weakly against a tree and waited for the strength to return to her legs. "Oh, Jig, how can I survive without you?" she whispered. She knew with God's help she would. That was another thing Jig had taught her—to lean on God.

She thought of her promise to Jig, and she moaned. Then she lifted her chin high. "I'll keep my promise no matter what it takes," she whispered hoarsely.

CHAPTER 2

♦ Lark wiped away her tears as she reached the driveway of Blue Creek Orphan Asylum. She'd helped Clay with Jig as long as she dared, but she had to return to the asylum to work on the books and teach deportment. She'd told Clay she'd see him late in the afternoon, then had run from the cabin to town. Maybe she could slip inside the small room she used for her office without Matron seeing her and docking her already low pay for being late.

Lark gripped the cudgel tighter as she walked toward the asylum. The large two story house with a full basement had been built years ago by a lumberman for himself, but he'd decided to move north with his business and had given the home to Blue Creek for an orphan asylum. Lark had lived there all her life, first as an inmate, then as an employee. The payment she received was room and board and a pittance of a salary. Fifteen boys and ten girls, ranging from infant to sixteen years lived there. In the past year Lark had been trying to have Matron Anna Pike replaced. She was too unbending and her punishments too harsh. Because she'd been at the asylum from its beginning, none of the board would listen to Lark, not even Jennet Havlick. Matron put on a good front with the board members and the townspeople, but she was entirely different with the orphans.

Lark walked between tall maple trees up the wide brick sidewalk that led to the big front porch. Once the yard had been covered with grass and shrubbery, but now was bare from too many children playing on it. A barn for two cows and the mare that pulled Matron's buggy and the chicken coop stood behind the house. The house had been a good distance from the residents of Blue Creek, but in the past few years people had built closer and closer until homes now stood on either side and across the road. Lark could hear a man whistling as he did his chores, and she could see a woman working in her garden.

Lark walked up the wide steps and stopped on the porch. Straight ahead were the wide double doors that led into the huge front hall where she'd had to stand in silence as punishment. Across the porch to the left a door led to the offices and across the porch to the right a door led into the large front room. Lark took a deep breath and carefully opened the door to the offices. Hot, closed in air rushed down the hallway. The smell of fresh baking bread drifted from the kitchen. Lark heard the muted sounds of teachers teaching in the classrooms and a baby crying upstairs. She knew Zoe Cheyney, an orphan girl who had just turned eighteen but had no where to go, was attending the children too young to be in the classrooms. Lark and Zoe were friends, but they weren't as close as Lark and Jig had been.

Lark opened the window at the end of the long hall, then walked to her office. Inside were two desks, hers and John Epson's when he came in. She stroked his desk, flushed, and jerked her hand back. John was an attorney with an office on Main Street and a desk at the asylum for the work there. He handled the adoptions and any other legal matters that arose. He was in his early thirties and a bachelor. Lark had been attracted to him at one time, but Matron had seen the interest and had cruelly nipped it in the bud by telling Lark she was too plain and too low class to set her sights on a man of wealth and social standing. But the attraction for him was still buried in her heart, waiting for a sign from him to spark it into a flame of love.

Lark stood her cudgel in the corner near the coat hooks and stuck her pouch and canteen in a bottom drawer of her desk. She pulled off her heavy boots and leggings and slipped on her regular shoes. From the heavy pitcher on a stand in the corner she poured a bit of water onto a cloth and rubbed her face and hands. Listlessly she dried off, then hung the rough white towel on the wire hook near the stand. She brushed her hair and retied the blue ribbon. She scowled in the looking glass on the wall beside the hook. Her brown eyes were red rimmed from crying. Her face was too narrow, her mouth too wide, and her nose too pointed to be attractive. Jig had always said true beauty comes from within. Oh, what would she do without Jig? The ache inside of her was so great she almost cried aloud.

She sat at her desk and slowly pulled out the heavy dark red ledger. She sighed. Would this be her entire life from now on?

Just then John Epson walked in, his straw hat in his hand. Her pulse quickened, but she didn't let it show. "Good morning, Lark," he said, smiling. He sailed the hat onto a hook, then leaned back on his desk as he studied her. He wore a black suit that fit well across his broad shoulders and a white shirt and collar. He fingered his neatly trimmed black beard. "Is something wrong, Lark?"

His kindness brought tears to her eyes. She blinked them quickly away. "My friend Jig died this morning," she said with a break in her voice.

John shot up. He'd been waiting to hear the good news, but he didn't let Lark see how pleased he was. "I'm sorry to hear that, Lark. Will you be all right?"

Lark nodded. "I guess I have to be."

"Ask Matron to give you the day off."

Lark shook her head. "She won't."

"When's the funeral?"

"Probably tomorrow morning," whispered Lark as she locked her hands together on the ledger. "The Havlicks are taking care of everything."

"I figured they would. Jig seemed more like family to them than an employee."

Lark nodded. She picked up her ink pen as a hint for John to stop talking. She didn't want to break down in front of him. She didn't want him to see just how ugly she looked when she cried.

Just then Zoe Cheyney ran into the room. Tendrils of red hair clung to her damp, pale cheeks. Her hazel eyes were wide with fright. She gripped Lark's hand and tugged. "Hurry, Lark! Matron is locking Linda and Maggie in the cellar because they were swearing. You know there're rats down there!" She had been locked in the cellar several times just as Lark had been. "The girls are terrified! Help me stop her!"

Anger shot through Lark and she jumped up and ran with Zoe down the narrow hall to the foyer. Silently Lark prayed for the wisdom and strength to handle the situation.

In the hallway Matron held two skinny, frightened almost into hysterics, little girls by the arms. Matron was short and plump, dressed in a black wrapper and black shoes with pointed toes. Her brown hair was pulled into a tight bun. With steel gray eyes she glared at Zoe. "You can't stop me! So don't try, or you'll be punished too."

Zoe whimpered and stepped closer to Lark.

"Don't do this, Matron!" said Lark. Inside she was trembling because of the years of punishment she'd received from Matron, but outwardly she looked calm and in control. "Locking Linda and Maggie in the cellar won't solve anything."

"Please don't!" begged the girls. They were sisters who looked like twins and had been at the asylum for about five months.

"I will not tolerate bad language. They must learn!" snapped Matron.

"I will go directly to the Havlicks with this," said Lark, struggling to sound firm. She could feel Zoe tremble.

"Hummmp! Just stay out of my way!" Matron tried to push past Lark and Zoe while the girls dragged their feet and screamed.

"Let them go!" cried Zoe.

"Move!" shouted Matron, her round face brick red.

Lark wouldn't budge and Matron was forced to stop. Lark looked Matron straight in the eye and said, "The girls will learn to stop swearing as I teach them deportment. Locking them in a cellar won't work."

"It won't!" whimpered Linda and Maggie.

Matron narrowed her gray eyes into slits. "It worked for you two and it'll work for them."

Lark shook her head. "Times have changed. This is 1890!"

"I won't change my mind!"

Lark took a deep breath. "I will go directly to the Havlicks and bring Jennet here to witness what you've done. You know Jennet Havlick doesn't abide such treatment."

Matron sputtered with anger, then shoved the two girls toward Lark. "This is not the end of this, Lark Baritt!" Matron turned on her heels and strode to her office, slamming the door hard behind her.

The girls clung to Lark, sobbing against her. She patted their thin backs and talked gently to them.

"Matron will make it bad for us," whispered Zoe.

"I don't care!" cried Lark. "It's time we stood up to her! We are adults." She tried to smile at Zoe, but failed. "You'd better get back to the babies. I'll tend the girls and see that they get back to class."

"We'll talk later," said Zoe. She ran lightly up the wide stairs to the nursery.

The girls looked up into Lark's face. "Thank you, Miss Baritt," they said together.

"You're welcome." Lark's voice was gentle and she tried to

smile as she wiped their faces with her hanky. "I don't ever want either of you to say bad words again. You both know better."

"We won't," said Linda solemnly.

"Not even if we get mad," said Maggie.

"Good. Now, get back to class."

Maggie looked at Linda. "We should tell her, Linda."

"We should," said Linda.

Lark lifted her brow. "Tell me what?"

The girls looked quickly around to make sure no one was listening. In a low voice Maggie said, "We know where Matron hid your box of stuff."

Lark's knees almost buckled and for a minute she couldn't speak. She didn't pretend she didn't know what "stuff" Maggie meant. For as long as she could remember she'd tried to find the things the man who'd dropped her off at the asylum had left with her. Lark had been told her mother had died when she was born and her father couldn't manage a baby alone. A man, maybe her father, had left her at the asylum with a box of things. She'd been only a few days old. She'd not known about the box until she was seven years old and some of the other orphans had talked about their stuff that Matron kept in a closet. Lark had asked about her box of stuff, but Matron had said she didn't have anything for Lark. Just the same, the other children had said they knew she did have something. Allie, an older girl who had moved to Grand Rapids about eight years ago had said she was outside Matron's door the day a man had left Lark with Matron. He had also left a box of things—photos, money to help pay for her keep, and baby clothes. Matron insisted Allie had lied just to stir up trouble. Now, Maggie and Linda were saying they knew where Matron had hidden the stuff.

"You okay, Miss Baritt?" asked Linda in alarm.

"I don't know," whispered Lark hoarsely.

"Don't you want to know where your stuff is?" asked Linda.

Lark nodded weakly.

"It's in Matron's room," whispered Maggie.

"In a trunk," said Linda.

"How do you know?" asked Lark.

The girls flushed and shrugged.

Lark's head spun and she couldn't think what to do.

"Want us to show you?" asked Maggie.

Before Lark could answer Matron's office door burst open and Matron snapped, "Aren't you girls in class yet?"

"We're going right now," the girls said as they turned and ran down the hall and into a room.

Lark felt like her head was packed with cotton and her eyes wouldn't focus.

"What's wrong with you, Lark?" snapped Matron.

"I . . . I don't feel well," Lark whispered.

"You look ready to pass out. Get to your room and lie down! You have Deportment Class in two hours." Matron spun on her heel and slammed her office door behind her.

In a daze Lark walked to the open stairs in the wide hallway. As she climbed she clung to the bannister, her legs almost too weak to support her. Why would Matron lie about her stuff and hide it in her trunk? Lark hesitated. Should she go to Matron's bedroom to look in the trunk? Numbly she shook her head. She couldn't walk that far without collapsing.

The long hall seemed to stretch on and on. Finally Lark stepped into the room she shared with Zoe. She didn't notice the sun streaming through the windows or the shabby white muslin curtains fluttering in the warm breeze. A fly buzzed at the window, but she didn't hear it as she sank to the double bed. The carved mahogany headboard stood about four feet high and the footboard about two feet. A patchwork quilt Lark had quilted herself during her twelfth year covered the bed. Unable to contain her emotions any longer, she burst into tears and her slender shoulders shook with sobs. All those years Allie had been right! A man had left some of her family's things so that someday she'd have a sense of who she was! Why had

Matron kept them from her? Should she take them from Matron's trunk? Lark pushed herself up, shivering as if it were twenty degrees below zero. A sudden strength coursed through her body. She had to get her stuff! But how could she? Matron always kept her door locked.

Lark paced from the bed to the tall chest, to the trunk, over to the chifforobe, and back again. Somehow Maggie and Linda had gotten into Matron's room. If they could, she could. She couldn't wait to tell Jig what she'd learned! Tears burned her eyes as she realized Jig wasn't there to listen to her! How could she survive the trauma of the day? Jig was gone! She was all alone! She stopped and shook her head, then looked up. "I'm not alone!" she whispered, a feeling of calm spreading through her. "Heavenly Father, you're always with me! With your help I'll be all right. Thank you!" Lark clasped her hands together at her throat. "Dear Father, I need to know what to do about Matron hiding my things."

Wild ideas on what to do flashed through her mind, but she quickly rejected them. Somehow she'd find a way to look in Matron's trunk, and she'd do it yet today!

Suddenly she remembered that she hadn't told the Havlicks about the two men she'd caught in the pines. She'd have to tell them immediately. She pushed thoughts of herself to the back of her mind where she'd carried her own problems for years and rubbed her hands together with agitation. Perspiration dotted her face. "How could I forget to tell the Havlicks? What shall I do?"

She walked to the window and let the breeze blow against her damp face. Maybe she could get someone to teach her class so she could run to the Havlicks now. "Kaitland will do it without getting me in trouble with Matron!" she whispered, then rushed downstairs to the history class. She arranged for Kaitland to teach deportment, then ran the two miles to the Havlicks' farm.

A white picket fence surrounded the three story white frame house Freeman Havlick had built for Jennet and their six children when Clay, the oldest, was a small child. Outside the fence behind the house stood two large barns, several small sheds, and the large shop where Free and his sons built buggies by special order. Chickens scratched in the farmyard along with turkeys, geese, and ducks. Cattle grazed in a big pasture on one side of a barn and sheep grazed on another side. Far enough away to keep the smell from the house was a pen full of pigs. Lark took a step toward the house, then heard Freeman and Clay talking in the shop, their voices loud.

Lark hurried back through the gate and across the farmyard to the shop. Her limp dress clung to her damp body. A fly buzzed around her head and tangled in the loose strands of taffy brown hair. Impatiently she swatted the fly away.

"I don't understand you, Clay!" Free snapped angrily.

Lark stopped short just outside the open door. An unfinished buggy stood behind Clay and Free. Tools hung on the back wall of the shop. Free's face was dark with anger. In all the years Lark had known the Havlicks, she'd never heard Free raise his voice in anger. Maybe she should call out and let them know she was there. The men looked very much alike, even in their anger, as they faced each other. They were the same height and build, with the same dark brown eyes. Clay wore dark pants held up by wide black suspenders and a blue plaid shirt cuffed to his muscled forearm. Free wore overalls, faded from many washings, and a blue chambray work shirt. He could afford to dress like a city man and he had enough money to keep him and his family for years to come, but he chose to work and to dress like a workman. He wasn't one to have idle hands nor were any of the members of his family.

"Pa, I have every right to make my own fortune!" cried Clay as he jerked off his straw hat and jabbed his fingers through his thick dark hair. He'd been talking about going into business for himself the past two years. Now the time for talking was past. "Pa, I am going to buy the two big warehouses in town and I'm going to build wagons. There's a market for them and there'll be a market for a *long* time."

Free scowled as he stabbed his fingers through his gray hair. "Why can't you keep working with me? We make quality buggies."

"There are men already developing a gas-driven buggy. There will come a time when people won't use buggies pulled by horses, but farmers and freighters will *always* need wagons. I have a contract to supply Midwest Freighters with three hundred wagons before fall."

"That's out of the question, Clay. How can you do that?"

"By hiring men to work for me."

Lark's stomach tightened as she stepped even closer. It was very embarrassing to hear the argument. Flushing, she cleared her throat. "Freeman, Clay, I must speak with you," she called out. Her voice quivered and she flushed even more.

The two men stepped from the shop, putting their anger and argument aside.

"Lark," said Clay. "Did you come about the funeral?"

"It's in the morning," said Free, smiling gently at Lark.

"I did want to know that, but that's not why I came. I must speak to you about two men I caught in the pines this morning."

"What's that?" asked Clay in alarm.

"Were you hurt?" said Free.

Lark shook her head as she stepped into the shade of the shop. She quickly told her story with questions and exclamations from Free and Clay. "They're in jail waiting for you to press charges."

"I'll tend to it right away," said Clay. "I'll need you with me to identify the men."

Lark hesitated, then shrugged. She'd have to deal with Matron's anger if she was found out. "All right."

"How about a drink of cold well water first," said Free as he motioned to the windmill twirling in the breeze. Cold water flowed from a pipe into a big tank for the animals.

"That would be nice. Thank you." Lark smiled at Free, but suddenly felt too self-conscious to look at Clay again.

Clay filled a dipper with cold water and held it out to Lark. She took it thankfully and their hands brushed. A tingle went through Lark.

Clay noticed the sudden flush on Lark's cheeks and wondered about it. He wasn't a lady's man like his twenty-two-year-old brother Tristan was already and like his sixteen-year-old brother Miles was on his way to becoming, but he could recognize a blush.

Just then Tristan drove up in the buggy with Jennet and his two sisters Hannah, eighteen, and Evie, eleven. The other sister was married and lived in Grand Rapids.

Tristan leaped from the buggy and helped his mother down while Hannah and Evie climbed out unassisted.

Lark smiled at the girls and then at Jennet and Tristan. Lark knew Zoe Cheyney would give anything to be there right then. Zoe was madly in love with Tris Havlick, and he barely knew she existed.

Jennet slipped her arms around Lark and held her for a minute. At forty-one years old, Jennet was still slender. She had graying chestnut hair and wide blue eyes that didn't seem to miss anything. She and Lark were the same height. She held Lark from her. "I'm so sorry about Jig. I know how much you loved him. I pray God will fill your heart with peace and comfort."

"Thank you," whispered Lark. It had been years since she'd been hugged by any adult except Jig. It felt good to have Jennet hold her and speak comfort to her.

"Can you come in?" asked Jennet as she released Lark's hands.

"She's riding to town with me," said Clay. "Pa will explain what happened."

"You must come to dinner here tomorrow after the funeral," said Jennet. "I won't take no for an answer!"

"Now, Mother," said Clay with a grin. "Don't force Lark to do anything she doesn't want to do."

"No, that's fine," Lark said quickly. She had to grab the

opportunity to fulfill her promise to Jig. "I'd like to have dinner with you tomorrow."

"Good," said Jennet with a smile.

"We must be going," said Clay, cupping Lark's elbow with his hand.

His touch sent a shiver through her, but she didn't let it show. She climbed in the buggy and Clay sat beside her. They said their goodbyes and Clay flicked the reins. The buggy rolled easily along the dirt road and across the bridge to the rough corduroy, a road built of logs laying side by side across the road to keep it from becoming rutted. They passed Red Beaver's large farm, then reached the outskirts of Blue Creek. They passed the lumber mill, the train depot, and the livery before Clay headed down Main Street to the sheriff's office.

Lark gripped her hands tightly in her lap as a plan leaped into her mind. But could she voice it? "Clay," she said hesitantly. "Who will guard the pines now?"

"I'll find someone from the mill," he said as he stopped at the hitch-rail in front of the sheriff's office.

"I want the job," said Lark in a rush.

Clay cocked his dark brow. "You?"

"Yes! I've walked the trail with Jig and I know how to do the job." Lark bit her bottom lip. "And I'd like to live in the cabin."

Clay thought about her years in the asylum. If he had his way he'd put all the children in homes and do away with the asylum, but he knew that was impossible. "What of your job at the asylum?"

"I could go there every day after I walk the line," said Lark. Suddenly this was the most important thing in the world to her. She'd thought she'd never get to leave the asylum, but now she had a way out. "Please, Clay! I want the freedom to walk the woods and to live on my own. I know there's no reason you should give me, a woman and an orphan, such responsibility, but Jig trusted me, and I think you would too if you'd give yourself a chance."

"I don't know," said Clay, pushing his straw hat to the back of his head. He watched a horse and rider walk down the sawdust covered street. "I don't like the thought of you being in such danger."

"I know how to take care of myself."

"From your story of this morning's happenings, I can believe that. But why endanger yourself for my trees?"

Lark looked at him squarely. "They might be your trees, but they're our heritage for generations to come! We can't let anything happen to the pines!"

Clay laughed. "You sound like my mother." There was something about Lark that reminded him of his mother. Perhaps it was the stories Jennet had told of her involvement with the underground railroad and how she'd made him think of a gutsy young woman—something that Lark seemed to be. It was funny, but he'd never thought such things about Lark before. She did seem to have a certain gutsiness about her. Why hadn't he noticed it before? "I don't know, Lark. A woman all alone?"

"This is 1890, Clay Havlick, not the Dark Ages." Inside Lark was leaping with excitement, but on the outside she looked calm. "I want the job!"

Clay saw her determination and smiled as he nodded slightly. "I'll ask the hired girl to clean the cabin today," he said.

Lark's heart leaped. Clay had given her the job! "Jig wouldn't want someone else looking at his stuff. I'll clean it before nightfall." She took a deep breath. "Can I move in tomorrow?"

Clay shrugged. "Yes . . . yes, I suppose you can."

Lark laughed right out loud. "Do you know how wonderful it will be to have a place of my own?"

Clay smiled at her excitement. "I'm glad you don't have to live at the asylum any longer. But then you'd be moving out when you marry."

"I will probably never marry," she said stiffly.

"Some young man will come along and you'll change your mind."

Lark shook her head. She wondered how he could be so dense. "And how about you? Do you have a young woman friend?"

He thought of Veda Thorne. She'd stayed in the same hotel as he had during his business trip in Detroit and had ridden back on the train this morning with him. Her beauty and her courage to speak to him even though she'd said her father had forbidden her to had touched him. "I have decided to start seeing Veda Thorne."

Lark froze. Jig had been right! "Veda Thorne? But isn't she Willie Thorne's daughter?"

Clay frowned. He knew exactly what his parents would say when they learned he was taking Veda to dinner tonight. "What if she is?" he asked gruffly.

"Jig told me about Willie Thorne."

"Veda is different."

"She's a Thorne," said Lark. "She might be using you to get the pines."

A muscle jumped in Clay's jaw. "I see Jig has been talking to you. She would never destroy the pines. She loves them as much as my family does."

Lark bit back a groan. "You will be careful, won't you?"

"There's no need to be," Clay snapped.

Lark lifted her chin. "I'm sorry if I offended you, but I would hate to see the pines lumbered."

"So would I!" Clay stepped from the buggy and reached up to help Lark out. "We'd best tend to business. I'd appreciate it if you didn't say anything about me and . . . and . . . Veda Thorne."

"Who would I say it to? It's not my place, is it?" Lark bit her lip. She had made it her place with her promise to Jig!

After their business at the sheriff's office was finished, Clay drove Lark to the asylum. "See you in the morning at the funeral," he said stiffly.

She nodded slightly. "Thank you for the ride. I hope those men don't make more trouble for you."

"They won't, thanks to you." Clay tipped his hat and drove toward the empty warehouses. He felt a great urge to turn and look back to catch one more glimpse of Lark. He scowled and shook his head. She meant nothing to him, so why was he feeling a special warmth for her? It had to be because of his promise to Jig.

A picture of Veda Thorne with her mass of auburn hair, sweet smile, and tall, slender body flashed across his mind and he flushed with pleasure. He was glad thoughts of Veda pushed away thoughts of Lark.

Veda had acted as if she'd found him attractive—something no other woman had ever done. He'd been able to carry on a conversation with her—something else he'd never been able to do with a woman. She was Willie Thorne's daughter, but he liked her.

Clay reined in the team near the warehouses. He'd made a sound judgment in using his pines as collateral. As a boy he'd spent hours of pleasure running through the pines, knowing someday they'd be his. He and Tris had built a fort of pine boughs and played "war." Often Jig joined in. Clay chuckled, then grew serious as he thought of the time he'd found two baby bobcats in a den. They had tan hair dotted with lots of black spots. He'd known better than to stay near the den, but the kittens were so cute, he couldn't help himself.

He crouched down before the kittens and said softly, "I'd like to take you home." His sisters would love them.

At a sound on a tree branch above he looked up and his heart leaped to his throat. The mother bobcat stood on the branch and growled, ready to spring on him. He leaped back just as it landed a few feet from him. Immediately it sprang at him again. Sweat soaked his shirt as he jumped aside. He grabbed a big stick and held it as a weapon in front of him. His stomach knotted, and he prayed Jig would come to his rescue. But Jig didn't come. The bobcat sprang again. Clay leaped aside and jabbed at it with the stick. It growled, showing sharp teeth. Slowly he backed up, brandishing the stick in front of him. The bobcat tensed, but didn't follow him. Finally it turned and ran to the den.

Chills running up and down his back, Clay had gripped the stick tightly as he backed further away until he felt safe enough to turn and run back to Jig and Tris. He had spotted bobcat dens again, but had never stopped to watch the kittens. Years later Clay had told Jig and Tris about the close call, and they'd all had a good laugh.

The pines had brought adventure, danger, and enjoyment to his life. Now they were providing money for his business.

Grinning, Clay walked inside the first warehouse and his steps echoed in the empty building. The workmen could easily build several wagons at once in the huge buildings. During nice weather they'd leave the row of wide doors open to let in sunlight. He'd already talked to several men and had hired fifty to start to work the minute he had the business set up. He'd called it *Havlick's Wagon Works*.

Slowly he walked back to his buggy. Why was Pa being so stubborn about him starting his own business? He'd started to tell Pa about putting the pines up for collateral when Lark had interrupted them. He still had to face both Ma and Pa with the news. He wasn't looking forward to that at all.

Clay stood beside his buggy and looked at the long warehouses. He'd heard the stories about how Grandpa Roman Havlick had kept Great-grandpa Clay's money from Free when he needed it desperately to become a lumberman. Clay knew someday he'd inherit a fortune from Pa, but he couldn't wait for that day. He'd had to have money now for the wagon business. All he had was the ten sections of white pines and he'd never sell them, but they were collateral.

"I had to do it!" he cried, making his team bob their heads. Now he had plenty of money for Havlick's Wagon Works.

Clay drove to the bank and within a few minutes the paperwork was filed with them. He'd borrowed the money from a Detroit bank that had a branch in Blue Creek. He'd do his business from the Blue Creek bank from now on. He knew he'd be able to make the first large payment in three months without any trouble. He'd already ordered the lumber he'd need and had hired blacksmiths. Several of the men he'd hired didn't know wagon making, but he'd promised to teach them quickly. He'd offered them each $9.00 a week with a bonus at the end of the first three months if the wagons were completed on time. The men had been glad for the good pay.

At home again in Free's study Clay told his parents what he'd done.

Jennet jumped up from her chair, her blue eyes flashing fire. "How could you do that, Clay? Do you realize the jeopardy to the pines?"

Clay stiffened. "There's no jeopardy."

Free sighed heavily. "Clay, if you can't finish the wagons in time and don't get paid, you'll be in a financial bind. The bank could easily take the trees."

"Then sell them to the highest bidder!" cried Jennet. "Like Willie Thorne!"

"He's not interested in the trees," said Clay sharply.

"He'll do anything to get his hands on them!" snapped Free as he stabbed his fingers through his gray hair. "He could sabotage your operation just so he could take over the bank note."

Clay shook his head. "He's going to be too busy with his own business to worry about ours."

"What do you mean?" asked Jennet as she sank to her chair again.

"Since when do you know Thorne's business?" asked Free as he leaned back against his heavy walnut desk.

Veda had told him, but Clay didn't want to say that. "I heard he's opening a tavern in Blue Creek."

Jennet shot from her chair again. "A tavern? How dare he? Doesn't he know Blue Creek is a dry town?"

Free slammed his fist into his palm. "That man will do anything to create havoc!"

"I won't have him bringing liquor into our area," said Jennet.

Clay slipped quietly away. He knew his parents would immediately jump into action to stop Willie from opening his tavern. Maybe it would keep them occupied so he could go about his business without further objections.

CHAPTER 3

♦ In the middle of the afternoon Lark stood before Matron's desk with her chin high, her shoulders square, and her stomach fluttering nervously. "I would like the things that were left with me when I was brought here twenty-two years ago."

Matron scowled, but her hands lay still on her desk. "If you had anything, it was long gone before I came here."

Lark shook her head. "I know I have a box of photos and clothes. I want them."

Matron slowly stood and smoothed down her black wrapper. "You are getting high and mighty all at once, Lark Baritt. I could toss you out on your ear, you know."

Lark shook her head. "You can't. The board hired me to do the bookwork and to teach. You don't have the authority to fire me."

"But I can make life miserable for you," snapped Matron.

"I'm moving out tomorrow," said Lark. "I have a place of my own away from here."

Matron's eyes widened in surprise. "And good riddance, I say!"

Lark took one step forward. "Get my box of stuff or I shall bring Jennet Havlick in to help me get it from you."

Matron turned scarlet. "I did happen to run across a box that might be yours. I'll see that you get it."

"Right now," said Lark firmly. She was surprised at her courage.

Matron sniffed as she sailed past Lark to the door. "I'll be back with it, but don't expect much."

Lark waited until Matron was out of sight, then she sank weakly down on a highback chair that stood to the left of the large maple desk. Finally she was going to get to see her stuff!

Just then Zoe Cheyney slipped into the room. Her red hair was combed back neatly and held in place with a narrow ribbon. She was wearing the cream colored muslin dress she'd had since she was fifteen, and since she'd grown it was too tight across the bust. "Lark! Are you really leaving?" she whispered in alarm.

"Yes." Lark knew Zoe had listened at the door, something they'd both done many times in the past when they wanted to learn what was happening. Quickly she told Zoe about her plans. "I will move in the cabin tomorrow."

"That is so romantic, Lark! You'll be right close to the Havlicks." Zoe trembled. "You'll get to see Tris every single day, won't you?"

"I don't think so, Zoe."

"But you might! Oh, Lark, let me stay with you! Please!"

"You can visit and spend the night at times, but you can't move in with me, Zoe. I need this time alone. You understand, don't you?"

"Yes," whispered Zoe with tears in her large hazel eyes. "If I had a chance to get away from here in a place of my own, I'd do it as quick as a bunny."

Just then Lark heard voices. "Zoe, Matron's coming. Slip out quickly. She's bringing my box of things."

"Be sure to show me everything!" Zoe squeezed Lark's hand and left quietly.

Facing the door, Lark steeled herself for Matron's return. Soon she'd get to see her box of things. Soon she'd know something about her past, about the mother who'd died in childbirth and about the father who couldn't care for her.

Matron walked in empty handed and Lark's heart dropped to her feet.

"Just as I suspected," said Matron with a smug look on her face. "There is no such box! I thought I'd run across one that might've been yours, but I was wrong."

With a cry Lark ran out of Matron's office and back to the kitchen where she knew she'd find Maggie and Linda helping prepare supper. "Girls, come here," she said, motioning from the doorway.

"What's wrong, Miss Baritt?" asked Maggie.

"Did Matron beat you again?" asked Linda.

Lark gripped the girls by the arms. "I asked Matron about my box of stuff. First she said she had it, then she said she didn't."

"We have it," whispered Maggie.

Lark gasped.

"We saw Matron take it to the cellar just after dinner and we got it and took it upstairs," said Maggie.

"How do you know it's mine?" asked Lark weakly.

"We saw your name," said Linda. "Lark Baritt. Your parents were Matthew and Meriel Baritt."

Lark bit back a cry. "I want to see the box now."

"We can't leave the kitchen yet," said Maggie, "but we'll tell you where to find the box."

"It's hidden in a safe spot," said Linda.

"It's in the big linen closet on the top shelf way in the back," said Maggie. "It's about as big as a breadbox."

Lark ran down the hall to the stairs and up. Blood pounded in her ears as she reached the closet and slipped inside. No one was upstairs yet, so she had time to look in privacy.

She stood on the stepstool and reached to the back behind a pile of worn sheets, found the cardboard box, and pulled it out.

In her weakness she almost dropped it. She carried it to her room and sank to the edge of the bed with her box held tight against herself. Dare she open it and see who she was?

Shouts and laughter from the orphans drifted in through the open window. The box on her lap smelled and looked old. Slowly she opened it and looked inside. Her hands trembling, she lifted out a tiny dress and bonnet that once had been white but were now yellowed with age. Had she ever worn the dress and bonnet? She held the dress higher. A piece of paper fluttered to the floor. She picked it up and tried to read it, but her hand shook so badly she couldn't focus on the words. Finally she found her name: Lark Louise Baritt, born January 28, 1868. PARENTS: Matthew Quenten Baritt and Meriel Louise (Jakaway) Baritt of Big Pine.

Giant tears welled up in Lark's dark eyes. "Matthew and Meriel Baritt," she whispered around the lump in her throat. She lifted out faded photos and studied the faces of her parents. They looked very young but well dressed. She could see her own resemblance to her mother and even to her father. She read two letters that her mother had written to her father while he was lumbering in the Saginaw Bay area, then pressed the letters to her heart. After a long time she looked in the box, but it was empty. There was no money, just as Allie had predicted, and no mention of money.

"Why would Matron take my things?" whispered Lark, shaking her head. Oh, what did it matter now? She had them and that's all that mattered. To be safe she hid them in her drawer, carried the box down to the cellar, and left it where the girls had found it. Now she could go to Jig's cabin to clean and get it ready to move in to tomorrow.

Lark wiped away her tears, brushed her taffy brown hair, then retied the narrow blue ribbon. Life had suddenly become almost perfect. What could go wrong now?

Lark laughed as she walked out the front door of the asylum. This morning she'd felt lost and without hope, but suddenly she had a life to look forward to.

At Jig's cabin Lark stopped outside the open door. Clay was cleaning! He wore the same dark pants and plaid shirt that he'd had on earlier, only now he was dirty from cleaning. "Hello," said Lark with a breathless laugh.

Clay turned and smiled. "I thought I'd lend a hand."

Lark stepped inside and looked around in surprise. The windows sparkled, letting sunlight flow in. "It looks like you lent two hands! You've cleaned the windows, the stove, and swept down the walls! You're much too busy to do this! I planned to do it."

Clay shrugged. "I don't mind a bit. It makes me feel close to Jig."

Tears stung Lark's eyes and for a minute she couldn't speak. Just then she noticed a wooden box sitting on the table. It was about fourteen inches square and ten inches deep. It had her name on it. She touched it, then looked questioningly at Clay. "What's this?"

"I found it in that box over there." Lark saw Jig's special box that he kept closed and covered with a lap robe sitting with its lid open. She bit her lower lip.

"Jig left this for you," said Clay softly as he tapped the box.

Lark touched the latch on the box. "I don't think I can open it," she whispered. "Would you?"

A desire to comfort Lark rose inside Clay, surprising him. He pushed the feeling away and released the leather and wood latch and lifted the lid. Inside was a photo of Lark when she was about eight years old. With a laugh he lifted it out and handed it to her. "You'll like this."

Color washed over Lark's neck and face as she took the photo of the frightened little girl with skinny braids and a scratch across her cheek. She remembered Jig having the picture made when a traveling photographer came through town. For some reason it embarrassed her to have Clay see the picture. She laid it upside down on the freshly scrubbed table, then looked in the box herself. She lifted out a framed delicate, blue-green moth with touches of lavender and light yellow and white body. "I mounted and framed this for Jig when I was twelve," she whispered.

"It's a real work of art," said Clay in awe as he looked at the moth.

"Would you like it?" asked Lark.

Clay smiled at Lark, then once again gazed at the delicate moth. "I used to take moths home to Ma just because she found such pleasure in them. I'd forgotten about that until just now. I would like this. Thank you."

"Here's a note," said Lark, lifting it out of the box and opening it, then read it aloud. "My girl, Lark, I never had much, but what I do have I give to you. Take it and know that I love you as my own. I never told you I had a family back in Sweden. They could all be gone. I don't know. I want you to send the letter to them that I wrote. I could never do it. You do it for me, please."

"A family," said Clay. "We never knew."

Lark stopped reading and looked in the box for a letter and found the envelope addressed in ink with Jig's sprawl. She studied the strange words on the address, then handed it to Clay. She continued reading Jig's letter aloud. "I have money put away. Give $100 to the Blue Creek Orphan Asylum for taking care of you all these years when your Dad couldn't. The rest of the money is for you. Remember, God cares more for you than I could. Always keep Him first in your life. Love. Jig."

Giant tears welled up in Lark's eyes and slipped down her pale cheeks. "He left me his things, Clay. I never knew. Why would he do that?"

"He loved you," said Clay softly.

"But why? I'm nobody!"

"How can you say that? You're Lark Baritt!" Clay had always been loved and couldn't comprehend how Lark felt. He could see she didn't have the strength to rummage through the box more. "I'll find the money for you."

Lark sank to a chair and nodded, the note still in her hand.

Clay lifted out an envelope marked Orphan Asylum and another one marked Lark Baritt. He opened Lark's and counted $1500.00.

Lark helplessly shook her head. "I can't believe it," she said weakly. "That's a lot of money!"

"I can't believe Jig didn't put this in the bank in town," said Clay.

"I could buy a house or start a business," said Lark.

"You could," said Clay.

"I could buy a horse and buggy."

"You could use one of ours," said Clay.

"Oh, Jig! You've given me freedom," whispered Lark.

Clay looked in the box again and lifted out a heavy, awkward cap and ball pistol. His name was written on a paper around it. "Look what he gave me," said Clay as sudden tears blurred his vision. He could remember admiring the pistol from the time he was old enough to remember.

Lark looked in the box again while Clay studied the pistol. She lifted out Jig's tattered Bible, several rocks he'd found and thought were pretty, two books written in Swedish, two gold coins, a crystal paper weight, and a copper kaleidoscope she'd often looked through in years past. Jig had given her his treasures!

The next morning Lark stood in the white pines with the Havlicks and Jig's other friends while Pastor James said the last goodbyes before they lowered the wooden box into the ground. She stood aside from the family, but Tris caught her hand and tugged her close. She smiled thankfully.

Clay frowned slightly as he saw Tris and Lark look at each other. Would Tris try to make Lark another conquest? Right then Clay decided to warn Lark about Tris. He was quick to love and just as quick to leave.

Lark wiped away her tears and forced herself to stop crying as Pastor James walked to his buggy and drove away, leaving three men behind to cover the casket.

Jennet slipped her arm around Lark and said, "I'm glad

you're having dinner with us. We who've loved Jig need to be together."

Lark's heart warmed to the special motherly attention from Jennet. "I will never forget him! Did you know he left me his special things and money too?"

Jennet nodded. "Clay told me."

Lark shook her head. "I still can't believe he'd do that."

"He loved you very much," said Jennet softly.

Just then Hannah and Evie walked up. Jennet handed Lark over to them. "Take her home with you, girls, and see that she rests for a while before dinner."

Lark smiled at the girls. Hannah was eighteen and looked a lot like Jennet with her chestnut brown hair and wide blue eyes. Evie, eleven, had almost white hair and striking brown eyes.

"Jig was teaching me how to shoot," said Evie sadly as they walked across the field toward the farm. "I'll miss him a lot."

"Me too," said Lark.

Hannah looked wistfully behind her. "Lark, do you really know Red Beaver?"

Lark looked at Hannah in surprise. Hannah sounded like a girl in love. "Yes, I know him," said Lark. "Some of the orphan boys work on his farm." Red Beaver was a Patawatomi who owned the farm to the west of the Havlicks. He had been at the funeral. "He's a very nice man."

"Pa says Hannah can't talk to Red Beaver," said Evie as she skipped on ahead. She glanced back over her shoulder. "Pa says Hannah can't marry an Indian."

"Evie!" cried Hannah, flushing scarlet.

Evie ran on ahead, leaving Hannah and Lark to walk alone through the tall grass and wild flowers.

"Could you fall in love with an Indian, Lark?" asked Hannah in a low, tight voice.

Lark shrugged. "I never thought about it. Red Beaver's a fine man."

"Pa likes Red Beaver and admires him for being such a hard

worker, but he says no daughter of his can marry a Patawatomi. I don't think that's Christian, do you?"

"You can't disobey your pa," said Lark.

"I'm full grown, Lark. My sister was married at my age. So was Ma!"

Lark watched a bee buzz around a patch of daisies. "Hannah, you can't want to marry Red Beaver or any man if you don't love him."

Hannah sighed heavily. "I'll tell you a secret," she said quietly. "I do love him. I can't look at the boys who come to call on me because my heart is full of love for Red Beaver."

"I don't know what to say," said Lark. "I didn't know you even knew Red Beaver enough to love him."

"We've talked together many times."

"How does he feel?"

"I think he cares for me," whispered Hannah.

Lark looked helplessly at Hannah. "You do have a problem, don't you?"

"I told Jig how I feel, and he said to pray for Pa and for Red Beaver. Jig said God would help me know what to do."

"He will," said Lark.

"Do you love a man, Lark?"

She thought of John Epson. "No." Clay flashed across her mind and she flushed hotly. Why think of him? She wasn't good enough for Clay Havlick or Tris or even sixteen-year-old Miles. If she ever married, it would be to a poor widower with kids who needed tending.

"Red Beaver's a Christian," said Hannah as they walked around a large hickory nut tree.

"I know."

"His ma isn't. Silent Waters. Do you know her?"

Lark nodded and forced back a shiver. Silent Waters was usually very quiet and seemed full of anger.

"She scares me," said Hannah. "She hates me."

"I don't think she likes anyone except Red Beaver."

"Maybe. But she hates me because I'm a Havlick." Hannah

fingered the cameo at her throat. "I don't understand why she hates my family. It doesn't make sense. Do you think?"

"No. Jig said your pa lumbered out all the trees around this area except the sections he saved. Maybe Silent Waters lived in the woods he lumbered out."

"Maybe," said Hannah. "Between Silent Waters and Pa I don't stand a chance with Red Beaver." Hannah stopped and turned to Lark. "I feel him watching me at church and when he comes to bring grain. Every time we talk it feels like my heart will float right out of my body."

Lark laughed. "You sound just like my friend Zoe."

"I've met Zoe at the asylum. I like her." Hannah picked a flower and held it between two fingers. "Is Zoe in love?"

"Yes." Lark knew she couldn't tell Hannah that Zoe was in love with Tris. "I'm thirsty, Hannah. Could we get a drink from the well?" Lark really wasn't thirsty, but she wanted to get Hannah's mind off Zoe before she asked who Zoe loved.

Several minutes later Lark sat between Hannah and Evie at the large cherry table in the Havlicks' dining room. Clay, Tris, and Miles sat across from them with Jennet at the foot and Free at the head. As Free asked a blessing on the food, the aroma of fried chicken, potatoes, green beans, and freshly baked bread made Lark's stomach cramp with hunger. She'd barely eaten in the past two days.

As they passed the food and talked, Lark glanced around the large room. A cherry buffet with chinaware stood between tall windows covered with white curtains. A cherry sideboard was on one wall and a matching corner hutch filled with fancy serving dishes stood in the corner near the kitchen door. Lark liked the elegant hominess of the room. She knew she'd never have a home like this.

Lark found it easier to talk during dinner than she'd thought it would be. She'd had no experience with small talk during a meal. At the asylum they were forced to eat in silence, but she'd carefully studied deportment so she'd know what to do if she was ever invited out. She knew the Havlicks were trying hard to make her feel at ease.

During dessert of apple pie and slices of cheddar cheese, Free said, "Lark, I'm pleased you want to guard the pines, but it's too dangerous for you."

Lark stiffened. Would he convince Clay not to hire her after all? "I know it can be dangerous, sir, but I've been doing it a long time."

"And she has angels watching over her," said Evie with a grin at Lark.

Free smiled and nodded. "That's right. I guess I should keep my objections to myself."

"When do you move in to the cabin, Lark?" asked Jennet.

"Today," said Lark.

"I trust Anna Pike didn't cause trouble for you," said Clay. He had heard things about the matron that he didn't care about.

Lark fingered her napkin. "Matron wasn't happy at all, but she didn't say much."

"I know you care for the pines as much as we do," said Jennet as she cut a small bite of pie. "I want you to look on us as family now, Lark. Come here any time you want."

Lark smiled at Jennet. Had her mother, Meriel Baritt, been like Jennet?

"Any time," said Free, smiling.

"Thank you." Lark glanced at Clay, then quickly away. What would the family say if they knew of her promise to Jig?

CHAPTER 4

♦ Lark set her box of clothes and things on the bunk, then looked around the clean cabin with a pleased look on her face.

"Are you sure you'll be okay here alone?" asked Clay from the doorway. He'd driven her from the asylum to the cabin so she could be settled in before nightfall.

Lark turned with a smile. "I know I'll be all right! It'll be different sleeping here all alone, but I'll like it. I have never, ever been by myself!"

"You might want to get leather clothes like Jig wore to protect your skin from the briars," said Clay.

"I'll see about it right away. I know Red Beaver tans hides, so I'll check with him tomorrow."

"Good. And I'm going to get you a dog."

Lark beamed. A dog! "That's not necessary, Clay."

"I'd feel a whole lot better if you weren't entirely alone."

"Thanks. I've always wanted a dog."

"Good. Then that's settled." As though he were checking off items on a list, Clay asked, "Did you put the money in the bank?"

"Yes," Lark said with a slight smile. "And I mailed Jig's letter."

Clay nodded. "I must be going," he said stiffly.

"Are you taking Veda Thorne to dinner again?"

"Yes." Clay smiled, remembering the good time he'd had with her the night before. They'd talked about many things and he'd enjoyed their conversation. She was a woman of intelligence as well as a real beauty.

Lark noticed his smile and turned abruptly away. She had to do something to stop Clay from falling in love with Veda Thorne, but she didn't know what. Could she get him to ask *her* to dinner? She rolled her eyes. *That's a joke,* she thought. At the asylum she hadn't learned how to attract a man even if she wanted to. Finally she turned back to Clay. "Tomorrow after I teach my afternoon class I'll probably see Red Beaver about the leather."

"Don't go alone. Take one of my sisters with you," said Clay.

"Maybe Hannah?" asked Lark, studying Clay for any reaction.

Clay shrugged. "Probably not Hannah. But Evie would enjoy the trip."

"Do you think Red Beaver is beneath you socially?"

"No. But for some reason Pa does, I'm sorry to say."

"That doesn't sound like your pa, does it?"

"No. No, it doesn't. I've questioned him about Red Beaver, but he won't give me a straight answer. I like Red Beaver. He's a fine Christian and he works hard and stays away from strong drink."

"Speaking of strong drink, I heard Willie Thorne is opening a tavern in Blue Creek," said Lark.

"I hope he doesn't, but I heard the same."

"I belong to the Temperance League," said Lark. "I know our group will try to stop Thorne at any cost."

"Ma said the same thing."

"Does Veda Thorne belong to the Temperance League?"

Clay flushed. He hadn't learned how Veda felt about drinking, but she didn't seem to think Willie was doing anything wrong by opening a tavern. "I don't believe she does," said

Clay stiffly. He didn't want to talk about Veda to Lark. They were two such different women but, each in her own way, both were interesting.

After Clay left, Lark walked around the cabin that had become very quiet. Even the crickets, the frogs in the creek, and the night birds were momentarily silent. In the distance Lark heard a dog. Once wolves had been in the area as well as wildcats. There were still bears and a few other dangerous wild animals, but nothing like there had been years ago. Jig had said there were even fewer rattlesnakes. A big one lived near the bog, and it frightened her every time she saw or heard it.

Lark opened the door and looked up at the twinkling stars and the sliver of moon. All the night sounds from the woods were like a special orchestra. She smiled, feeling at great peace. This was her first night ever of not having to go to bed at a set time with sounds of children shouting or laughing. She didn't have to listen fearfully for Matron's footsteps or think Matron would punish her for something she'd done by accident or neglected doing, or because she blamed her for something she didn't do.

"Heavenly Father, thank you for this wonderful haven," Lark said, smiling up at the sky.

She closed the door and lit the kerosene lamp. The smell of kerosene and smoke waved out, then disappeared. She couldn't leave the door or windows open or moths would swarm in. She sat at the table and opened her Bible to read in Ephesians. Jig had shown her how to study her Bible. She knew her faith grew when she studied and heard God's Word. She also knew she could not survive without faith and trust in God. She thought of her blessings and smiled. She knew she'd once had parents who had loved her. She'd had Jig who had loved her and taught her many, many things. Now she had a home she didn't have to share with anyone unless she chose to. She had money in the bank and the guard job she loved.

When she was too tired to keep her eyes open, she crawled into the bunk, between the clean sheets Jennet had given her.

It felt strange not to have Zoe beside her, whispering to her as long as she could stay awake. Usually they both fell asleep within minutes of going to bed, dead tired because of their long work day.

Lark turned on her side and smiled in the dark. In the morning she'd walk the pines as the hired guard. She would be paid once a month and would live in the cabin free. Jennet had said that every day she'd send fresh fruit, vegetables, and meat over to Lark. "This will be a good life," said Lark. Her voice sounded loud in the great silence.

The next morning just after dawn Lark walked out of the cabin with her revolver in a holster and her canteen strapped to her belt, her cudgel in her hand, and wearing her boots and leggings. One of Jig's old hats sat on her head. At the thought of Jig the deep ache of missing him surfaced and tears filled her eyes. She brushed them away as her lips quivered with sobs.

She glanced up toward heaven and whispered, "Heavenly Father, thank you for your comfort! I'm glad I'm your child and that you love me. You're God Almighty, yet you know all about me. You are the God of the universe, yet you watch over me. Thank You, Father! I love you! Thank you for your protection. Please take care of the Havlicks today, and help Clay to see the truth about Veda Thorne. Keep these pines safe. In Jesus' name. Amen!"

Lark's heart felt light as she walked away from the cabin toward the trail in the pines. She swung the cudgel high in the air, then caught it. It had taken her a lot of practice to use a cudgel as a weapon, but with Jig's help she'd learned.

As Lark walked along the pine needle covered path, birds twittered in the trees and a crow cawed. Frogs and peepers blended with the sounds of small animals running under the thick carpet of needles.

Lark walked up the long hill and through the briars, using the cudgel to hold them back until she had passed through. The peaceful river was flowing down below. In the distance she could see a raft floating down stream. She looked up ahead to the spot where the tree poachers had waylaid her and her nerves tightened. Was someone hiding behind the giant uprooted tree? She walked past it without a mishap, then relaxed slightly as she walked up to the northernmost tip, then on to the cutacross.

Just then some sound or smell sent a chill down Lark's spine. She slowed her steps on the narrow path and listened intently without appearing to do so. Jig had always said to act natural in case anyone was watching. She couldn't allow her actions to give away her sudden awareness of danger.

The birds were quiet and a squirrel deeper in the woods scolded loudly. Lark tightened her hand around the cudgel and rubbed her arm over the butt of her revolver. The feel of it reassured her and she walked just a little faster.

Suddenly a bear cub walked out on the path ahead of Lark. She stopped short, blood roaring in her ears. She knew the cub's mother was nearby. Lark turned slowly, studying the underbrush, the bushes, and the trunks of the trees. The sow could easily be hidden from view by the trunk of a pine. The cub stood on its hind legs and batted the air, then sniffed as if it had caught Lark's scent.

Lark took a deep breath as she silently prayed for protection and a way out of the situation. Should she leave the trail and try to walk around the cub? Lark looked across the trail to the swamp. Jig had warned her many times never to walk in that part of the swamp no matter what the time of year because she'd sink right down in it never to be seen again. He'd watched a deer disappear before his eyes. No, she couldn't take that way out.

Just then Lark heard a movement behind her. The hairs on the back of her neck stood on end. Her calico dress felt as hot as a wool coat. Slowly she glanced over her shoulder. Shivers shot up and down her spine and fear pricked her scalp. A massive black bear stood on the trail on all fours! If it weren't for the cub, Lark knew she could get away without any problem.

Black bears usually left humans alone, but they were fearless when protecting their young.

Lark looked to her left and knew she couldn't walk into the swamp, nor would the bears. Lark looked to her right. She could walk off the trail to go around the cub, but to get back she'd have to fight her way through masses of wild roses that stood ten feet high and several feet thick.

The sow roared and reared up on its hind legs. Sweat soaked Lark's skin. The bear stood almost six feet tall. It looked around, then dropped to all fours and ambled along the trail toward Lark, sniffing with a snout that resembled a pig's.

Lark frantically eased her way toward the cub who was eating grubs from under a rotted log beside the trail. The cub stood half on the trail and half off. Maybe she could get around it and run like lightning away from the bears.

"Father, thank you for your help," Lark whispered as she drew closer and closer to the cub. She glanced back and could almost feel the sow's breath on her. She knew that was her imagination. She also knew that if she started running the sow could easily overtake her. Black bear could run fast and they also could climb trees.

The cub squealed in pain. The sow roared. Lark's heart stopped, then pounded so hard she could barely breathe. Her legs felt like two stumps held fast in the ground.

The sow roared again and ran awkwardly toward Lark. Lark leaped forward, startling the cub. She ran at a dead run, brushing past the cub. The sow roared fiercely, but Lark willed herself to keep her eyes on the trail ahead. She dared not stumble and fall or the sow would be on her in a flash and tear her to pieces.

Suddenly a shot rang out, missing Lark's ear by a hair's breath. Her cudgel gripped in her hand, she dropped to the ground, playing dead until she could analyze the situation. Dust tickled her nose and she held her breath to keep from sneezing. Her canteen felt like a hard lump under her. She heard men's voices, but she didn't twitch a muscle. An ant crawled over her cheek, tickling it, but she forced herself to ignore it.

"You got her, Bub," a man said gruffly.

"Or she's playin' possum," said Bub. "Go check, Dicky."

"Not me," said Dicky. "I heard how quick she is with that club of hers."

Lark's stomach tightened and her mouth felt cotton dry. She wanted to leap up, but she knew if she moved a hair the men would shoot her dead. Silently she cried out for God's help.

"Take a rock and bash in her skull," said Bub. "We don't dare shoot again for fear somebody might hear and check it out."

Bile rose in Lark's mouth and she almost gagged. She had to make a move. She heard footsteps coming toward her. Could she spring up, disarm the man, then move quickly enough to use him as a shield against the other man's bullet?

Further up the trail Clay Havlick crept forward. He'd heard the shot and wanted to make sure Lark was safe. He'd decided to walk with her on her first day, but she'd already left when he'd arrived at the cabin. Up ahead he could see two men and Lark face down on the trail. Shivers ran down Clay's spine. Was Lark dead? Why had he agreed to let her guard the pines? Why hadn't he brought his gun?

One of the men stepped closer to Lark, a large rock in his hand. Clay's heart caught in his throat. Silently he prayed for wisdom in dealing with the frightening situation. He knew he couldn't wait a second longer. In a loud, commanding voice he cried, "Drop your weapons and get your hands up before I shoot you both!"

Lark's heart leaped at the sound of Clay's voice. She peeked through her thick lashes at the boots a short way away. She saw the boots turn and she sprang to her feet. With a quick glance she saw Clay was not armed and that the men knew it now. Lark struck the man near her with her cudgel, dropping him to the ground in a heap, then she threw the cudgel at the other man, striking his arm and sending the gun flying from his grasp.

Clay sprang forward and scooped up the gun, then aimed it at the man still standing. "Are you all right, Lark?"

"Yes." Lark felt tears rising and she forced them back.

Clay smiled shakily. His relief was so great that she was unharmed, he couldn't speak for a while. Finally he ordered, "You men walk ahead of me. Lark, you keep your gun ready in case there's a third one waiting."

Lark nodded grimly.

Several minutes later they came across two horses tied to a bush. There wasn't a sign of an axe or a crosscut. Lark frowned. "They didn't come to steal the timber," she said, suddenly shivering.

Clay jabbed one of his prisoners with his gun barrel. "What brought you fellows out here to the woods this morning?"

"Sight seein'," snapped Dicky.

"We came to take care of her," said Bub gruffly, motioning to Lark.

Lark fell back a step. "Me? Why?"

Clay's heart almost stopped. Fear stung his skin. He had sent Lark into danger! "Why do you want her dead?" asked Clay harshly.

"We don't," snapped Dicky. "We got hired to do a job."

"Shut up!" snarled Bub.

"Keep talking!" commanded Clay. "Who hired you and why?"

Lark holstered her revolver and lifted her cudgel high. "I want answers now before I use this to break some bones."

Dicky rubbed the base of his skull and Bub rubbed his arm where she'd already hit him.

"A man at the mill asked us if we wanted some extra money. We said yes and he told us to get rid of the guard," said Dicky in a defeated voice.

"What man?" snapped Clay.

"We never saw him before," said Bub. "And we didn't get his name."

"Describe him," said Lark.

Bub shrugged. "Ordinary lookin'."

Lark swung her cudgel and the men cried out, but couldn't give any more information.

"You spread the word that I'm guarding the pines and that I'm not easy to kill," said Lark grimly. "And I won't let anyone steal a single tree!"

Clay looked at Lark in admiration. She was full of a fire he hadn't noticed before. He wouldn't be able to convince her to quit the job and go back to the asylum, but when the time was right, he'd try.

Later Clay rode one horse while the two men rode double on the other. He had left Lark to finish walking the line so she could get to her other job at the asylum. Once in Blue Creek he took the men to the sheriff, then checked at the mill for someone who might've seen Dicky and Bub with a man. Nobody knew anything.

Clay walked away from the mill in defeat. He glanced toward the asylum, then headed for the warehouse. Today the lumber and tools he'd need for building the wagons were coming by train. The men were already on hand to start to work.

Later in the day Lark forced away the dangers of the morning, changed her clothes, and walked to the Havlicks to get someone to go with her to see Red Beaver. The hot sun burned through her bonnet. A grasshopper landed on her arm, then jumped off onto a tall weed.

As Lark reached the Havlick yard, Tris stepped out of the shop and ran to meet her. He wore brown pants, brown suspenders, and a tan shirt without a collar. A straw hat covered his dark hair. Lark smiled as she thought what Zoe's reaction would be if she were there.

Tris tipped his hat and smiled. "Good afternoon, Lark. Clay said you'd be coming." Tris sobered. "He told us about this morning. I wish I could've been there!"

"You like excitement, don't you?" Lark laughed, then glanced around. "Is Clay here?"

"No. He had urgent business." Tris lowered his voice. "I

happen to know it has something to do with a woman named Veda."

Lark gripped her handbag tighter. "Doesn't it bother you for him to be seeing a Thorne?"

Tris shrugged. "Some. But he thinks Veda is prime, so how can I object?"

Lark let the subject drop, but she tried again to think of a way to keep Clay from continuing to see Veda.

Tris led Lark toward the barn where the buggy was already hitched to two matching sorrel geldings. "Evie," called Tris. "Lark's here and ready to go. Evie wants to get buckskin breeches and shirt too. She thinks she'll get to guard with you like she did at times with Jig."

"But of course she can!" Lark nodded, pleased to think she could teach Evie what Jig had taught her.

Her flowered skirt flipping around her stocking covered legs, Evie ran to Lark and caught her hand. "I'm glad you're taking me with you! Hannah wanted to go too, but Pa said she couldn't."

Tris tapped Evie on the head. "Don't tell all of our secrets, Evie."

Evie tossed her head and her white-blonde braids danced around her thin shoulders. "I never tell secrets!" She climbed in the buggy and smoothed her skirt over her knees, then impatiently rubbed at her puffed sleeves. "I just might get two buckskin suits! Pa said he used to dress that way because Great-grandpa Clay did when he was a fur trader. I wish I was a fur trader."

Tris helped Lark in, then started to climb up beside her.

"You can't come with us, Tris," said Evie sharply.

"Don't be obnoxious," snapped Tris as he settled in place and picked up the reins.

Her lower lip out in a pout, Evie turned to Lark. "Tell him to stay home."

"It's all right if he goes with us," said Lark, patting Evie's hand.

Evie shook her head hard. "He'll start making eyes at you and sweet talking you like he does all the girls, then you'll forget I'm even here."

Flushing, Tris jabbed Evie. "Stop that!"

Lark laughed softly. "Evie, I know what Tris is like. You don't have to be concerned about him sweet talking me. I won't let him. I don't like that kind of thing."

"You don't?" asked Evie in relief.

"You don't?" asked Tris in surprise. "But all girls do!"

"Not us," said Evie, taking Lark's hand. "We don't like sweet talk."

"We like straight arrow men," said Lark. "Men who don't flirt. Men who love from the heart in deed as well as in word."

"Like Pa," said Evie.

His face red, Tris jumped from the buggy with a self-conscious laugh. "I won't go with you. I'm just not straight arrow enough."

"You are in your heart," said Lark softly, looking deep into Tris's eyes.

"Thank you," whispered Tris, touched more than he thought possible.

He stepped back and waved them on. Lark flicked the reins and urged the horses over the dirt road that led to the corduroy. A short time later she drove up the long lane to Red Beaver's farmyard.

Cattle grazed in a field to the north of two large red barns and sheep grazed in a pasture to the west. Turkeys, chickens, ducks, and geese walked noisily around the yard. A short white picket fence circled the comfortable looking, well-kept white farm house. Several giant oaks shaded the yard.

As Lark stepped from the buggy, Red Beaver walked from the nearest barn. He was dressed like a white man except for a rolled red and gray scarf around his forehead to hold back his straight, shoulder-length hair. He was about Clay's age, but had a medium build where Clay was tall. Lark had heard Red

Beaver was part Patawatomi and part white, what most people called a *half-breed.*

Evie jumped down beside Lark. "Hello, Red Beaver."

Red Beaver smiled. "Hello, Evie. Hi, Lark. What brings the two of you to my place?"

"We came to get tanned hides for clothing to wear in the woods," said Lark.

"I have plenty of hides," said Red Beaver. "My mother, Silent Waters, could sew your clothes if you want. She is good with a needle and very quick." He named the price and Lark quickly agreed.

They walked to the house with Evie chattering happily beside them. A turkey gobbled and a donkey brayed. Flies buzzed around a bucket of slop near the back door. Red Beaver shooed away the flies and quickly opened the door, let Lark and Evie walk in, then he followed.

With Evie close at her side Lark stopped just inside the kitchen door beside a tall white cupboard that held white dishes. A tea kettle was boiling on the cookstove, sending steam whistling out. Silent Waters sat at the round oak table, a cup in her hand. She was slender, attractive, and dressed in white woman's calico with a rolled scarf around her forehead to hold back her long black hair. She glanced at Lark and Evie, then quickly down at her cup.

Red Beaver rested his hand lightly on Silent Waters' shoulder. They both had the same high cheekbones, wide foreheads, and deep brown eyes. Red Beaver's hair had a red cast to it while Silent Waters' was so black it almost looked blue. "Mother, this is Evie and Lark. I said you would sew leather breeches and shirts for them."

"I will," said Silent Waters with a curt nod.

"Thank you," said Lark, smiling. She'd seen Silent Waters in town, but had never spoken to her before. She had heard the gossip about her being a white man's squaw and Red Beaver their child. She was a woman who kept to herself.

"I'll go back to work while you women discuss the clothing," said Red Beaver. He squeezed his mother's shoulder, smiled at Evie, and walked out.

Lark felt at a loss for words as Silent Waters sipped from her cup. Should they sit down or remain standing?

"I want to look like a fur trader just like my great-grandpa," Evie said excitedly as she walked to the table to stand across from Silent Waters.

Lark stepped to Evie's side and slipped her arm around her.

Silent Waters pushed herself up, eyeing Evie, then Lark.

"Your son said you are quick with the needle," Lark said when she couldn't think of anything else to say.

"Can you make me look like a fur trader?" asked Evie.

Silent Waters carried her cup to the dishpan at the back of the stove, dipped it in the soapy water, then faced Lark and Evie. Her eyes narrowed as she studied Evie. "Where have I seen you before?"

"I guess in town," said Evie, stepping closer to Lark.

"Where did your great-grandfather live?" asked Silent Waters sharply.

"All over lower Michigan, but his home was south of Grand Rapids," said Evie.

"He died years ago," said Lark. "You wouldn't know him."

Silent Waters flashed an impatient look at Lark. "Are you her mother?"

Lark shook her head as a shiver ran down her spine. The look on Silent Waters' face and the hatred in her eyes made her want to run to the buggy and drive quickly back to the Havlicks. Did Silent Waters hate all white people? Lark forced herself to say, "I'm Lark Baritt from the Orphan Asylum."

Silent Waters glared at Lark. "*You* I have seen in the pines where my grandfather's people once lived. You were with the old woodsman, Jig."

"I didn't know anyone ever lived in those woods," said Evie.

Silent Waters drew herself up haughtily. "We lived there

from the beginning of time. But the white man stole it from us."

"We didn't steal anything," said Evie sharply. "My great-grandfather bought it."

"And who is your great-grandfather?" asked Silent Waters sharply.

"Clay Havlick," said Evie, smiling proudly. "My big brother was named after him."

Silent Waters' face darkened with rage. "You leave my house now! I will not sew for a Havlick! Havlicks are evil!"

Lark gasped in surprise.

"Havlicks are not evil!" cried Evie, shaking her head hard.

"Evil! Wicked!" snapped Silent Waters. She shook her finger at Evie. "Get out of my house and never step foot in here again!"

Evie burst into tears and ran from the house.

Lark started to follow her, then whipped back around. "How could you hurt her? She hasn't done anything to you!"

"She's a Havlick!" spat out Silent Waters.

"She's an innocent child!"

"She's a Havlick!"

"But they're respected people in the community. They wouldn't harm anyone."

Silent Waters doubled her fists at her sides. Her breast rose and fell. "Freeman Havlick ruined my man! Freeman Havlick broke up my home!"

Lark stared at Silent Waters in shock. Free was never cruel. "What are you talking about?" asked Lark weakly.

"My man, Willie Thorne!"

Lark bit back a cry of surprise.

"Willie Thorne is father to Red Beaver, but Willie walked away from us and married a white woman to be part of the social community. He wanted to compete with Freeman Havlick!" Silent Waters spit the words out as if they'd been locked inside her for a long time.

Lark's head spun with what she'd learned. Did Free know

Red Beaver was Willie's son? Was that why he kept Hannah from Red Beaver?

Silent Waters jerked open the door. "Get out and don't set foot inside my house again!"

Trembling, Lark walked past Silent Waters, then ran to the buggy. She wanted to leave as quickly as possible. She stopped short. Evie wasn't in the buggy! Did Red Beaver have the same anger as his mother, and had he taken it out on Evie? Lark cupped her hands around her mouth and called, "Evie! Where are you?"

With a laugh, Evie stepped from the barn with Red Beaver beside her.

Lark ran to her and caught her hand in a tight grip. "Why didn't you go to the buggy?"

"She wanted to see the donkey," said Red Beaver. "She is safe with me."

Lark relaxed. She should've realized Red Beaver wouldn't harm anyone, not even a Havlick.

"You're my friend, aren't you, Red Beaver?" said Evie.

Red Beaver pulled a beaded band from his pocket and tied it around Evie's forehead. "We're friends forever. This will prove it to everyone."

"Thank you," said Evie in awe.

"If you ever need me, I'll come," said Red Beaver as if he were swearing a pact with Evie.

Evie pulled a pink ribbon off the tip of her braid and tied it around Red Beaver's wrist. "We are friends forever! If you ever need me, I'll come," she said as seriously as he had.

Lark smiled. Would Freeman Havlick object to the pact between Willie Thorne's son and his little daughter?

CHAPTER 5

♦ Late in June on a Wednesday after Lark finished teaching deportment, she walked to the only dress shop in Blue Creek. Sally Smith, a girl her age who Lark had seen in church, was the clerk. Lark knew she could trust Sally to help her find what she needed. She pushed open the door and the bell tinkled. The store smelled like new fabric and wild roses.

"Hello, Sally," said Lark with a hesitant smile. She'd never in her life bought a dress already made.

"Lark!" Sally was short and plump with a wide nose and mouth. She was kind to everyone and always thought the best of others. "What brings you in? Not that I'm not glad to see you! It's just you've never been here before."

Lark laughed. "I came to buy a nice dress."

"That's wonderful! What kind of dress?" Sally waved her hand around at the different displays. "Do you see anything that interests you?" Sally's voice dropped to a whisper. "How much do you want to spend?"

"I really don't know. You show me what the latest fashion is," said Lark. "I want to look like Hannah Havlick does when she's dressed up."

Sally showed Lark several ready made dresses, shirtwaists,

and skirts. Finally Lark chose a puffed-sleeved shirtwaist of medium green and white print with a black background and a black silk moire skirt lined with silk-finished taffeta and interlined throughout with canvas and extra fine velvet binding. Sally tied a hip-pad bustle on Lark, then helped her on with the waist and skirt. Lark marveled at the way the skirt hung straight down in front and swept wide in back. She stared at the puffed sleeves, the high collar, and the bustle.

"It looks so different from my old limp calico!" whispered Lark, hardly believing she was the attractive woman in the looking glass.

"The skirt has a full four-and-a-half yard sweep. It looks handsome on you, especially with that waist." Sally handed Lark a pair of fine kid shoes. "These will be perfect with it."

Lark pulled off her high top shoes and slipped on the others. How dainty her feet looked peeking from beneath the skirt!

Sally swept Lark's hair up and pinned it on top of her head. "See how wonderful you look? You're gorgeous!"

Lark wished it were so. "I'm as plain as a post, and we both know it, Sally. But these clothes do help."

"Here's a hat that would be perfect on you." Sally held up a small, medium green hat with three black feathers.

Lark tried it on, then gasped. She didn't look like Lark Baritt, the orphan! She looked as if she'd come from the Havlick's household. She pinned the hat in place and turned to Sally with a laugh. "I'll take it. I'll take the skirt and the waist and the shoes and the hat. And even the hip-pad bustle!" Lark patted her flushed cheeks. "And I'll leave them on and wear them home."

Sally laughed. "Good for you! You'll turn heads just like Hannah Havlick does."

Lark flushed with pleasure. "I don't know about that, but I do feel elegant." She thought of the money in her handbag and laughed breathlessly at her daring decision. "Sally, I want some other things too."

Lark bought a small looking glass, two fancy combs for her

hair, stockings, a flowered nightgown with a matching robe—the first new nightgown and robe she'd ever owned, a plain white shirtwaist, and a dark blue skirt. Sally showed her a variety of underclothing and she added some to her pile.

"That will be $22.50," said Sally.

Lark pressed her hand to her racing heart. She'd never spent that much money in her entire life.

"If you want to put something back, you may," said Sally softly.

"No. I can pay for it." Lark pulled out some of the money Jig had given her. How she longed to show him what she'd bought! Would he think she looked pretty all dressed up?

Lark handed the money to Sally, then silently watched as she wrapped the selections in paper and tied them securely. Lark considered throwing away her old dress, then decided to use it for a rag. She chuckled. A few days ago she had about one dollar to her name, now she was rich enough to buy ready made clothes.

A few minutes later Lark walked outdoors, the bundle in her arms and her head held high. Just then Clay Havlick left the bank and they almost collided. He tipped his straw hat and smiled, then his mouth dropped open. "Lark?"

She laughed breathlessly. "It's me, Clay."

"You look fantastic!" He couldn't believe this was the same Lark Baritt.

"Thank you." Lark flushed with pleasure. She was glad he'd seen her. It was as much a shock to him as it had been to her.

"Forgive my rude stare, but I can't get over it. I don't think I can let you guard the pines after seeing you like this."

Lark frowned. "I'm still the same woman, Clay Havlick! Clothes don't change who or what I am!"

"No . . . no, I realize that. I'm just . . . well . . . taken back." Clay ran a finger under his white collar, then checked to see that his dark blue plaid suit coat was buttoned.

"I'd better be going," said Lark, but she didn't move.

"Do you know Abe Nester?"

"Yes. His farm is near Red Beaver's." Lark considered telling Clay what had happened to them at Red Beaver's farm, then dismissed the thought.

"He has a Dalmatian for sale. I thought you might like him. He's a beautiful dog."

Lark had always wanted a big spotted Dalmatian. "I'll check into it."

"We could both go right now," said Clay. "My buggy's there." He motioned to the buggy and the gray mares hitched to it.

Lark hesitated only a fraction of a minute. "Let's go."

Clay took Lark's bundle and stuck it under the seat, then handed her in. She seemed small and frail and feminine. When he walked around the buggy and climbed into the driver's seat, she sat stiffly beside him, her hands clasped in her lap over her handbag. The canvas top of the buggy blocked the sun from her. Clay drove the team down Main Street, over the bridge, and onto the corduroy that led past Nester's farm.

For once Clay was at a loss for words with Lark. She seemed like an elegant, attractive stranger, not the little ragged orphan who'd hung around Jig. Lark peeked under dark lashes at Clay. She couldn't understand why he was suddenly so quiet.

She looked out at the farmland they passed that once had been the growing place of giant white pines. Jig had told her that before the lumbering began the entire area had been covered with trees. Off in the distance she could see a section of small pines about thirty years old. Jig had said it took eighty years for a pine to grow enough to be harvested for lumber.

Clay turned into Abe Nester's drive and stopped outside the fence near the barn. Nester walked out of his barn, wrapping his big, work-roughened hands around his wide blue suspenders. "How do, Clay. And who's the fine lady with you? A stranger in these parts?"

Lark laughed. "It's me, Lark Baritt. You know me."

Nester's eyes almost popped out of his head. "Well, I'll be dad-blasted! You clean up real good."

"Thank you," said Lark. She sat still in the buggy until Clay held up his hand to help her out. She stepped to the ground and stood with Clay. She thought they looked like they'd both just stepped from a catalog.

"We came for a Dalmatian for Lark," said Clay. He explained that Lark had taken over Jig's job as guard. "We want a dog that'll be of help to her."

"I got just the one," said Nester, nodding hard. "His name's *Sears* because he was always a tearin' up the wife's wish book when he was a pup. She swore she'd get rid of him first chance she got. He's trained well and would be a right good dog for Lark."

"Bring him out and we'll take a look at him," said Clay.

The *we* wrapped around Lark's heart and set her pulse fluttering. She couldn't look at Clay for fear he'd see her reaction. She watched Nester walk to his kennel, calling to Sears. He came back with a wide chested, spotted dog with pointed ears slightly flopped over. The minute Lark saw Sears, she knew he was the dog for her. She held out her hand and Sears licked it, then wagged his tail hard. She took his head between her hands and pressed her forehead to his. He wriggled all over, squirming until he was able to lick her face.

Clay paid for Sears and Lark stiffened. She would not allow Clay to pay for Sears and lay claim to him because of that.

"He's a fine dog," said Nester as he put Sears in the buggy.

"I'm sure he is," said Lark, holding her hand out to Sears. The dog sniffed her and flipped his white rope of a tail. Lark scratched Sears around the ears and down his spotted side.

"You got a friend for life," said Nester with a chuckle.

They said their goodbyes and Clay handed Lark into the buggy. When they were out of earshot Lark said, "I'll pay for Sears from Jig's money."

"No need," said Clay with a quick look at her. For some reason it had pleased him a lot to buy Sears for Lark.

Lark took a deep breath. "Clay, I will not allow you to pay for my dog! It's not your place to buy him for me."

"My place?"

"You're not my husband or my beau!" Lark flushed scarlet.

"Nor will I ever be!" snapped Clay, suddenly angry. "I gave you a gift and you throw it in my face."

"I didn't mean it that way," she said stiffly. "I just know I don't want you to pay for Sears."

"I can't imagine why."

"I don't want you to!"

"That's not a good reason," Clay said impatiently.

Lark lifted her chin stubbornly. "But that's the way I want it."

"You are a stubborn woman, Lark Baritt!" Clay slapped the reins on the team and they stepped forward so fast the buggy rocked hard, sending Lark bouncing against Clay. She flung her arm around him and gripped his muscled arm to keep from flying out of the buggy. Her touch burned into him, sending a shock through his body like he'd never felt before.

Her face on fire, Lark pulled away from Clay and braced her feet to keep from touching him again.

Even after she had righted herself, Clay felt the warmth and softness of her body. Finally he said, "Have it your way. You pay for Sears."

"Thank you," Lark said weakly.

They didn't speak again until Clay drove past Red Beaver's farm. "Did you and Evie get your tanned leather?" Clay asked in what he hoped was a normal voice.

"His mother refused to sew for us," said Lark.

Clay shot Lark a surprised look. "Why?"

Lark started to tell Clay, then shrugged. "She just said she wouldn't, that's all." Maybe he didn't know Red Beaver was Willie Thorne's son. She didn't know if she should tell him. "Are you as prejudiced against Indians as your pa?"

"No, I'm not prejudiced against Indians or anyone else. I

don't believe whites and Indians should marry each other, but I'm not prejudiced."

Lark bit back a sharp answer. He sounded prejudiced to her.

Clay drove Lark to the cabin and helped her stake out Sears until he got used to his new home. "I'll bring a dog house over tomorrow," he said, his voice quite stiff and formal.

"Thank you," said Lark, her voice equally stiff and formal.

Clay smiled. "I was almost afraid to offer."

Lark chuckled. "I'll pay for it."

Clay threw up his hands and let them fall in defeat. "I might've known."

Lark reached for her bundle under the buggy seat, but Clay took it from her and carried it into the cabin.

"Thank you," said Lark.

Clay tipped his straw hat and smiled. "You're very welcome."

Her eyes locked with his and she couldn't move or speak. His heart fluttered strangely. Abruptly he strode to his buggy, flicked the reins, and drove rapidly across the field to the Havlick farm.

Lark stood in the cabin doorway and watched Clay until he disappeared from sight behind a cluster of oaks. Sears barked and Lark dragged her gaze off Clay to see about her dog.

Several minutes later Lark stood at her table and unwrapped the bundle she'd brought from the asylum. She took a deep breath and once again looked through her things. She re-read the letters her mother had written to her father, then studied the photos a long time. Was her father alive or dead? If he was alive, why hadn't he come for her? How could she know if he was alive or dead? What steps could she take to find out? Maybe John Epson would know since he was a lawyer.

The next morning after her trip around the trail she hurried to the asylum, dressed in the new white waist and blue skirt. As she stepped inside the asylum, Matron was walking down the hall.

"May I help you, ma'am?" asked Matron with a polite smile. Then she recognized Lark and her face hardened. "Lark Baritt! My, aren't we putting on airs."

"Good morning, Matron," said Lark, determined not to lose her temper or be hurt by the cutting words.

"Jennet Havlick is in my office to see you," said Matron. "I allowed her to meet you there today, but don't let it happen again."

"What does she want of me?"

"Something about the Temperance League."

Lark knew Matron was totally against drinking liquor. "Did you hear Willie Thorne is opening a tavern on Main Street across from the dress shop? In fact, it's today!" Lark hadn't realized the time had crept up on her. She'd been too busy thinking about her own life and what was happening to her.

Matron clicked her tongue and shook her head. "We'll have him out by next week if I have anything to say about it! I'll set the children making posters to hang around town and a big one to stand right in front of his place."

"That's a good idea." Lark followed Matron to her office.

Jennet stood and walked forward. "Lark! You look wonderful!"

Lark blushed. "It feels good to have nice clothes."

"Clothes do make a nice covering, but Lark, we both know clothes can't change the person," said Jennet, squeezing Lark's hands. "You're the same fine young lady no matter how you dress."

Lark tipped her head slightly in agreement. She knew she was the same, only it did help her self-confidence to look better.

"I suppose we'd better get to the business at hand," said Jennet.

"Please have a seat," Matron said as she walked behind her desk, her black skirts billowing out behind her.

Lark sat on the chair beside Jennet and waited expectantly.

"We must discuss how to get the tavern out of town," said Jennet with a frown.

"I say one of the first steps to take is having a talk with Mayor Greene. How is it he agreed to give Willie Thorne a permit to have a tavern? It's in the bylaws of Blue Creek to be a dry town."

"That's a very good point, Anna," said Jennet.

Lark knew Jennet was the only person ever to call Matron by her given name.

"My husband has already spoken to Willie Thorne, but it didn't do any good. We'll contact Mayor Greene yet today," said Jennet as she jotted down a note on the pad of paper on her lap.

"I think we of the Temperance League should go right to Willie Thorne too," said Matron crisply.

"And his wife," said Lark, suddenly thinking about her promise to Jig. Maybe she could learn something from Mrs. Thorne about Willie's plan for Veda to marry Clay as well as learn Mrs. Thorne's feeling about the tavern. She'd read in the newspaper that other tavern owners' wives belonged to the Temperance League. Maybe Mrs. Thorne could help stop Willie from opening the tavern.

"Good," said Jennet, nodding. "Lark, you visit Agnes Thorne. Take someone with you if you want. Anna, you take a couple of women and visit Willie Thorne. I'll find someone to go with me and we'll see the mayor." Jennet stood to her feet, smiled goodbye, and walked out.

Lark glanced at Matron, and walked out, too, before any argument. She'd see Mrs. Thorne first, and then she'd come back to work.

A few minutes later at the Thornes' the maid answered the door. Lark gasped in surprise. It was Gert, the woman who had once been the housekeeper at the asylum. She was short and plump and wore a black apron over a gray dress and a black cap. She didn't look any older than when she and her husband,

Ray,had left the asylum six years ago. "Gert! It's good to see you! I thought you were in Grand Rapids."

"Lark Baritt, I believe!" Gert hugged Lark, then stepped back from her. Tears filled Gert's eyes. "You look like a real lady! It looks like Matron let you have some of the money left to you."

Lark gasped. "What money, Gert?"

Gert clamped her hand over her small round mouth.

"Please, tell me! I got my photos and papers and baby clothes, but there wasn't any money."

Gert fingered the brooch at her high collar. "It's not for me to say, Lark. But I will anyway! Matron does like to help herself to money not logged in. To my knowledge yours wasn't, and she more than likely took it and used it herself."

"How much was it?"

"That I don't know. But it was enough to keep you clothed and fed until your father could come get you."

Lark sagged against the heavy front door. "My father?" she whispered.

"Matthew Baritt. He was a naturalist and also worked in the lumber camps. He couldn't tend you, so he left you at the asylum to be taken care of."

"Where is he now?" whispered Lark.

"Last I heard he was in the Upper Peninsula, I believe."

"How could I get in touch with him?"

Gert frowned thoughtfully. "You might send a letter to Brackton at Driscoll's lumber camp. That might reach him."

"I'll do it," said Lark, barely breathing. Things were moving so fast she could hardly take it in.

"Are you all right, Lark?" asked Gert in concern.

"I don't know." Lark looked around the hallway, then remembered why she'd come. "Gert, I do thank you for the information. I almost forgot why I came."

"Did you come to call on Miss Veda?"

"Is she here?"

"No. You just missed her."

"I really came to see Agnes Thorne."

"Oh, I don't know," said Gert, suddenly nervous.

"Is there a problem?" asked Lark softly.

"She's in one of her vacant moods," said Gert. She lowered her voice. "I don't ever tell folks that, but I guess I can tell you. She's got a lot of strain on her what with that husband of hers treating her bad, I believe."

"I'm sorry about that."

"Me too. Mrs. Thorne is a nice lady. Gentle. Not like that Veda and Mr. Thorne. If I was a judging person, I'd say they're bad to the heart."

"Does Mrs. Thorne object to the tavern Willie Thorne is opening?"

"Yes, when she's in her right mind. But he doesn't care a whit about her feelings. He says he'll open it, and he will." Gert wrung her plump hands and looked ready to cry. "Me and my man don't drink and no liquor will ever touch our lips. If we could work somewhere else, we'd leave the Thornes tomorrow."

"You could go back to the asylum to work."

"Not as long as Matron is there," said Gert, shaking her head hard. "My man won't go back either. She accused him of selling a cow and keeping the money. No, he won't go back either."

"I'm sorry. You were always good with us kids."

"I never had none of my own, so you all became mine."

Lark brushed a strand of hair off her cheek and glanced toward the open door and the wide stairs. "May I please speak with Mrs. Thorne. I won't do anything to hurt her."

Gert nervously smoothed her black apron and touched the black cap covering most of her gray hair. "I suppose you can sit with her a while. But when she's in her vacant mood she doesn't talk to anyone."

"That's all right," said Lark. She had to try to speak to her anyway about Veda, about the tavern, and about the plans for Clay and Veda and the white pines.

Gert led Lark up the polished stairs to the first door on the right. The room was spotlessly clean and smelled like a flower garden. Agnes Thorne sat at the open window in a blue overstuffed armchair. The hot sun streamed in over her embroidery work and the breeze ruffled her gray hair. She looked up vacantly, then bent back over her work.

Gert fluffed a blue flowered pillow beside Mrs. Thorne and drew her footstool an inch closer to her chair. "Mrs. Thorne, dear, this is Lark Baritt. I've known her since she was little. She came to visit you."

"Hello, Mrs. Thorne." Lark smiled down at the woman, then turned to Gert. "I can sit with her if you have an errand you want to run."

"I do have some things I need to do. But it's asking too much of you to stay, I believe."

"I offered, Gert." Lark hugged Gert and turned her toward the door. "Come back in an hour."

"Thank you, Lark. You've always been such a dear!" Gert beamed with pleasure as she hurried out.

Her nerve ends jangling, Lark pulled a heavy oak armchair with a high back across the flowered carpet. She set it in front of Agnes Thorne next to her footstool, then sat down with her hands folded in her lap over her small pocketbook. She tried to appear calm.

"Mrs. Thorne, I want to speak to you about . . . Veda . . . and about Willie Thorne." Lark watched for a movement from Mrs. Thorne. None came.

"I promised my friend Jig that I'd save Clay Havlick and save the white pines. Does your husband still plan to lumber the Havlicks' pines?" Lark waited, but still there was no sign that Mrs. Thorne heard.

"Is Veda going to try to marry Clay to get the pines for Willie Thorne?" Again Lark waited, but Mrs. Thorne continued to embroider.

"Maybe Silent Waters would know," Lark said softly.

Suddenly Agnes Thorne jerked and her hands grew quiet on

her wooden hoop. Lark's heart raced. She'd said something that got through! She leaned forward and said, "Silent Waters. Willie Thorne's squaw."

Agnes Thorne looked up at Lark. "What does Silent Waters know of love?" Mrs. Thorne said sharply.

Lark almost jumped out of her skin. "I don't know. What does Silent Waters know of love?"

Mrs. Thorne flung her embroidery from her and jumped to her feet. "She knows nothing! If she did she would never have let Willie take her baby from her and give her to me!"

Lark pressed her hand to her heart. "What baby?" she whispered.

"Veda. My baby! But Silent Waters named her Laughing Eyes. Veda thinks she was born to me. That's what Willie wants her to think." Mrs. Thorne tapped her small bosom. Her black sateen wrapper with a small pointed collar made her skin look washed out and sickly. "Born to me? Ha! I couldn't have babies. Couldn't have babies!" Mrs. Thorne dashed away a tear. "But Silent Waters could. She had Red Beaver, then she had Veda."

Lark sat in speechless silence.

Mrs. Thorne tore at her gray hair, then dropped her hands to her sides, leaving her hair in wild disarray. "Willie Thorne was married to me, but he visited Silent Waters often." Mrs. Thorne folded her arms across her thin breast and rocked back and forth, back and forth on her heels. "Do you know how that made me feel? I wanted to kill both of them!" She spread her hands hopelessly. "But what could I do? I'm only a weak woman."

Lark knew Mrs. Thorne didn't expect an answer, and she didn't give one for fear of stopping the flow of words.

"Veda was born. Laughing Eyes." Mrs. Thorne moaned. "Willie loved her to distraction. He couldn't bear to be apart from her, but he couldn't go live with his squaw and still have the respect he wanted. So he brought her child to me." Mrs. Thorne tugged at her collar as if it was too tight against her wrinkled throat. "We lived in Grand Rapids and he took Veda from Silent Waters and he brought her to me. As a gift! A *gift!*"

"Does Veda know?"

"No! Willie says no one can know. He and I and, of course, Silent Waters know, but no one else." Mrs. Thorne stared through the window for a long time. A fly buzzed at the glass; the house creaked. "I'd been ill. So Willie just told everyone I had given birth to Veda. We hired a wet nurse to tend her. We raised her as ours."

Lark's breathing was so shallow she felt as if she couldn't get air into her lungs. "What did Silent Waters do?"

Mrs. Thorne turned to face Lark. She looked dead. "She came to take Veda, but Willie wouldn't let her. He said if she didn't leave us alone, he'd take Red Beaver from her too. So, she left us alone until we moved back here."

"Why did you move?" Lark waited, not moving, not blinking an eye.

"So Willie can destroy Freeman Havlick."

"How?" whispered Lark.

Mrs. Thorne sank to her chair and locked her hands in her lap. "He told Veda she must marry Clay Havlick, get the pines, and let him lumber them. Destroying the pines will destroy the Havlicks."

Lark knew it would hurt them deeply, but it wouldn't destroy them. "Can't you stop your husband and your daughter?"

"No, I can't. I'm too weak to do anything," Mrs. Thorne whispered.

"I'll help you," said Lark softly.

"You will?" Mrs. Thorne studied Lark questioningly. "But why?"

"Because I promised Jig I would do what it takes to save Clay Havlick and the pines."

"You can't do it. Willie is too strong for you too."

"No. I have the Almighty God helping me."

Tears spilled down Mrs. Thorne's pale cheeks. "What will

Willie do if he doesn't get his own way this time?"

"He will move away."

"He will keep trying. I know him."

"We'll pray for God to show us a way to stop him," said Lark softly.

"Yes. Pray. I once prayed. But it's been so long!"

"It's never too late to start again," said Lark. "Talk to God. He'll help you. He's always with you, Mrs. Thorne. He has comfort and peace for you. Just receive it from him."

Mrs. Thorne leaned back in her chair and closed her eyes.

Just then the door opened and Gert walked in. She looked flustered. "Willie Thorne just got home, Lark. You must leave before he sees you."

"Yes. Leave," said Agnes Thorne weakly.

Lark squeezed Mrs. Thorne's hand. "God is with you. Don't forget!"

Mrs. Thorne picked up her embroidery without answering.

Gert tugged on Lark's arm. "Hurry! Go out the kitchen door so Willie won't see you. Come with me. I'll show you the way."

Lark's stomach knotted as she followed Gert. And it stayed knotted long after she had slipped out of Willie Thorne's house through the kitchen door. She didn't breathe easily until she was almost at the asylum. As she walked along the dirt road all that Mrs. Thorne had revealed came back piece by piece until she sorted out the whole sordid story. She closed her eyes and moaned. Somehow she would have to think of a way to save Clay and the pines. She didn't have a moment to lose. Then she remembered what Gert had said about her father.

All thoughts of Clay and the pines left Lark's head as she wondered if her father was still alive. "If he is, how can I find him?" she whispered hoarsely.

CHAPTER

6

♦ After a fine supper that he couldn't enjoy, Willie Thorne paced his front room, his hands clenched at his sides, his graying red head bent. His dark suit fit snug across his shoulders and thickening waist. He'd always wanted to be tall and muscled like Free Havlick. Oh, how he despised Freeman Havlick! He seemed to have it all—an inheritance, a good wife, six children he could be proud of, and respect. Willie had a wife he didn't love and two children by a squaw.

Willie's pulse quickened as he thought of Silent Waters; then he frowned. How could he still love her? She was Patawatomi! With her he'd been able to relax and enjoy living without thinking about getting rich or making a name for himself. But that wasn't the real world. In the real world he had to have a name and he had to have wealth.

When he was young he'd been the timber walker for George Meeker, a lumberman without scruples. Willie smiled as he thought of those exciting days. He had been paid well to find the timber Meeker lumbered, and had been paid even better when he managed to find a way to get trees that another walker had already marked for someone else. Free Havlick had walked the woods with him to learn the business, but when Free had seen how dishonest he and Meeker were, he'd quit. Willie doubled his fists and narrowed his eyes in anger. Later Free had told what he'd learned about Willie, and from then on he hadn't been able to work in the lumber business.

He'd tried many things and finally had settled on living off Agnes and bootlegging liquor whenever possible. He'd already gone through most of Agnes's inheritance. She didn't know it yet, but soon she would. He'd tried to keep the truth from her. He didn't want Agnes or Veda to know how destitute they really were. It looked now that he'd be forced to tell her, unless he could get his hands on some money very soon.

The only way he knew to get rich quickly was to get Clay Havlick's trees and lumber them. Then he'd be *rich*. Then everyone in town would look up to him. Then he'd have the respect he deserved. He'd planned to open a tavern in order to tide him over until his plans could work out, but the Temperance League had delayed that and made him lose money. He slammed his fist into his palm and swore under his breath. Somehow he had to speed up his plans to lumber the Havlicks' white pines.

He'd tried stealing a few trees at a time during the past few years, but Jig had stopped him, and now Lark Baritt was standing in the way. But he'd get rid of her soon. No orphan girl was going to keep him from those trees. Still just getting rid of her wouldn't be enough. Stealing a tree or two now and then was not the answer. He needed to get *all* the trees.

For several months he'd toyed with the idea of having Veda marry young Havlick to get at the pines. Finally he'd concluded it was the only answer and without much trouble had convinced Veda to entice Clay into marriage. She didn't have to stay with him if she didn't want to, but she needed to get him to fall for her, and she needed to get him to give her the pines. Her charms seemed to be working on young Clay. Soon he'd get those trees—all of them. Soon he'd get the wealth he deserved.

Willie stopped at the wide window and looked out on the

flower gardens and the lush sweep of green lawn. He'd paid a small down payment on the place and struggled to make the bank payments each month. The price was much more than he could afford, but he'd had to keep up appearances. He growled deep in his throat. Free Havlick owed him for ruining his name and forcing him to live off a wealthy wife. "He'll pay for it all," muttered Willie as he paced from the sofa to the tall plant near the door and back to the overstuffed chairs.

Just then the door opened and Veda walked in. Her white and green shirtwaist was tucked in at her narrow waist. A silver and sapphire brooch was pinned at the high collar. Her dark skirt hung down straight in front and poofed out in the back over her bustle. Her dark eyes lit up as she smiled at Willie. "I wondered where you were, Papa."

Willie pulled her close and held her tightly. She was so much like Silent Waters he wondered how Veda could not notice. But she had no idea Agnes wasn't her real mother, so she wasn't looking.

"You are as beautiful as ever, Veda," said Willie against the rich auburn hair that smelled like lilac. He held her from him and studied her oval face, wide dark eyes, and perfectly shaped red lips. He and Silent Waters had produced a beautiful daughter! He pushed the thought aside and smiled. "Have you seen Clay today?"

"No." Veda pouted prettily. "He was too busy today, *again*. He isn't as easy to conquer as other men I've admired."

"He has his mind on his wagon business, but you keep at it. One of these days he'll see what a fine woman you are."

"Papa, are you sure you want me to marry him?"

Willie caught Veda's smooth, well-shaped hands in his. "He will make a fine husband for you, Veda. His family has a name and they have wealth. You'll want for nothing when you're his wife."

"I do think he's a fine looking man," said Veda. "And I could learn to care for him."

"Good girl!"

"Are you sure he'll want to give me the pines as a wedding gift?"

"Veda, since when has any man denied you anything?"

Veda laughed, then sobered. "Won't he hate me when I sign the pines over to you?"

Willie shrugged. "He might for a while, but with his Christian upbringing, he'll get over it. He won't hold a grudge or stay angry."

"I hope you're right, Papa." Veda kissed Willie's cheek, then sat on the edge of the sofa with her hands folded in her lap. Her dark skirt fell in graceful folds to the carpeted floor. "Already Clay and I have been out to supper several times since I rode the train with him last month. Tomorrow night we're going out again. But I don't know how to make him even consider marriage."

"Then you bring it up, Veda. You can do it without seeming to be forward. But you must act quickly. I've seen Clay with Lark Baritt on a few occasions. She doesn't have your grace or beauty, but she's a woman to reckon with. John Epson says she has a quality about her that's most attractive."

Veda waved her hand impatiently. "Lark Baritt is not competition for me even though she has learned to dress well!"

"Just be aware of her." Willie started to run his fingers through his carefully groomed hair, thought better of it, then dropped his hand at his side. "You talk marriage with Clay Havlick tomorrow night."

Veda nodded, then looked thoughtfully at Willie. "Maybe you should give up your plan for lumbering the pines."

Willie shook his head as he forced back his anger. Veda was the only person alive who could question his actions without knowing the sharp side of his tongue. "I told you I won't. *We must have them!*"

Veda sighed heavily. "Then I will do all I can to see that you get them."

The grandfather clock in the hall bonged seven times, and Willie glanced out the window just as a buggy stopped in the drive. "John Epson is coming to talk business. Don't let him turn your head with his sweet talk."

Veda laughed softly. "He is a fine man, but I wouldn't marry any man you didn't approve of."

"Spoken like a true daughter," said Willie as he kissed Veda, then sent her out of the room. He couldn't let even Veda know about the plans he and John Epson were making against the Havlicks.

The next evening in the best restaurant in Blue Creek just after ordering the salmon dinner, Clay smiled across the table at Veda Thorne. Her auburn hair was piled becomingly on her well-shaped head. She was tall and slender and wore a floral design, black grenadine dress lined with yellow taffeta. Every time she moved he heard the soft rustle of the taffeta. There was something about the way she looked at him tonight that stirred his blood and made him very aware of her.

"You look very beautiful tonight, Veda," said Clay softly. He'd never said that to a woman before, so the words didn't slip off his tongue easily like they would have Tris's.

"Thank you, Clay." Veda smiled as she leaned slightly forward. "I know I'm not supposed to say this, but you look very handsome tonight. Any woman would be proud to have you as a companion."

Clay flushed and suddenly felt like a schoolboy. "Thank you." He wanted to run his finger around his stiff white collar and straighten his tie, but he kept his hands in his lap. Building the wagons was going so smoothly that Clay felt more relaxed than he had in a long time. Even Pa was starting to think he could meet the deadline.

"I still can't believe you're unattached, Clay." Veda widened her dark eyes and smiled. "I'm sure all the young ladies of the area have been making eyes at you. You're a fine looking, strong, intelligent man."

Clay liked to hear flattery, but he wasn't used to a woman saying nice things to him. Women usually stayed away from him. Ma said it was because he was too formal and unapproachable. He wanted to reach out and run his finger down Veda's smooth, rosy cheek. He wanted to cup her face in his hands and kiss her full lips. He hadn't kissed a girl since the time he'd stolen a kiss from Tillie Rousch when he was sixteen. Tris couldn't count the number of girls he'd kissed, and Miles already had kissed quite a few. Suddenly Clay wanted more from life than working hard all day at the Wagon Works. His business was important, but he didn't want it to be his whole life.

"I'm glad you had time for me tonight, Clay," said Veda in a low husky voice. "I hope we can do it again."

"Tomorrow night," said Clay quickly before he lost his nerve.

Veda nodded, looking very pleased. "Tomorrow night. I would invite you home, but you know Papa would be very angry with me. I have to sneak out of the house to meet you." Veda patted her cheeks, then folded her hands in her lap. "Maybe you could invite me to your home sometime."

Clay hesitated, then nodded. "I'll see Ma about it."

"I know it's hard on your family because I'm Willie Thorne's daughter." Veda sighed heavily. "I trust that someday they'll accept me for myself like you have."

"They will in time," said Clay. But would they? Just then he glanced across the dining room and caught sight of Lark at a table with Zoe Cheyney. Lark was listening intently to Zoe but glanced up. Before Clay could look away, his eyes locked with hers. He felt as if he'd been caught with his hand in the cookie jar. He frowned and forced his attention back to Veda.

"Is something wrong, Clay?" asked Veda, glancing around.

Clay shook his head as he rubbed his damp palms on his pant legs. "Not a thing." Why was he so upset all at once? He glanced toward the kitchen. "I wonder what's taking the waiter so long."

"It doesn't bother me a whit." Veda sipped her water, then daintily patted her lips with her white linen napkin. "Time passes quickly when I'm with you. You always know just what to say and how to treat me. You make my heart beat faster and leave me light-headed."

He smiled, but didn't feel as good about her flattery as he had before he noticed Lark watching him, condemning him for spending time with a Thorne. "How do you feel about your father opening a tavern here in town?" Now, why had he asked that? He hadn't planned to, but seeing Lark had flustered him.

Veda lifted a slender shoulder and let it fall. "I can't stop Papa from starting a business. I'm against strong drink, of course, but Papa won't let me stop him."

Clay breathed easier. "I thought you'd be against it. I know the Temperance League stopped him for a while."

"I know. So does Papa, but he's ready to fight for his rights. He said the men around here are buying their liquor somewhere, so it might as well be from him."

Clay didn't feel like arguing the point. He was glad to see the waiter bring the plates of food and serve first Veda, then him. Steam rose from the salmon, sending out an aroma that made him realize he was very hungry.

Across the restaurant Zoe leaned toward Lark and whispered, "Why don't you walk over and say hello to Clay?"

Lark shook her head, sipped from her glass of water, and dabbed her lips with her napkin as her thoughts returned to her father. He was never far from her mind since Gert had told her in great detail about him. She'd said he was Matt Baritt, a man working his way up in the logging business. Lark laid her napkin in her lap and absently rubbed her hand over it. She'd sent off a carefully worded letter just after she'd spoken to Gert and had finally received a letter from Grant Evans in Saginaw, a man she'd never heard of, who said Brackton from Driscoll's lumber camp had forwarded her letter to him. He said Matt Baritt had worked for him five years ago after leaving the Upper Peninsula. Mr. Evans had suggested she contact Lucas Gotia in Grayling and had given her the man's address, but she'd been too impatient to send a letter. She had run to the telegraph office and had sent a telegram. That had been days ago. So far she hadn't received an answer.

"Lark," said Zoe impatiently. "Will you listen to me?"

"Sorry." With great effort Lark forced her attention back to Zoe.

"I wish Tris would come in. I'd say hello to him. I do think I would." Zoe stroked the sleeve of the new light blue shirtwaist Lark had bought for her. "And I wouldn't be ashamed to have him see me, now that I have this beautiful waist and skirt. Oh, Lark, it was so nice of you to buy me new clothes!"

Lark smiled. "If I could, I'd buy new clothes for all the kids at the asylum." She laughed softly as a great idea popped into her head. She should've thought of it sooner. She grabbed Zoe's hand and said, "I know what we'll do! I'll see that the money Jig gave to the asylum goes into the clothing account!"

"If Matron will allow it."

"Well, she'd better," said Lark grimly. "I'll fix it so she'll have no choice but to allow it." Once again she glanced toward Clay and Veda and all thought of clothing and the asylum vanished. Would Clay believe her if she told him what she learned from Agnes Thorne? She'd wanted to tell him, then all of her thoughts had been on finding her father and she hadn't mentioned any of it to him. She had to be careful how she told him. She didn't want to anger him and have him take her job away and send her back to the asylum. She couldn't give up the cabin after all those years of living in the asylum.

About an hour later Lark watched Clay and Veda walk through the heavy door of the restaurant. Clay's hand rested lightly on Veda's back. The sight of it made Lark grip her linen napkin so tightly she was certain there would be permanent wrinkles in it.

Zoe leaned over and whispered in Lark's ear, "Shall we follow them?"

Lark shook her head, though without meaning to she bunched her muscles to spring up and run after Clay. "They'd see us," she said stiffly. She had to admit to herself she really didn't want to see them together in the privacy of a buggy.

Outdoors Clay handed Veda into his buggy and drove slowly down the street toward her house. Unlike the first time he'd seen her in the hotel lobby in Detroit, he didn't want the evening to end. But he didn't know what else to do other than take her home. He could not take her for a long ride on such a bumpy road, and he would not park somewhere to spark like Tris always did.

The evening was pleasantly cool with a bright moon. The aroma of roses in bloom almost covered the odor of the river. Piano music drifted out from the house just before Veda's. A dog barked and another one answered. Clay stopped the team in the driveway. The harness rattled and the team snorted. Lights from the windows and the bright moonlight made it possible to see the flowers in the yard and the cat walking toward the barn. Clay stepped from the buggy, then helped Veda out. He moved away from her, suddenly at a loss for words—just as he had been at their first meeting in Detroit.

She'd stepped right up to him and said, "Clay Havlick, I know we aren't allowed to have anything to do with each other, but I think fate wants differently. Why else would we be in the same hotel at the same time? I've seen you the last two evenings and I couldn't walk away without speaking. I hope you don't mind. We shouldn't let our parents stop us from doing something we really want to do, should we?"

He'd felt a flush creep up his neck and over his face. "I suppose not."

"Can we sit and talk a while?" Taking his arm, she'd tugged him to a brocade sofa where they sat side by side. She'd done most of the talking, but he'd found himself actually relaxing and enjoying her company.

Tonight he'd enjoyed her company more than any other time.

Veda touched Clay's hand and he stiffened slightly. "I don't want the night to end," she whispered. "You're a dear, dear man and I care deeply for you."

Clay's pulse leaped. No woman had ever said that to him.

Veda leaned against him and looked into his face. "Do you care for me . . . just a little?"

"Yes," he said hoarsely. Oh, why couldn't he be as free with his speech as Tris?

"You may kiss me if you want," said Veda softly, lifting her lips to him.

Suddenly Clay wanted to do just that. He felt awkward as he slipped his arms around her and pulled her close. But before he could touch his lips to hers, she kissed him, and a shock went through him. Then he took control, kissing her as if he were accustomed to such things. Startled at his bold action, he pulled away slightly.

"You make me weak all over," Veda whispered against his ear. "Do I do that to you?"

"Yes," he said hoarsely.

"Could you ever care enough for me to marry me?" she asked softly.

"I might," he whispered.

"You could?" She kissed him again and he returned her kiss with a growing passion. Finally she pulled away, but kept her hands on his chest. "I know we haven't known each other very long, but I care enough for you to marry you."

He didn't know what to say.

"Do you think I'm too forward? Do you think less of me for saying that?"

"I like an honest woman." Her lips were so close to his he could smell her sweet breath. He pulled her closer and kissed her passionately. Desire stirred in him and he didn't want to let her go. He trailed kisses down her cheek and to the pulse throbbing in her throat, then kissed her moist lips again. "I can't get enough of you," he whispered against her soft hair.

"I know," she whispered. "If I had the courage, *I'd* ask *you* to marry *me*."

He hesitated a fraction, then held her away enough to look

into her face. "Will you marry me?" His question surprised him, but it felt right.

"Oh, Clay! Are you sure? Your family!"

"I don't care!" He was sure now. "I want you!"

"And I want you!" Veda's voice was low and whispery.

Clay felt a rush of emotion he'd never known before. He pulled Veda close and kissed her again. Finally she pulled away.

"I must go in," she said breathlessly. "I don't want you to get the wrong idea about me."

"I wouldn't."

"When shall we marry?"

"I'll let you decide."

She laughed breathlessly. "I don't want to live another day without you! Should we marry in August?"

"That's next month!"

"Then how about September?"

That still seemed too soon to Clay. "Let's have a Christmas wedding."

"But that's so far away! I don't know if I can wait that long." Veda ran her hands over Clay's chest. "But if that's what you want, then that's what it'll be."

Clay laughed softly. "Maybe we'd better make it sooner."

"Maybe we should elope so we don't have to listen to our families trying to break us up."

"Maybe so."

"Tonight?" she asked against his lips.

It was tempting, but he shook his head. "We'll think about the date and decide later."

Veda shook her head and pouted as she trailed her finger down his cheek and across his lips. "You said I could decide. And I will take you at your word. I say August."

Clay laughed. "All right. August it is. But it'll have to be late in the month to give me a chance to work on the wagons."

"Leave it to your men to do! I want a month's honeymoon in Europe."

"I can't be gone a month. Maybe next year, but not now. Maybe we should get married next year."

"I won't wait!"

"I can't be away from my business."

"I guess I understand." She tapped his lips with her fingertip. "But I don't like it a teeny bit."

"I'm sorry. My business is very important to me."

"I hope it's not as important as I am."

He didn't know what to say to that and he was feeling uncomfortable. "I'll walk you to the door."

Clay slipped an arm around Veda and walked slowly to the lighted front door. He kissed her one more time, waited until she slipped inside, then ran to his buggy. He slapped the reins on the team and drove away from the Thorne home. His head spun as he thought about the change in his life. He had his own business and soon he'd have a wife. His stomach knotted and he trembled. A month ago he'd never considered a personal relationship with a Thorne; now suddenly he was planning to marry one. Was he doing the right thing?

He slowed the team as he drove through Blue Creek, across the bridge, and onto the corduroy that led home. What would Ma and Pa say about his engagement? He hated to think about their anger. Borrowing against the pines had been the first thing he'd ever done in his life that they'd objected to. Marrying Veda would be the second.

Just past Red Beaver's farm, Clay spotted a buggy at the side of the corduroy. He stopped beside it and called, "Hello? Is there trouble? Could you use a hand?"

In the darkness Lark's heart leaped at the sound of Clay's voice. She stepped around the back of the buggy where she could see him. "Clay!" she said. "It's me, Lark. I'm so glad to see you! The lug nut fell off the wheel and I can't find it. Will you help me?"

Clay stared at Lark in surprise. He'd never expected to see her on the road alone after dark. "How long have you been out here?" he snapped. "Don't you know what could happen?"

She bit her lip, but didn't answer.

He jumped from his buggy and reached for the lantern in the back. He lit it and walked with Lark to look for the lug nut. He noticed she was still dressed in the finery that she'd worn in the restaurant. "What're you doing out so late alone?"

"Going to the cabin," she said. "I visited too long with Zoe."

"You could be in danger," said Clay sharply. "You can't forget the enemies you've made since you've been guarding the pines. This is no place for you to be by yourself."

"I have my revolver and cudgel in the buggy," she said stiffly.

Clay scowled as he walked back the way Lark had come, holding the lantern high to shed light on the log road. How could she think a cudgel and a revolver in the buggy would keep her safe while she was on foot?

Lark walked along beside him, her steps unsteady on the road. She could walk easily in her heavy boots, but her new shoes with the small heel made walking harder. Suddenly she tripped. With a startled cry, she flung out her arms and caught Clay's arm.

He stumbled slightly and almost dropped the lantern. The touch of her hands seemed to burn through his clothing and into his flesh. "What's wrong?" he asked sharply as he looked down on her.

She regained her balance and released her death grip on his arm. "Sorry," she muttered, barely able to breathe with him so close. "I tripped."

"Are you hurt?"

"No." There was a slight pain in her ankle, but not enough to mention.

"This is ridiculous. We'll leave the buggy here for the night and find a nut in the morning. I'll unhitch the team and tie them behind my buggy."

"I can't leave your pa's buggy for someone to steal!"

"He'll understand. He wouldn't want you to risk your life for a buggy. Get in mine while I unhitch the team." Clay's voice sounded angry even to him.

"I'll get my things," she said stiffly. She walked back to the buggy and lifted out the pouch carrying her revolver and her cudgel.

A few minutes later Lark sat beside Clay as he drove down the corduroy. Blood pounded in her ears and tingles ran over her body. "I'm sorry for ruining your night," she said with her hands locked in her lap over her pouch.

"You didn't ruin it. It just so happens this is a *fine* night for me." Clay hesitated a fraction. "Veda and I are engaged."

"What?" cried Lark in alarm as she turned to stare at him. "You're going to marry Veda Thorne? You mustn't! What about Jig's warning?"

Clay turned onto Havlick property and pulled the team to an abrupt stop. He glared at Lark as his temper rose even higher. The moonlight was bright enough for him to see her wide eyes and shocked look. "I told you Jig was wrong about Veda!"

"He was not! Even Agnes Thorne knows the truth!"

"Mrs. Thorne isn't well."

"She can't tolerate her life! She doesn't like to see what her husband and daughter are doing." Impatiently Lark told him what she'd learned from Agnes. Ordinarily Lark would've told the news carefully, but she was too upset at the moment to use care. Brutally honest words poured from her. She ended with, "If you don't think it's right to marry an Indian, then you won't marry Veda Thorne."

Clay gripped the reins so tightly his knuckles hurt. The team moved restlessly. An owl screeched. Surely Agnes Thorne was out of her mind and wasn't telling the truth!

"I *know* Veda wants the pines!" cried Lark.

"You're wrong!"

Lark struggled to calm herself. "I can't believe you've already decided to marry Veda. You met her only a short time ago."

"We've spent enough time together to know our feelings."

"And have you prayed about it?"

A muscle jumped in Clay's jaw. He hadn't prayed. "I know I want to marry her."

"And what will you do when she has your pines lumbered out?"

"She won't do that no matter what her mother said," Clay said grimly. He was angry enough to shake Lark until her teeth rattled.

"What if she does?"

"Drop the subject, Lark Baritt. It's not your affair."

"The pines are my affair! I won't let them be lumbered! I'll do anything to stop that from happening."

Clay gripped her arms and pushed his face close to hers. "Just what does that mean?"

"Just what I said." She felt his anger even as hers mounted. "You know Veda Thorne pushed herself on you."

"She did no such thing."

"She made the first move to speak to you in Detroit or on the train. She suggested you have dinner together. She probably even suggested marriage."

Lark spoke the truth, but just hearing her say it set Clay's blood boiling. "I suppose you don't think I can get a wife without my precious white pines."

"I didn't say that. I said Veda Thorne is after them."

"Don't say another word!"

"I suppose you'll kick me out of the cabin and take away my job."

"I'd like to, but I won't." Clay abruptly released Lark and flicked the reins against the horses. The buggy jerked, then rolled along behind the clip-clop of the horses. "I'll leave you at the cabin. If you say another word against Veda, I will fire you on the spot."

Lark clamped her mouth closed into a tight, straight line as she stared off across the field toward the cabin. She would not give up the cabin or her job as guard. Only in the woods could she find release from the tension she felt when she thought about looking for and finding her father. "You could settle it all by not giving Veda the right to the pines when you marry."

"I don't intend to give her the pines," said Clay stiffly.

"She'll ask for them."

"You don't know what you're talking about!" Clay braced his feet to keep from swaying with the movement of the buggy. He was afraid he would lose his temper if he so much as brushed against Lark.

Several minutes later Clay stopped the team outside the cabin. The smell of pine was heavy in the night air. Sears barked and strained against the rope holding him to the stake beside his dog house. "Quiet, Sears!" commanded Clay sharply.

Sears immediately stopped barking and whined a welcome.

Lark stepped from the buggy and retrieved her cudgel and her pouch. "The pines are as important to me as they are to your mother and as they were to Jig. I won't let them be lumbered. Not by Veda or Willie Thorne. Not by anyone."

Clay bit back the angry words burning his tongue, turned his team, and slapped the reins down hard. The buggy swayed dangerously as he drove toward the farm.

Lark slowly walked to Sears and patted his head. "Sears, we'll keep the trees safe, won't we?"

Sears licked Lark's hand as he wriggled his back end.

Lark looked toward the pines and said in a loud, ringing voice, "Willie Thorne, not you or anyone else will lumber the pines!"

At the edge of the pines a shadow moved. Lark held her breath as she watched. Was it her imagination or had she seen someone lurking among the trees? She shivered and hurried inside the cabin and locked the door.

The next morning at the Havlicks, Clay sat at the breakfast table with the family. They always ate breakfast in the kitchen around the round oak table. Wood burned in the cookstove.

The hired girl slipped outdoors to leave the family alone to eat the hash browns, fried eggs, bacon, thick slices of fresh bread, and applesauce, with coffee and milk to drink. Clay looked at his parents, his two sisters, and two brothers, and almost lost his nerve. He had to tell them before they heard it from someone else—especially Lark Baritt.

Jennet laughed as she looked at Clay. She knew something was on his mind. She straightened the collar of her brown calico dress. She wasn't wearing a bustle. She liked dressing plain when in her own home. "Out with it, Clay. You look ready to burst."

Clay took a deep breath, ran a finger around his collar, then blurted, "I am going to marry Veda Thorne next month."

Jennet fell back against her chair and stared speechlessly at Clay. The others sat in shocked silence.

Free pushed his chair so hard it fell backward as he jumped up. "You'll do no such thing!" he roared. "No son of mine will marry a Thorne!"

Clay leaped up, sending his chair flying. Sparks shot from his dark eyes. "I'm twenty-five years old, Pa. You can't tell me what I can or can't do."

"Stop it, you two!" cried Jennet as she ran to Free's side and caught his arm. "Don't say anything you'll regret later. We can't let this tear apart our family! Let's be calm. Don't we need to talk?"

Free shook his finger at Clay. "I'll go directly to Willie Thorne and tell him you won't be marrying his daughter."

"You can't do that, Pa," said Clay in a tight voice. "Veda is afraid he won't approve of the marriage as it is. But she won't listen to him. Just leave it alone and let me handle it. We'll marry no matter what anyone says."

"Then Jig was right," said Jennet hoarsely.

"No. No, he was not," said Clay between his teeth. "I don't intend to give Veda the rights to the pines. But I will marry her even if we have to elope." Eloping was beginning to sound like a great idea. He grabbed his hat off the peg near the back door and stormed out of the house. He couldn't listen to another word. He glanced across the field to Lark's cabin. She would already be walking the trail, but she'd be plotting ways to stop him from marrying Veda. More than ever he wanted to grab Lark and shake some sense into her.

"Nobody will stop me," he whispered grimly. His heart felt like an icy stone but he ignored it and ran to the barn to saddle Flame.

CHAPTER 7

♦ Clay stood at his desk and listened to the noise around him in the shop. July heat made the building hot even with the doors open. He watched Jay trim an axle, then smiled down at the new contract he'd signed to build a hundred more wagons for a company in Kansas. Clay advertised that they built wagons that would last. The wooden pieces were hand hewn out of white oak with an axe, an adze, and a drawing knife. The coupling poles were made from well seasoned hickory he'd bought from his uncle Wex. Clay's blacksmiths forged the standards, hound plates, and other metal parts, but he bought the actual nuts from a company in Chicago. He was certain that in the future someone would invent tools to make the building of wagons easier and quicker and he wanted to be in on any new method that would work.

As Clay dropped the contract back in the folder, he wondered where he'd find enough seasoned wood. Uncle Wex had said he didn't have any more and the mill in town didn't either. Clay scratched his head in thought. If he couldn't find it, he'd be in big trouble. Without more wood he couldn't build enough wagons to fill the order. He'd sent a man around to different mills to find more lumber. Was there a way to season wood quickly? He'd have to check into it. Pa might know. Clay sighed. Pa was still worried about losing the white pines. The memory of Pa's angry words and his warnings made Clay's stomach tighten. He knew if he couldn't fulfill the contracts and pay back his bank loan, he could indeed lose the pines. If he had to, he'd hire additional employees. He already had sixty men working. There wasn't a chance he'd lose the pines to Willie Thorne. He was certain of that but Pa didn't believe it.

Just then Tris walked in, his straw hat in his hand. He wore dark work pants and a black and white striped cotton shirt. He looked hesitantly at Clay. Clay stiffened. Tris hadn't spoken to him since he'd announced his engagement yesterday morning.

"Morning, Clay," said Tris.

Clay glanced quickly around to make sure his men weren't able to hear the conversation. They were all deeply involved with their work and making too much noise to hear. Clay nodded to Tris. "Don't try to talk me out of marrying Veda Thorne."

Tris grinned and shrugged. "I thought about it, and I wanted to. Then I decided against it. You get stubborn when anybody opposes you."

Clay scowled. "I do not."

Tris shrugged again. "I came to see what I could do to help you with your wedding plans."

"Why would you want to help? You're against it as much as Ma and Pa."

"I know. But you're my brother and I don't want hard feelings between us."

A lump filled Clay's throat and he couldn't speak for a moment. He clamped his hand on Tris's strong shoulder. "Thanks, brother. I won't forget this."

Tris grinned and settled his hat in place. "Could I help run your business while you're on your honeymoon?"

Clay considered the offer, then shook his head. "I'll have to delay the honeymoon until later. I just got a new contract for more wagons. I'll probably have to hire more workers. Know of any available men?"

"Not offhand. You could check in Big Pine or Grand Rapids. Maybe put an ad in the paper."

"I'll do that. . . . You could work for me."

"I would if I could, but I'm helping Pa finish the buggy he's working on and I have bookwork to catch up on." Tris leaned back against the wooden desk. "Who's doing your bookwork?"

Clay rolled his eyes. "Me. I tried to get Bob Jenkins, but he's too busy."

"What about Lark Baritt? She's good."

Clay hesitated, then nodded. He had thought about her, but immediately rejected the idea. She didn't approve of him seeing Veda. Now that he was engaged to Veda, having Lark work for him at the Wagon Works could cause a real problem. It was bad enough that she was guarding the trees and he had to see her about that.

"She's changed a lot in the past few weeks," Tris said.

"Really? I hadn't noticed." Clay tried to sound disinterested.

"Her appearance has changed and she's more sure of herself." Tris pushed his hat to the back of his head. "I heard from Zoe that Lark is trying to find her father." Zoe had been with Lark at the cabin when Tris had stopped by with fresh vegetables. He'd been surprised he hadn't noticed that Zoe had grown up. On impulse he'd invited her on a Sunday school picnic and she'd quickly accepted.

"I didn't know Lark's father was still alive. I thought, since she was raised at the asylum she was an orphan."

"Me too. Zoe told me what she knows about it." Tris looked out the open door to the street beyond. "Lark has had a lot of unhappiness and deserves to be happy. I hope she does have a father out there who wants her and will love her."

Clay didn't want to think about Lark. "How about dinner?" he said. "It's almost noon."

At the orphan asylum Lark closed the books with a frown. Why wasn't there an entry of Jig's hundred dollar donation. She'd given the money to Matron just after Jig died. At first Lark had thought she'd overlooked the entry since she was a little distracted. Her mind was full of plans to find her father—if he was to be found—and she could think of little else. Even the news of Clay's engagement to Veda Thorne had alarmed her only for a short time. Clay would have to take care of himself and his trees. She had to find her father before she could think about anything else.

Lark looked down at the books. Regardless of what was on her mind, she had to take care of the business at hand right now and see what Matron had done with Jig's gift. With a determined look on her face Lark walked to Matron's office.

Matron stood beside a bookshelf and scowled at Lark. Her office smelled like coffee and cinnamon rolls. She had a dab of white frosting at the corner of her mouth. "I'm very busy," she said.

"I can't find the record of Jig Bjoerling's donation."

Matron smoothed the skirt of her black wrapper, then fingered a pearl brooch at her throat. "Why are you speaking to me about it? You're in charge of the books."

"You took the money from me. I assumed you deposited it in the bank."

Color stained Matron's round cheeks. "What are you implying, Lark Baritt?"

Lark trembled at the tone in Matron's voice. "I want to know what happened to the money."

"I did deposit it. Check at the bank." Matron waved Lark from the room. "Don't bother me about it again."

Lark wanted to argue the point, but she slowly walked from the office. She would check at the bank. Just then the front door opened and Sally Smith from the store burst in, looking very angry.

"What's wrong, Sally?"

Sally's round face was red with anger and perspiration glistened on her wide forehead. "I just learned that Glenna must give Matron a percent of the money she earns from me." Glenna was the orphan who swept up for Sally. "Glenna says Matron forces her to hand over part of her money to help pay her own way in the asylum."

"So that's what she's been doing!"

"Glenna said the boys who work at the mill have to do the same thing. She said Matron told them if they tell anyone she'll lock them in the cellar for a whole week." Sally's breast rose and fell and her blue eyes blazed with fury. "I want to know what we can do about it."

Lark narrowed her eyes thoughtfully. "This is my chance to get her out of here. I'll talk to the kids and we'll call an emergency board meeting for this evening."

"Are you sure that's the right thing to do? I know how Matron has treated you."

Lark shivered, but nodded determinedly. "I won't let her continue to be cruel to the children!"

That evening Lark looked around the front room of the asylum at the board members she'd sent messages to about the emergency meeting. Her heart jerked when she saw Clay sitting with his mother. Lark hadn't expected to see him at the meeting. Was he still angry with her? She knew she didn't want to deal with him or his problems right now. Just then he looked up and his eyes locked with hers. She tried to look away, but couldn't. Her lungs ached from not being able to take in air. Finally he turned back to his mother and Lark was free.

Clay tried to concentrate on what his mother was saying to him, but he couldn't get his mind off Lark. She looked drained and her eyes haunted. Was she having trouble at the pines that she hadn't reported? He saw Lark stiffen as Matron walked into the room.

Smelling of talcum powder, Matron stopped beside Lark. "Call off the meeting or you'll never learn about your father," hissed Matron so low only Lark could hear.

Lark's heart zoomed to her feet. She pressed her trembling hand to her throat. "What do you know of him?" she whispered hoarsely.

"I know where he is."

Lark gripped Matron's arm. "Tell me!"

Matron pried Lark's fingers loose. "I'll tell you if you call off the meeting."

Frantically Lark glanced around the room. If she called off the meeting, she might not have another chance to remove Matron from her position. But if she didn't call it off, she might never learn her father's whereabouts. Lark trembled. Her blue plaid shirtwaist and dark skirt felt too hot.

"Tell them you made a mistake," hissed Matron close to Lark's ear.

Lark caught a glimpse of Sally with the orphans standing outside the door. Lark moaned. She wanted to call off the meeting, but she couldn't hurt the children. "I won't call it off," Lark said weakly.

"You'll be very sorry," said Matron, stalking to a chair, her black skirt rustling loudly.

Jennet walked to the front of the room and faced the others sitting on sofas and the chairs Lark had had the boys carry in. Jennet smoothed down her gray skirt and touched the cameo at her throat. "Shall we pray?" She bowed her head and prayed for God to help them. She lifted her head and smiled at Lark. "This is a special meeting called by Lark to settle an issue with Matron Anna Pike. You may have the floor, Lark."

Lark walked to the front and stood beside Jennet. Lark had so much she wanted to say, but she couldn't remember a thing. She saw the questioning look on Clay's face and felt Jennet beside her. Lark took a deep breath, but still she couldn't find the words she'd planned to say against Matron. "Sally Smith has something to report." Lark sat down while Sally walked in, the bustle of her black skirt swaying. Her face was flushed and her eyes bright.

Clay frowned slightly. What was wrong with Lark? She looked ready to pass out. He forced his gaze to Sally.

Sally stopped beside Jennet, smiled stiffly, then turned to the board members seated in front of her. "Glenna works for me and is paid every week. When she gets paid, Matron forces her to give her most of the money." Sally waited, letting the news sink in. Jennet gasped and Mrs. Pepper sucked in her breath. "Les and Joe work at the mill and Matron forces them to do the same. Even the boys who work at the Wagon Works have to give her some of their earnings."

Matron jumped up. "It's only right they pay for their own expenses!"

"Sit down, Anna," said Jennet firmly. "You'll have a chance to speak later."

Clay scowled at Matron's back. He'd always known there was something about her he didn't like.

Lark locked her icy fingers together. Had she lost all chances of finding her father?

"Come in, children," said Sally, motioning to them.

Lark moved restlessly as she watched the children file in and stand in a line in front of Sally and Jennet. All the children had on their best clothes and were scrubbed clean. Lark tried to listen to them tell what Matron had forced them to do, but her mind was on what Matron had said about her father. Had Matron lied or did she really know where Matt Baritt was? Lark's stomach cramped and the room seemed to spin.

When Matron stood to defend herself Lark wanted to shout at her to tell her about her father, but she clamped her mouth closed.

"The money these children earn must be used for their clothing and food," said Matron. "It's only right when we're so short of finances."

"But why are you short of money?" asked Mrs. Pepper. "The community supports the asylum."

"What about the money from Jig?" asked Clay. "That should've helped for a while."

Matron shrugged. "That money was used wisely."

"That money wasn't recorded," said Lark.

"Then how can I be expected to remember?" asked Matron.

"I don't think the children should give their money to Matron," said Sally. "They work hard for their wages."

"I agree," said Jennet. "And I will check to see what did become of Jig's money."

Just then two sisters, Linda and Maggie, ran to Jennet. The girls wore patched dresses and their faces and hands were dirty. Linda held her soiled apron close to her chest. Maggie pushed an envelope in Jennet's hand. "We found this in Matron's room," said Linda, her face red.

Lark recognized Jig's envelope and her eyes widened.

Matron gasped.

Jennet looked inside the envelope and saw several bills that added up to $100, then she glanced at the front. "This is Jig's writing," Jennet said, looking at Matron.

"I don't know anything about that money!" cried Matron. She glared at Linda and Maggie. "Those girls had no business being in my private room."

Maggie pressed against Linda.

"Here's more," said Linda, dumping the contents of her apron on the table in front of Jennet. Bills and coins scattered across the smooth surface and a few coins fell on the floor. "We found it all in a box in Matron's trunk."

"There's my special silver dollar!" cried Les as he picked up a silver dollar with a hole through the center. "Somebody stole it right out of my bag."

Just then Gert and Ray Moline walked into the room and stepped to the front of the room. "We heard about this meeting and we wanted to have our say," Gert said, wringing her hands as she looked at Jennet. "We worked here several years and we know Matron took money that didn't belong to her." Gert glanced at Matron and looked quickly away.

"I never!" snapped Matron angrily.

Gert swallowed hard and moved closer to Ray. "She accused my man of stealing, but he never stole anything. Matron took from the kids and kept donations when she thought she could get away with it."

Ray nodded, but didn't speak. Matron glared at Gert.

"Why didn't you tell us before now?" asked Jennet softly.

"Because it's not true," said Matron icily.

"We didn't have the nerve," said Gert, flushing. "It was wrong of us, I believe, not to report her. But we're telling now."

"She punished the kids even if they didn't do any wrong," said Gert. "And she never let me have enough to see the children got enough nourishing food."

"You're lying!" snapped Matron.

"We'll see who's lying," said Gert, looking smug as she walked to an empty chair and sat down. Ray sat next to her.

"Anna, there's a good bit of evidence against you, but I want to hear what you have to say," said Jennet softly.

Her face ashen and her chin held high, Matron crossed her arms over her ample breast. "I worked hard all these years."

"I know," said Jennet. "But did you steal from the orphans?"

Matron's face hardened. "Steal from orphans? You can't steal from someone who doesn't have anything." She waved her hand at the children. "Look at them! Why would I steal from them? I do admit I take the money they bring in, but it goes to pay for food and clothes for them. Why do they need cash money? All their needs are met."

"But the money was theirs to keep," said Jennet. "The county pays for food and clothing for them."

Matron patted her hair and cleared her throat. "You just don't understand, do you? I work hard. What do these kids do? Nothing! And they're mean, dishonest, little nothings! If I did happen to take their money, it's because I deserve it."

Lark sagged in her seat. Now the truth would come out and

Jennet and the others would finally learn of Matron's abuse, meanness, and dishonesty through the years. Now they'd know how the children had suffered. She had accomplished what she'd set out to do!

"Did you take their money?" asked Jennet firmly.

Matron's eyes blazed. "Yes! But I told you why. I need it and they have no use for it. They are nothings! They deserved every punishment I gave them!"

"How did you punish them?" asked Jennet, her face white.

Lark listened as Jennet pulled the confession from Matron. The room was very quiet as the others listened to the sordid details, their faces showing shocked surprise. The silence was broken only occasionally with a murmured "Oh!" and the sound of a gulp of air.

"Ask her about my father," Lark said in a weak voice.

"Your father?" Her eyes large and questioning, Jennet turned quickly toward Lark.

Clay leaned forward with interest.

"She knows where he is," said Lark around the hard lump in her throat.

"Tell Lark everything you know about her father," said Jennet, nudging Matron.

Matron shook her head. "I don't know anything. She's an orphan. There's nobody that wants her! Nobody ever wanted her!"

Lark trembled and bit back a cry of outrage.

Clay jumped to his feet. "That's a cruel remark, Matron Pike! If you know anything about her father, tell her now." Tears stung Lark's eyes at Clay's surprising intervention.

Matron lifted her chin. "Lark Baritt's been nothing but trouble for me from the day she arrived. Her father brought her here and left her and that's that." Matron turned and stalked from the room.

Lark trembled. Then she ran after Matron and caught her arm. Lark's breast rose and fell and for a minute she couldn't speak.

"Let me go!" Matron slapped Lark's hand away. "I have nothing to say to you!"

Clay hurried from the room after Lark and Matron. He saw the anguish on Lark's face and the anger on Matron's.

"Please, you must help me," said Lark with a sob.

Matron lifted her hand to slap Lark's face, but Clay caught her arm and jerked her back.

"Don't ever do that again to her," said Clay grimly.

Lark bit her lip to stop her sobs as she stared helplessly at Clay.

Clay leaned down to Matron. "You tell Lark all about her father right now or we'll press charges against you and you'll spend the next several years in jail. What'll it be?"

Shivering, Lark waited as she watched the anger drain from Matron to be replaced with defeat.

Matron leaned weakly against the paneled wall in the hallway. "The last I heard he was in Lansing."

"Lansing," whispered Lark. "So close!"

"When did you hear last?" asked Clay, surprised at the news.

"About a year ago," said Matron hesitantly.

"Last year?" cried Lark, her hand at her throat.

"Did you hear from him before that?" Clay's voice was even and hard.

"Occasionally," Matron said.

"How did you hear?" Clay asked. "Letters? Did he write?"

"Some," Matron said weakly.

"My father wrote letters and you didn't tell me?" Lark's voice was filled with pain.

"Did he ever come here?" asked Clay.

Matron shook her head. "No. Never."

"Why didn't he come here at least to visit if he's kept in touch?" asked Clay.

Matron trembled.

Lark struggled against fresh tears. "Does he want me?"

Clay narrowed his dark eyes. "We want the whole story, Matron."

"Did he ever say he would come for me to take me away from here to be with him?" whispered Lark.

Matron shook her head.

Lark sagged weakly. Suddenly she didn't want to hear what Matron knew.

"But he did write," said Clay. He hated to see the agony Lark was suffering.

Matron nodded.

"Where are the letters?" asked Clay.

"I destroyed them," said Matron weakly.

"What did he say in them?" asked Lark just above a whisper. She reached for Clay's hand. He held it out to her and she clung to him with all her might. He could feel her rapid pulse as she gripped his hand. The agony in her eyes made his heart ache.

Matron swallowed hard. "He . . . ah . . . he thinks you don't want to see him. And . . . each time he wrote, he . . . ah . . . he sent his address for you to write to him."

Lark leaned weakly against Clay. The room began to spin and she gripped Clay's hand even tighter. Her father had wanted to hear from her!

"Give Lark the latest address," said Clay in a tight, hard voice.

"I burned it," said Matron.

With a moan Lark pressed her face into Clay's arm, and it seemed natural to him to put his arm around her shoulders and hold her close to him.

"You must remember something," said Clay.

Matron shrugged.

"Jail? Is that what you want, Matron?" snapped Clay. He gently patted Lark's back, but his eyes were hard and locked with Matron's.

Matron sighed. "He was in Lansing finishing a book. He's a

writer. It was a book about plant and insect life in lower Michigan."

"Was that last year?" asked Clay.

Matron nodded. "He said he wouldn't write again."

Lark turned to Matron. "Why not?"

"He thought you didn't want to see him and didn't want to hear from him again," said Matron.

"Did you tell him that?" cried Lark in horror.

Matron nodded.

"Why?" asked Clay.

Matron clamped her mouth closed tightly.

"You'd better tell me or you'll go directly to jail," snapped Clay.

"I couldn't let him find out about the money and all the letters he'd sent and why you hadn't answered."

"I'll go to Lansing," said Lark, trembling. "I'll find him and talk to him! I'll tell him I never knew."

"Lansing's a big city," said Clay.

"You can help me, Clay," said Lark. "You can help me find him. You promised Jig you'd watch out for me. You promised!"

"It isn't wise for us to go there since we couldn't begin to know where to look. But I will telegraph a man I know in Lansing and ask him to hire a detective to find your father."

"I want to go myself. You could hire someone from the mill to guard the pines for a few days."

Clay shook his head. "It's not safe for you to travel alone."

"I'm not a child or an invalid, Clay Havlick."

"Let her go," said Matron sharply. "Maybe we'll finally be rid of her. She's nothing but trouble anyway."

Clay frowned at Matron. "Go to my mother, Matron, and wait with her. I'll tell the board of the deal I've made with you. Then you'll have to find somewhere to live, somewhere away from Blue Creek."

Matron walked slowly away and into the front room. She stood quietly beside Jennet.

Clay turned toward Lark. He couldn't understand why he

wanted to help her or to protect her, but he knew he had to. It was probably because he had promised Jig he would. "Please, let me send a detective after your father first. Then if he doesn't turn up anything, you can do what you want."

Lark considered his advice and finally nodded. "But I'll only wait a week."

"Make it two weeks."

Lark sighed heavily and nodded. "All right. Two weeks."

Later at dusk Clay drove Lark home in his buggy. He hadn't wanted her to go alone. She'd sat quietly all the way from town. At the cabin he stepped from the buggy, then reached for her. Sears whined a welcome, but didn't bark.

Just then Lark noticed the cabin door stood open. Fear pricked her skin as she caught Clay's hand and gripped it tightly. "The door," she whispered, motioning with her head.

The hairs on the back of Clay's neck stood on end. Was this more trouble for Lark? "Wait here," he whispered.

Lark hesitated, then jumped down and followed Clay. He looked inside the cabin and frowned at the mess he saw. The pillow and quilt had been slashed into ribbons. Feathers covered everything like a first snow of winter. Jig's Bible lay on the floor with several pages wadded up on the floor beside it. Chairs were overturned and the pots and pans knocked from the cupboard.

"Who would've done this?" she whispered.

"I'll find out," said Clay grimly.

Lark ran to the bunk and dug out her cudgel and revolver and laid them on the ruined quilt on the bunk. The box Jig had left her was untouched in the corner where she'd put it. She opened the lid, then jumped back with a shriek as a rattlesnake rattled inside it.

The snake struck just as Clay pulled Lark aside, and the fangs missed them both. Clay grabbed up the cudgel and hit the snake a death blow before it could coil again.

Lark shivered, her hand at her throat. With a whimper she

sank to a chair and watched as Clay lifted the rattler with the cudgel and flung it out the door. He rested the cudgel next to the door and stood looking down at Lark, then looked back outdoors at the pines.

"What do you see?" she whispered fearfully.

"Come and look," he said around a lump in his throat.

Lark looked to where he was pointing and she cried out in alarm. An uneven ring of bark had been chopped off all the way around a giant pine near Jig's grave.

"Four giant pines have been ringed," said Clay gruffly.

"Whoever did that didn't want to lumber those pines. He wanted to kill them," whispered Lark as she walked toward the trees. She knew if chips had been chopped off the trees in one spot, rosin would ooze over the wound and eventually the bark would grow and cover the bare spots, healing itself. But a ring all the way around caused the tree to die.

"We'll have to get the crew to lumber them tomorrow," said Clay as he balled his fists at his sides. "I'll get someone else to guard the pines."

Lark whirled to face Clay. "What do you mean? You can't take this job from me!"

"It's too dangerous, Lark."

Lark's lip quivered. "Clay, please don't take this job from me! I can't go back to the asylum! I love the cabin and the pines!"

"It's for your own good."

Lark burst into tears and gripped Clay's arms. "I can't go back to my old life. I can't. Please don't make me, Clay."

His heart melted at the sight of her tears. Against his better judgment he said softly, "All right. We'll try it a while longer and see what happens."

"Thank you," she whispered, struggling to control her tears.

The temptation to take her in his arms made him tremble. How could he want to do that when he was going to marry Veda? Was something wrong with him?

Slowly Lark lifted her eyes to Clay. "When will they lumber the pines?"

"Tomorrow. It's better to put the lumber to use instead of letting it rot and fall later."

"You're right, of course."

The next afternoon Clay and Lark stood beside the mill foreman in charge of seeing that the trees were cut and felled to the best advantage.

"It won't be long now," said the foreman. "The saw is almost through. The tree will fall there." He pointed to an open spot where it wouldn't damage Jig's gravestone or the cabin. Immediately following his words there was an ominous grinding at the base of the tree. The powerful trunk trembled, then shivered. "Timber!" shouted the sawers.

Lark caught Clay's hand and gripped it with both of hers as she watched the top of the tree sway. "Oh, Clay," she whispered, close to tears.

Clay swallowed hard. He hated to lose any of the precious white pines. Cutting even a single one caused him grief.

Slowly the tree toppled, gained speed, and with a mighty crack the trunk broke from the stump. Sweeping limbs snapped against other trees, and the giant pine whooshed to the ground with a loud thud, sending dust high into the air. Broken limbs and twigs fell nearby.

Clay felt Lark tremble as she swayed against him. He thought she might fall too. He turned her to him and pressed her face into his chest, his hand spread across the back of her head. Her hair felt soft under his hand and she smelled like bayberry soap.

Lark felt Clay's heart thud against her forehead and she trembled harder, this time from the feelings that leaped inside her because of being held by Clay Havlick. She pulled away and said, "I can't watch the others fall."

Clay turned her away and they walked to the far side of the cabin where Clay had tied Sears out of the way. He barked a welcome and Clay patted his head.

"I'll find out who ringed the trees," said Lark grimly.

"Oh, no, you won't!" Clay caught her hands and held them tightly. "I won't let you put yourself in more danger. We'll leave it up to the sheriff. I mean it, Lark Baritt!"

She sighed heavily and finally nodded.

CHAPTER 8

♦ Clay held up a spoke and eyed it to see if it was oval-shaped instead of perfectly round. Oval-shaped spokes gave the wheels a tremendous amount of strength. Bailey and Timmers carved out the best spokes he'd ever seen. They used oak that had seasoned two years, and with a drawing knife shaped the base of each spoke to fit the slots in the hub. There were twelve spokes to a wheel. For the past week Clay had had Timmers training other men to carve spokes the way he did. And he demanded perfection. Timmers sometimes lost his patience if a man said a spoke was good enough when it wasn't really perfect. Clay was glad Timmers wanted the very best work, but at times Clay worried about perfection slowing production.

Just then a blond haired, blue eyed man about Tris's age called to Clay. Clay nodded, laid the spoke down, and walked to the wide doorway. A pleasant breeze blew in the door, making working easier on the men.

The man stuck out his hand. "I am Dag Bjoerling. From Sweden." He spoke with a heavy accent, but plain enough for Clay to understand him.

Clay stiffened, then shook the man's work-roughened hand.

"I had a friend with your same name, but we called him Jig."

"He is my grandfather."

"Did you receive his letter?" asked Clay.

"Yes. It was hidden away for many years, but I found it, and came looking for him." Dag nodded and smiled.

Clay frowned slightly. "Don't you know he died in June?"

"No!" Dag paled. "I came too late." Dag leaned against the doorway. "My grandfather left Sweden as a young man. He was deeply in love, but couldn't marry the girl he loved. They had a son, Erik. Her family put Erik in an orphanage." Dag swept a hand over his blond hair. "Erik was my father. As long as I can remember he's been looking for his father. He learned the story and he discovered my grandfather had come to the forests of Michigan. My father accidently found a letter written by his mother telling about a letter from Grandfather Dag. Father searched for the letter but did not find it until after he was married and had children. At that time he couldn't leave his family to search for his father in another country. He put the letter away and several months ago I found it. I came to America to find my grandfather."

Clay thought about the letter Jig had left for Lark to send to his family after he died. Dag would've been here in America by then. Clay decided not to say anything about that letter. "Where are you living?"

"I've been sleeping under the stars."

Clay thought Dag didn't look like a man who'd spent his nights outdoors. "There's a boarding house here in Blue Creek."

"Ah, but I have no job." Dag looked around. "I know much about making wagons."

Clay cocked a brow. "You do? Can you carve spokes?"

Dag walked to the men who were working on them, picked up a piece of oak and a drawing knife and carefully carved the beginnings of a spoke.

Clay watched him and knew he'd found a man he could use. "You have a job, Dag, if you want one. When can you start?"

"Right now," said Dag with a wide smile.

Clay introduced him to Bailey and Timmers, then walked away to supervise the men making the bolsters.

Dag watched Clay through his long lashes and hid a smile. It had been easy to get Clay Havlick to give him a job! Tonight he'd report everything he could learn about Clay's business to Willie Thorne and tomorrow their plan to start the workmen drinking and fighting would begin. Willie had not made a mistake in bringing him here to Blue Creek. He had been in Grand Rapids and Willie had seen him. Because of his looks, accent, and knowledge of wood, Willie had hired him to pose as old Jig's relative and to set himself up to do serious damage to the Wagon Works. His job was to see to it that Clay Havlick had so many problems he couldn't fill his contracts. The funny thing was although he was only posing as Dag Bjoerling, his name really was Dag. He had been given the surname of Gotland, but he had no idea what his real name was. He was tired of having nothing, so Willie's offer had been a godsend. Dag nodded. He wanted his own home, a business, and a wife and family. After his job was finished here, he'd have enough money to go back to Grand Rapids and get everything he wanted.

The next morning in the forest Lark sang as she strode through the briars and across the bog that sucked at her boots. Sears followed, coming out with muddy stockings. He was good company and never left the trail to chase an animal.

Suddenly Sears growled deep in his throat. Lark gripped her cudgel and rested her hand on Sears as they kept walking. She listened for any signs of an intruder, but heard nothing. Up ahead was the spot where she'd run into the bears. She brushed her hand over the butt of her revolver. Sears growled again and Lark silenced him with a gentle tap on the head.

From the corner of her eye Lark caught a movement in the woods to her left. Her nerves tingled, but she started another song, singing as if she didn't have a care in the world. She passed the huge root where she'd been waylaid, but no one jumped out to stop her. The movement had probably been her imagination. Or had Clay sent someone to guard her? She didn't know whether she should be angry or pleased if he had. She did know she was thankful he'd hired a detective in Lansing to find her father. Maybe by tomorrow they'd have word. She'd thought *maybe by tomorrow* for the last three days.

Lightning began to flash and thunder rumbled. Wind whispered in the pines. In the clearing Lark looked up through the trees at the gray sky. She didn't like being in the woods with lightning flashing so close. It could strike a tree and knock it down or even cause a fire. "We'd better hurry, Sears," she said, sprinting forward.

Thunder boomed closer and the sky grew darker. Lark listened for sounds of the intruder, but heard nothing other than a loud clap of thunder. She reached the cabin without mishap and her nerves tightened more. She tapped the bell once to signal the Havlicks all was fine, but longed to strike it hard twice to call someone to the cabin to keep her company during the storm.

Lark filled a pan with water for Sears and set it beside his doghouse. "Sears, I'm glad it's Saturday and I don't have to go to the orphan asylum." Thunder clapped and Lark jumped. Lightning zigzagged across the sky above the field. The wind whipped tall grasses and flowers and bent down the tops of the trees.

Lark ran into the cabin just as the rain began to fall in giant drops, soaking into the sandy soil. She closed the door against the storm, then sank to the chair to pull off her high top shoes. She pulled off her leather pants and tunic and slipped on the limp calico dress that she'd planned to use as a rag. It felt soft and comfortable against her warm skin. She looked longingly at her bunk. She hadn't slept well for several days, and she felt very tempted to take a nap. Finally she walked to the bed and sank down on it. She couldn't remember the last time she'd slept during the day. She closed her eyes and listened to the rain on the roof and the thunder cracking farther and farther away. The sounds of the storm became comforting as the thunder moved away. She drifted off to sleep with her arm resting across her forehead.

Silent Waters opened the cabin door and slipped inside. She crept to the bunk where Lark lay sleeping and carefully laid a rag soaked with chloroform over Lark's mouth and nose. When she was sure Lark was unconscious she removed the rag, tied on Lark's shoes, then eased Lark on her shoulder like a sack of potatoes, and carried her outdoors. The rain had turned to a steady drizzle and the temperature had cooled slightly.

Sears barked and strained at his rope, but no one heard him. Silent Waters had counted on that.

She carried Lark deep into the forest to a place near Red Beaver's farm where she would wait until nightfall to finish the last part of her journey with her unconscious prisoner. Willie would be glad to see she'd brought Lark Baritt to him. He'd been plotting a way to get rid of her. Now he'd have her at his mercy. Silent Waters smiled slightly. Maybe Willie would be so pleased that he'd let her see Laughing Eyes any time she wanted to.

Lark squirmed and moaned. The taste in her mouth made her gag, and the ground felt damp and cold under her. Where was she? Was it a bad dream? She forced open her eyes but couldn't see anything. She felt a cool breeze against her face and heard someone breathing beside her. She lifted her head, then moaned.

"You are awake," said Silent Waters.

Fear pricked Lark's skin. "Where am I?"

"Don't talk."

"Who are you? . . . I know you, don't I?"

"I am Silent Waters."

Lark gasped. "What do you want of me?"

"No more talk."

Lark clumsily pushed herself up and sat with her knees

drawn to her chest. She wanted to leap up and run, but she knew she wouldn't be able to get away while her brain was foggy and her legs trembling.

A bobcat screamed and Lark shivered. A great horned owl fluttered from a tree and swooshed up into the sky.

Without warning Silent Waters covered Lark's nose and mouth with the rag. Lark struggled, but the chloroform overpowered her. Once again Silent Waters flung the unconscious form over her shoulder and walked through the woods to a shed at Red Beaver's farm. She slipped inside, bound Lark's wrists and ankles and tied a rag around her mouth to gag her when she awoke.

Silent Waters eased open the secret door that she'd discovered a few years ago and pushed Lark inside. Silent Waters smiled, then closed the door and moved a potato planter enough to partially cover the door.

Much later Lark whimpered and tried to move to get comfortable on the chilly dirt floor. The rag in her mouth choked her and the ropes around her ankles and wrists bit into her soft flesh. Silently she prayed for Clay or Red Beaver to find her. Tears welled up in her eyes and she blinked them quickly away. It wouldn't do any good to cry.

When she heard a voice and saw a tiny flash of light she tried to yell, but the sounds wouldn't pass through the rag in her mouth. She bucked, but couldn't move enough to make a noise. Her pulse raced and perspiration soaked her face and blue calico dress. Again she shouted, but only a low sound came out, too low for anyone to hear. She whimpered and closed her eyes. How long would it take Clay to know she was missing? Would he even consider Silent Waters as the culprit? Lark moaned. Probably not. He'd assume it had been someone who wanted to steal the pines.

Lark's eyes widened. Had Silent Waters taken her to turn her over to Willie Thorne? Maybe he'd learned his wife had told her everything. Silently Lark prayed for someone to rescue her.

She heard a scratching sound and froze. Was it a rat? She bucked again and frantically tried to pull her arms free. Pain shot up her arms and down to her fingertips and she stopped struggling. She listened again, but couldn't hear the sound. She couldn't survive if rats came in to chew on her. She felt like the terrified child she'd been when Matron locked her in the cellar room when she was six years old. She balled up as tight as she could and waited for someone to come for her.

His stomach a tight, cold ball, Clay knocked on the cabin door again. A warm breeze ruffled his black striped shirt that was tucked into his dark work pants. The heavy walking boots felt awkward today after not wearing them for so long. He glanced at Sears straining at his rope. If Lark had left to walk the trail, why hadn't she taken Sears? If she was still here, why wasn't she answering the door?

"Lark? Open the door, Lark." Clay pulled off his straw hat, leaned his head against the heavy door, and listened for movement inside. None came. "It's me, Clay. I'm coming in." He hesitated a moment longer, then opened the door and looked inside. It was empty. "Lark?" He frowned as a shiver ran down his spine. "Where are you? Where is she?"

Clay glanced around the cabin. Lark's buckskins were draped over a chair, the cudgel and revolver lay on the table, and the bed was rumpled. "Something happened to her," he whispered as his heart turned over. She had a lot of enemies. Had someone who wanted to steal the trees killed her and carried her off? Would Willie Thorne take her? Or had Matron hired someone to get rid of her out of spite?

"Clay!"

He jumped, then hurried to the door to find his sister calling to him. She wore a heavy shirtwaist and skirt, leggings, and high top boots instead of the Sunday clothes he'd expected her to be wearing. "Hannah, do you know where Lark would be?"

"No." Hannah pushed her bonnet off her head to dangle

between her shoulder blades. "I saw Flame and wondered why you were here."

"Lark's gone." Clay showed Hannah the cabin. "She'd never leave without her revolver and cudgel or her work clothes."

"I was going with her this morning," said Hannah, fingering the long braid that hung over her slender shoulder. "I said I'd keep her company, then we were going to church together afterward."

"I came to tell her I'd walk the trail today," said Clay. "She's been under a lot of pressure and I wanted to give her a day off."

Hannah bent down and picked up a small red bead from the floor. Had Red Beaver been here? Her pulse leaped, then she shook her head. He'd never take Lark. But Silent Waters might. "Look, Clay." Hannah held out the bead on the palm of her hand. "Let's go talk to Red Beaver to see what he knows."

"He and his mother aren't the only Indians around here, Hannah."

"I know. But it's a beginning. And Silent Waters hates us. She might want to harm Lark."

Clay groaned as he stared off into the pines. Was Silent Waters really Willie Thorne's squaw? Was that why she hated the Havlicks? Had Agnes Thorne told the truth when she'd said Red Beaver and Veda were the children of Willie Thorne and Silent Waters?

"We'll take Sears with us," said Hannah as she walked toward the wide-chested Dalmatian. "He'll help us find Lark."

"We'll go get the wagon," said Clay, forcing himself into action after the paralyzing thoughts that plagued him. Could he still marry Veda if she really was part Patawatomi?

With Sears running beside them, Clay and Hannah rode double on Flame back to the farm. Clay hitched up the wagon, lifted Sears into the back while Hannah climbed on the high seat, then climbed in himself.

At Red Beaver's farm Hannah jumped from the wagon, her heart racing. The sun was bright in the sky already drying yesterday's rain. Chickens, turkeys, ducks, and geese walked around the yard looking for bugs or worms. A cow mooed and a donkey brayed. Wind whirled the blades of the windmill, pumping water into the big round tank in the barnyard. Hannah looked around for Red Beaver, then saw him run from the barn with his hired man, Dave Legg, behind him. Red Beaver looked tall next to the short, round hired man. Hannah's heart leaped at the sight of Red Beaver. She saw his eyes light up when he saw her, but he quickly masked his feelings.

"Is there trouble?" asked Red Beaver, looking from Clay to Hannah and back again. He couldn't trust himself to look too long on Hannah. He might give away his feelings for her.

"Is it me Cora?" asked Dave, rubbing a pudgy hand over his round face. Cora was Jennet Havlick's hired girl and Dave's oldest daughter.

"Cora's fine," said Hannah.

Dave breathed a sigh of relief.

"We're looking for Lark Baritt," said Clay. "Have you seen her, either last night or this morning?"

"No," said Red Beaver while Dave Legg shook his head. "Is something wrong?"

"She's missing," said Clay, stabbing his fingers through his hair. Sears whined from the back of the wagon.

"We found a small red bead on her cabin floor," said Hannah. "We thought you might know something."

Red Beaver frowned. "Do you suspect my mother?"

Hannah barely nodded.

"She hates the Havlicks," said Clay.

"I know and I'm sorry," said Red Beaver. He glanced at Hannah, then quickly away. White woman or Indian, he'd never met one he'd wanted to be his wife except Hannah Havlick. Silent Waters would object as much as the Havlicks, so he'd kept his feelings to himself. He knew Silent Waters' anger and bitterness were eating holes in her spirit and turning her into a woman he didn't know, but she wouldn't give up her hatred. "I'll speak to her. Wait here."

Hannah watched Red Beaver run easily across the yard to the white fence. Instead of going through the gate, he leaped the fence as if he'd done it thousands of times, ran to the back door, and disappeared inside.

"He won't find her," said Dave Legg with a long, tired sigh. "He don't know it, but she left last night and ain't returned yet."

"Why didn't you tell him?" asked Clay, frowning.

Dave shrugged his thick shoulders. "She disappears at times. But she always comes back."

His hands locked behind his back and his head down, Clay nervously paced the length of the wagon and back. Why did everything have to take so long? Lark could be hurt or even dead. Silently he prayed for her, but the weight stayed in his heart. He should've insisted she leave the cabin and the job. The asylum might not be a nice place to live, but she would've been safe there.

Her fingers laced together in front of her, Hannah watched the back door for Red Beaver. How she hated to see him hurting! It would be terrible to live with a hate-filled mother. Jennet Havlick was a wonderful mother, full of love and gentleness. She taught and lived the fruits of the spirit that Jesus had taught. Hannah bit her lip. Someday she'd be a mother just like her.

Finally Red Beaver walked back, his shoulders bent in defeat. "She's not in the house. If she knows anything about this, she could be hiding anywhere so she won't have to answer questions."

"I'm sorry," said Hannah softly.

Red Beaver glanced at her, but the love he saw in her eyes made him look quickly away.

"We brought Sears to help us find Lark," said Clay, helping Sears jump to the ground. "Can we look around?"

"Yes," said Red Beaver. "But Dave and I have been in most of the buildings already this morning."

"She's not here or we'd a seen her," said Dave, nodding hard.

Flags of red flew in Hannah's cheeks. "We'll take Sears and look anyway."

Red Beaver flushed hotly and nodded. He hated to think his mother had stolen Lark away, but he knew it was possible. Silent Waters knew the pines as well as she knew the woods around his farm.

Clay ran with Sears to the big barn. The others waited in the doorway as Sears zigzagged down the aisle, then back to Clay's side. He ran to the next building and the next, waiting just inside each one long enough for Sears to sniff it out. In the shed next to the chicken coop Sears ran to the back corner and scratched against a board.

"There's nothing back there but maybe a rat," said Red Beaver. "Dave, finish the chores while we look."

Dave nodded and walked reluctantly away.

Clay stepped around some stored machinery to where Sears was sniffing and scratching. "Did you find something?" Clay said.

"There's nothing there, Clay," said Hannah, her shoulders drooping with disappointment. She felt Red Beaver beside her and she wanted to reach out and touch him, but she kept her hands at her sides.

Sears barked and scratched at the rough board.

Behind the board Lark tried to shout and tried to kick, but she couldn't. Tears of frustration rolled down her face as she lay curled on her side unable to make a sound Clay and Hannah could hear.

Clay studied the board as Sears scratched harder. Clay patted Sears on the neck. "There's nothing there, boy. Let's look in the other buildings."

"We have to find her," whispered Hannah.

Clay began to walk away, but Sears wouldn't move.

"Red Beaver, what's behind that board?" asked Clay.

Red Beaver looked and shook his head. "It's only the siding."

"Can you pull off just that one board and see?" asked Hannah.

Red Beaver hesitated, then nodded. He'd tear down the whole shed if Hannah asked him to. As he started to pry it off he suddenly saw the hidden door. He pulled aside the potato planter.

"A door!" Clay bent to open it. Inside was a small hidden room, the kind that could've been used to hide runaway slaves. As his eyes adjusted to the darkness inside, he saw Lark bound and gagged. "It's Lark," he whispered hoarsely as he reached for her.

Hannah held Sears aside to leave room for Clay to move. "You found her, Sears," said Hannah with tears in her eyes as she patted Sears on the neck.

"Forgive my mother," said Red Beaver in a ragged voice.

"It's not your fault," said Hannah softly.

Red Beaver turned his head and bent his shoulders in anguish and shame.

Clay eased Lark out and pulled the gag from her mouth. Tears blinded her eyes as she looked into Clay's face. He gently untied her wrists and rubbed the red welts on her wrists. He untied her ankles. He lifted his head and tears stood in his eyes. "I'm sorry, Lark."

She wiped the tears from her eyes. "It was Silent Waters," she whispered. "Somehow she was able to drug me."

Red Beaver cried in agony as he knelt beside Lark and Clay on the dirt floor. "I'm sorry! Forgive my mother! Hatred has overcome her."

"You know I'll have the sheriff after her for this," said Clay in a hard voice.

"Clay!" cried Hannah. "Don't hurt Red Beaver more than he is already!"

"Let it be, Hannah," said Red Beaver. Her name fell off his tongue as easily as if he'd called her by name often. But always he'd called her Miss Havlick to her face. He'd spoken *Hannah* only in his daydreams.

"Don't blame Red Beaver," said Lark, struggling to her feet. She stumbled and Clay caught her and held her until she felt steady enough to stand.

"*I* blame myself," said Red Beaver sharply.

"Please don't," said Lark as she pulled away from Clay. Her taffy hair hung in wild tangles around her head and shoulders. She pushed it back off her face, leaving a dirt streak from her hand. "It doesn't do any good to talk of blame." She turned to Clay. "Please take me home. I must make sure the pines are safe."

A muscle jumped in Clay's jaw. "You'll do no such thing, Lark Baritt! I'll check *my* pines while you rest."

Lark cringed at his stress of the word *my*. She knew the pines were his, but at times she felt they belonged to her too. Finally she nodded. "All right. I'll rest for a while." She patted Sears on the head, then bent down and hugged him. "Thanks for finding me."

Clay swallowed a lump in his throat and blinked moisture from his eyes.

Outdoors Hannah turned to Clay. "I want to speak with Red Beaver. Take Lark home and I'll walk."

Clay frowned. "Pa wouldn't want you to stay by yourself."

Hannah lifted her chin. "I'm staying, Clay. I'll explain to Pa later."

"Go home with your brother, Miss Havlick," said Red Beaver sharply. "There's nothing for you to say to me."

"I will stay and I will speak my mind," Hannah said with more courage than she felt.

Lark smiled at Hannah, then let Clay help her into the wagon. Sears stuck his nose against her cheek and she patted his shoulder.

Clay slapped the reins on the team and they stepped forward.

"I'm sorry I worried you," said Lark.

"I'm just thankful you're alive," said Clay. "I am going to tell the sheriff." Clay shook his head. "But if Silent Waters doesn't want to be found, he won't find her. She's spent her entire life in the woods around here."

"She frightened me. I've never seen anyone with so much anger."

"She won't do anything to you again. She won't have another chance. You're moving out of the cabin and back to the asylum."

Lark turned on Clay. "No! I can take care of myself. I won't let her capture me again."

"I don't understand you, Lark. The pines don't even belong to you."

Tears blurred her eyes. She felt like the pines did belong to her! Around the lump in her throat she said, "I know, but I love them. I will do anything to keep them safe."

Clay heard the same passion in her voice that he heard in his mother's when she spoke of the pines. "I don't want anything to happen to you," he said with his eyes on the team and the road ahead.

Lark blinked away her tears and lifted her chin. "Someday I want my children and my grandchildren to see your white pines! I want them to have a part of what Michigan once was when Jig first came. I want the habitat left the way it is."

The passion she felt blazed in her eyes and through her speech. He knew he couldn't take the pines from her. She did indeed love them the way he and his family did. With a sigh he said, "I won't take them from you."

"Thank you," she whispered. Relief left her limp, but she held herself erect to keep from leaning against Clay.

At Red Beaver's farm Hannah squared her shoulders and turned to face Red Beaver. They had kept their love for each other locked inside long enough. It was time to speak up. After what had happened to Lark, she felt frightened about losing more valuable time. The sun felt hot against her head.

The fire in her breast felt even hotter. "We must talk freely about our feelings for each other, Red Beaver," she said with a catch in her voice.

Red Beaver groaned. "We dare not."

"I need you to tell me how you feel about me, Red Beaver," she cried.

A muscle jumped in his cheek. Behind him he heard the bray of a donkey and the squeak of the windmill. His heart pounded at the thought of speaking the words to Hannah that he'd only said in his daydreams. He shook his head. "I can't, Hannah, not after what Silent Waters has done to Lark."

"She doesn't blame you. Nor do I." Hannah clasped her hands to her heart. "I care for you." She saw his eyes darken. "Do you care at all for me?"

Red Beaver gripped her arms. "You don't know what you're doing, Hannah."

"I do! I want you to tell me how you feel about me. I've waited too long already."

Red Beaver moved closer to Hannah, but he dropped his hands to his sides. "What I feel for you is a love so intense it would frighten you. I want you as my wife. I want you in my bed, in my house, on my farm, at my side for as long as we live."

Hannah trembled and her heart soared at his words. She leaned forward until they touched. "I love you."

Red Beaver held her fiercely to him and she clung to him as if she'd never let him go. He smelled the clean smell of her hair and skin. She felt his heart thud against her and smelled his earthy smell. Finally he pushed her at arm's length and looked deep into her eyes. "But I can never take you as my wife. I will live out my days alone with the shame of what Silent Waters did to Lark and to the Havlick family."

Hannah shook her head. "No!"

"I am a man of honor."

"Red Beaver, I can't survive without you." Tears welled up in Hannah's eyes and slipped down her ashen cheeks.

"Nor I without you. But my shame is too great." Red Beaver knew how Freeman Havlick felt about him. Now there was one more reason for him to despise him. "You find a white man to love and marry."

"Never! I too will live all my days alone. You are the only man I want as my husband, the father of my children, my companion until we die. You have brought a lifetime of loneliness on me because of your pride."

A groan rose from deep inside Red Beaver. "You must forget about me."

Hannah lifted her chin and flames shot from her eyes. "Never! Do you hear me? I will love you forever."

With a low moan Red Beaver cupped Hannah's face between his work-roughened hands. He looked deep into her eyes, then slowly lowered his mouth to hers and kissed her with all the pent up passion in him.

Hannah clung tightly to him, returning the kiss while her heart raced.

Finally Red Beaver held her from him and said softly, "I love you."

"And will marry me before winter comes," she whispered.

Red Beaver shook his head. "I can't."

Hannah leaned weakly against him. "Then I shall die an old maid."

CHAPTER 9

♦ Clay leaned against the top rail of the fence beside Free and absently watched Evie train her pony to jump. Dust billowed out behind the pony's hooves. Clay's mind was on Veda and Silent Waters and Agnes Thorne's story. What was the truth and what was a sick woman's ranting?

Free chuckled. "Evie's like her ma. She won't quit even when she's tired." It was almost time for Evie to go inside for the night, but she wanted to take the pony around one more time.

Clay moved restlessly.

"What is it, son? You've been on edge since Sunday. Are you brooding about Lark's experience? She seems to be fine. Surely something like that won't happen again."

"She's a strong woman," said Clay. "I'm learning not to worry about her." He was amazed that she'd gone right back out Monday morning to walk the line, then had gone to work at the asylum as if nothing had happened to her.

"Then what's on your mind, Clay?"

"Red Beaver."

Free stiffened. "I'm not blaming you for Hannah's disobedience."

Clay faced Free. "Are you against Red Beaver because he's Patawatomi or because he's Willie Thorne's son?"

Free's eyes widened and he shot a look at Evie before he turned back to Clay. "I didn't know you knew."

"I found out a few days ago." Clay steeled himself to ask the next question. "Do Silent Waters and Willie Thorne have other children?"

"No. Willie went off to marry Agnes and left Red Beaver and Silent Waters on their own."

Relieved, Clay leaned back against the fence. Agnes Thorne hadn't been thinking clearly when she'd told Lark about Veda. He'd stayed away from Veda to try to sort out his feelings, but now it didn't matter. Veda wasn't Patawatomi. Clay cringed as he realized how prejudiced he was. He hadn't realized it before.

"Have you heard anything from the Lansing detective?" asked Free. He had been trying to find a way to help Lark find her father, but first he wanted to see what the detective discovered.

Clay shook his head. "He said he found a copy of the book he'd written, but couldn't find him."

"I think I'll send word to the lumbermen I know and see what they can find."

"Thanks, Pa. Lark will be glad to hear that."

"She's a fine woman, Clay."

Clay nodded. He knew Free was getting ready to compare her with Veda and he didn't want to hear it. "I have business in town, Pa. I'll be late getting home." Veda had stopped at the Wagon Works earlier in the day and wanted to have supper again tonight, but he'd said he couldn't until tomorrow night. She'd pouted at first, then she'd kissed him and walked away to shop for things for the wedding. He waved to Evie, then ran to the buggy he'd hitched earlier and drove away.

At Blue Creek Clay heard the last train of the day pull away from the station. The loud hiss, rattle, and clank covered all other sounds in the town for a while. He stopped the team to the side of the street and waited. He watched two boys race their bicycles along the street. The wheel was becoming very popular around the country because it was cheaper than keeping a horse. He knew Miles wanted a wheel more than anything else. Pa said as soon as the roads were better he could get one. It was hard to keep a wheel upright on the corduroy.

Clay sighed. Sometimes he liked change and other times he didn't. Probably the wheel would take the place of riding horses and the gas buggy the place of a horse drawn buggy. Would anything ever take the place of a wagon?

Just then Willie Thorne stepped out of his tavern. It still wasn't open for business, but Clay knew men sneaked in from time to time for a "drink on the house." The Temperance League was still hard at work to keep the doors closed and locked. Clay frowned. Would Willie Thorne ever give up and leave town?

Just then Willie spotted Clay. Willie waved and strode down the wooden sidewalk to where Clay was stopped. Willie puffed out his chest and wrapped his hands around his suspenders. He wanted to ask Clay about Lark Baritt, but since no word had gotten out about her abduction, he couldn't. He'd told Silent Waters to let him handle the problems, but she'd wanted to do something to please him. Just seeing her pleased him, but he couldn't tell her that or she might take it on herself to get rid of Agnes.

Willie shook his finger at Clay. "I don't want you seeing my daughter again, young Havlick!"

Clay tightened his grip on the reins. "I'll see her if I want, Mr. Thorne."

Willie hid a smile. He'd already figured out Clay was the type who would try harder if he was told not to do something. "She won't get a dime of my money if she marries you."

"I have enough money without taking any of yours," snapped Clay.

"I won't have you eloping with her," said Willie gruffly. The wind ruffled his graying red hair.

"We don't plan to elope," said Clay.

"See that you don't!" Willie turned on his heels and stalked away. Suddenly he turned back and shouted, "And don't you marry my girl until winter!"

Clay wanted to shout that he'd marry her any time they decided, but he saw others listening. He slapped the reins on the team and drove to the Thorne house. He had a mind to elope with Veda that very day. His straw hat in his hand, he knocked on the door and Gert answered.

"Well, Clay Havlick, it's a real pleasure to see you, I believe," said Gert, opening the door wide enough for him to enter.

He heard the tick of the grandfather clock beside the tall green plant in the big hallway. He smelled oil soap and could tell someone had recently been at work cleaning and polishing the open stairway and the carved newel posts and bannister.

"How's your dear mother and father?" asked Gert with just a hint of nervousness in her voice.

"They're fine," said Clay, smiling down at Gert.

She touched the little black cap on her head and rubbed the black apron tied around her thick waist. "What brings you here?"

"To see Veda Thorne."

"But she's not here. She and Mrs. Thorne went to Grand Rapids on the afternoon train, and won't be back until tomorrow."

"I didn't know that."

"It was one of those spur of the moment things."

Clay fingered the wide brim of his straw hat. "I heard Mrs. Thorne wasn't well."

Gert spread her hands and shrugged. "She has her days, but she was fine today."

Clay watched Gert closely. "Lark said she came here and visited with her."

Nervously Gert rubbed her plump hands together. "It was to be a secret between me and Lark."

"I won't tell."

"Mr. Thorne would get up in arms if he knew his wife talked with Lark."

A shiver ran down Clay's spine. "Why?"

"Mrs. Thorne says things. Things that he doesn't want said, I believe." Gert patted her flushed cheeks and again rubbed her hands over her black apron.

Clay wanted to ask more questions, but he knew Gert wouldn't answer them. He talked a while longer, turned down the piece of apple pie she offered him, and walked back to his buggy.

He stopped at the Wagon Works and to his surprise found Dag still at work carving spokes.

Dag grinned. He enjoyed the work and he knew it wouldn't hurt to do extra work to get on Clay's good side. Dag wanted a key to the shop to give him the freedom to come and go as he wanted. He glanced toward a case of liquor partly hidden near the workbench, then smiled at Clay. "Caught me," said Dag.

Clay shook his head. "You should've stopped at six like the other men. Six to six makes a long day."

Dag carved off another strip of wood. "I think while I work, Clay. I have no family. What do I have to take up my nights? I don't drink and I don't gamble."

"Neither are allowed in Blue Creek."

Dag laughed. "Then it's good I don't do either." What would Clay do when he found his men drinking on the job tomorrow? Willie had dropped off the case of whiskey just a few minutes ago. If the men were drunk, they couldn't work well, and Clay wouldn't be able to fill the contract.

Clay picked up the spokes and eyed them one by one. They were perfect. "I'm glad you happened in when you did, Dag."

"It's like it was planned," said Dag.

"Ma says to bring you to supper one night. She and Pa want to meet you. Jig was like family to us."

The offer surprised but pleased Dag. "You name the day and I'll be there." Dag laid the drawing knife down and brushed shavings off his plaid work shirt and dark pants. "I would like to see the cabin my grandfather called home."

"I'll arrange it."

"If I can, I would like to live in it."

Clay shook his head. "The guard for my pines lives there."

"I didn't know. I would like to see it and touch what my grandfather touched."

Clay thought about Jig's muzzleloader, but he couldn't bring himself to offer it to Dag. There was plenty of time. Clay was sure he was being overcautious, but there was something about Dag that kept him from totally trusting him. Maybe given time he'd learn to trust Dag as much as he'd trusted Jig. "Sunday afternoon we could take a ride out there together."

"I could work Sunday."

"No. We don't work Sundays." Clay smiled. "But I like your attitude." Clay clamped a hand on Dag's shoulder. "Call it a night and I'll lock up."

"Timmers said he'd be by later to lock up," said Dag as he put away his tools and quickly cleaned the area. "I'll stop by his place and tell him you locked up."

"Thanks, Dag." Clay watched Dag walk to the main street and turn toward the boarding house. Clay started out the door, then remembered he hadn't logged in the wages. With a sigh he pulled the book from his desk. Suddenly the job seemed too much for him. Maybe now was the time to ask Lark to keep the books. "She's probably still at the asylum," he muttered as he quickly locked the large doors and walked to his buggy. Since Matron had left, Lark had taken over many of her duties until the board could hire a new superintendent. Often she stayed late. He flicked the reins against the horse, then frowned. Why was he suddenly excited about seeing her? It had to be because it would be so much easier to run his business if she kept the books.

A few minutes later Clay walked into the asylum and stood a moment in the wide front hall. Laughter floated down the stairs. The smell of cookies drifted out from the kitchen. He turned toward Matron's office that Lark had taken over until the replacement arrived. The door stood open and he saw her sitting at the big desk with her head in her hands. He frowned. Was she already too overworked to take on another job?

He tapped on the door and stepped into the room, taking off his hat as he did.

The color drained from her face as Lark jumped up and ran to him. Her waist and skirt were slightly wrinkled and the button at her throat was unbuttoned. Tendrils that had pulled loose from the pile of taffy brown hair on her head hung around her face. She clasped her hands at her throat and tried to steady the wild beat of her heart. "Did you hear word of my father?" She was sure that was the only reason he would come to the asylum looking for her.

"No."

Lark drooped just like a flower with no water. "What is taking so long?" she whispered brokenly.

Clay awkwardly patted her shoulder. "Don't give up," he said gently. He told her what his pa planned to do and she brightened.

Absently Lark brush her hair from her cheek. "All my life I thought I had nobody of my own. Now that I know I do, I want to find him and get to know him. But oh, the waiting is agony!"

"I wish I could help." Suddenly Clay grinned. "I just might be able to."

Lark lifted a dark brow. "How?"

"By keeping you busier than you already are."

"I use that on the children here. Busy hands make time pass faster." Lark leaned back against the desk and smiled at Clay. Just having him stop in had brightened her day. "What do you have in mind?"

"I need someone to do the bookkeeping for the Wagon Works. Would you like the job? The pay is good and . . . the boss is nice." Clay chuckled and Lark laughed. He liked the sound of her laughter.

"I'll do it. When shall I start?"

"I'm already behind."

"Then I'll start tomorrow if that's all right with you. I can do it here or at the shop."

"Here would be better. I don't have an actual office there and you'd be a big distraction to the men."

Lark flushed. She knew Clay was only teasing. She was as plain as a post and wouldn't distract any man. "Does it look like you'll make your contract?"

"Yes. Thank the Lord."

Mrs. Pepper knocked on the door and ushered in a middle aged woman with light brown hair and big blue eyes. She was short and slight and looked on the verge of laughing. "Lark, Clay, I'd like you to meet the new matron, Mercy Kettering. Mercy comes highly recommended and is willing to start immediately."

Lark stepped forward with her hand out. "I'm happy to meet you, Matron."

"Call me Mercy." She shook hands with Lark, then with Clay. "I like your town and I know I'll like the Home." She smiled brightly. "I would rather call it a *home* instead of an *asylum.*"

"That is better," said Lark, liking Mercy immediately. "I've been using your office, but I'll move my things to leave it free for you."

"That's very kind of you."

"Welcome to our town," said Clay, tipping his head slightly.

"Thank you," said Mercy.

"I've told her about the tavern," said Mrs. Pepper.

Mercy squared her shoulders and her eyes twinkled. "I've walked into many a tavern with my tambourine in my hands and a hymn on my lips to stop demon rum from destroying folks. I look forward to doing it again here in your pleasant town."

"My mother will be right with you," said Clay.

"And so will I," said Lark with a firm nod. So far she'd never stepped foot in a tavern to close it down, but she would if she had to.

They talked a while longer, said goodbye, and Clay helped Lark carry her things to her office. The evening breeze ruffled the curtains at the windows. The room seemed small to Lark after being in Matron's office the past few days.

"I'm thankful we have a matron again," said Lark. "I like her, don't you?"

Clay nodded. "She's different from Anna Pike, and thank the good Lord for that. I think she'll be wonderful with the kids."

"I had the same impression. She has a soft glove covering a hand of steel." Lark put her things away and closed the windows for the night.

"I'll drive you home if you're ready," said Clay.

Her heart gave a strange little jerk. "No need. I can walk. I'm sure you have more important things to do."

"Not at all."

"What about Veda?"

Clay shrugged. "She's away tonight."

"Oh." Lark pinned her small hat in place and picked up her handbag. She suddenly remembered the feel of Clay's arms around her when he'd rescued her and she flushed. She would not let herself care for Clay Havlick! She was not good enough for him even if he had been available. "I'm ready," she said in a small voice.

The next day after Clay left the building with the bookwork under his arm, Dag "accidentally" discovered the case of whiskey. He held up a bottle. "I don't know who this belongs to, but I say we break it and pour the foul drink on the ground."

"Hold it!" cried Clarence, grabbing the bottle from Dag. "You can't throw away good whiskey."

"You can't drink on the job," said Dag. "It's not right." He knew that was like saying "sic 'em" to a bulldog. He stepped away from the whiskey and watched the men crowd around it. Some of them tried to stop the drinking, but couldn't without a fight. Quietly Dag slipped to the other building. There he "found" another case of whiskey, pretended shock and outrage, and stepped aside so the men could greedily break open the bottles. By the end of an hour, about fifteen men were too drunk to work. A few others could work, but not up to the standards Clay had set.

Inside Dag was laughing, but he didn't let it show on his face or in his eyes. He'd learned that in the orphan asylum in Grand Rapids. While the drinking continued and the noise grew louder around him he carefully slipped a tenon he'd carved then shaped into the mortise. "A perfect fit," he muttered, pleased with himself. When he finished, the slope of the mortises in the hub automatically created the required dish shape. The dish curved toward the inside of the wagon so when the wagon was fully loaded the hubs were forced outward and the spokes would straighten up rather than bow out. If the wheels weren't dished, then as the load shifted, the wheels would bow outward and split apart. "Well done," he said. "Well done." He liked doing a job well.

Dag glanced up just as Clay walked in. Dag tensed, but he didn't let his tension show.

Clay looked at the men in horror. Several of them were sprawled across a crate, singing and laughing. Two had passed out on the ground. "Who brought drink in here?" Clay shouted angrily.

"Not me," said Higgins with a slurred laugh.

"Me kind angel did it," said O'Brian, lifting a bottle high.

Clay looked at the sober men and questioned them, but no one could tell how the whiskey came to be in the buildings. "You men go home and sober up so you can work tomorrow. If you ever drink on the job again, I'll fire you on the spot."

"But you can't meet your contract if you do that," said Mullins.

"I'll hire men from out of town," said Clay. "I will not allow drinking on the job." His head ached with anger. He'd report the whiskey to the sheriff, but he knew it wouldn't do any good. Had Willie Thorne brought the whiskey here? If the sheriff could prove that, he'd be able to kick Willie out of town. What would Veda think of that? Clay's head spun. Maybe Willie didn't have anything to do with bringing the whiskey in.

His fists clenched at his sides, Clay watched the men leave the shop. The ones left couldn't begin to meet production, but he'd keep them working anyway.

Dag watched Clay's control and was astonished. He'd expected Clay to rave with anger and maybe break a few bones or bloody some noses. If Willie Thorne expected to break Clay, he'd have to try harder.

Late in the afternoon Lark stepped from the dress shop where she'd stopped to talk with Sally and bumped into John Epson. "I'm so sorry," said Lark with a laugh as she stepped away from him.

"That's quite all right, Lark." John stroked his well trimmed beard and chuckled. He'd been waiting ten minutes already for Lark to come out of the dress shop. He pulled off his straw hat and held it between his hands. A slight breeze ruffled his black hair. "I don't get run into by a fine lady very often."

Lark straightened her hat and brushed a damp tendril of hair off her cheek. "I usually don't go around hitting men. Unless it's with my cudgel when they jump me in the pines."

"Would you leave your cudgel behind and join me for supper?" John smiled and his white teeth flashed through his black beard and his blue eyes crinkled at the corners.

Lark bit back a gasp of surprise. She'd never been invited to eat with a man. Several months ago she would've given anything to be with John. Even now she felt a flash of excitement as she nodded.

In the restaurant Lark looked around the crowded room.

She knew several of the people and she knew John did too. They spoke to several people as they walked around the square tables to an empty one near the back.

Smiling, Peg took their orders of perch for Lark and roast beef for John. She served them tall glasses of cold water, then hurried to the kitchen.

"I'm glad I decided to come to Blue Creek to live," said John. "I considered Lansing for a while."

"This is a nice place," said Lark. "The lumber mill and the farms provide good incomes. The economy is stable right now."

John cocked his dark brow. He hadn't realized Lark would know such things. "Do you approve of President Harrison?"

"He's a fine republican."

"What about the Sherman Antitrust Act?"

"A monopoly is harmful to the people. Competition keeps prices fair."

John leaned forward with interest. It had been a good while since he'd had a debate and he was looking forward to it. Willie had said to spend time with Lark and he hadn't wanted to, but now he was pleased he had agreed to it. He'd do anything to get her away from the pines so Willie could steal them. And a portion of every dollar Willie made belonged to him. Willie had first hired him to manipulate Agnes's wealth so he could have free access to all her funds, then when Willie couldn't pay him, he'd become a partner in stealing the Havlicks' trees. Maybe it wouldn't be so bad to work toward a close relationship with Lark Baritt. They'd been casual friends for a couple of years now, but he'd never considered her for more than that until Willie had made it part of his plans.

Over dessert of cherry pie John said, "I don't know how you can continue to guard the Havlicks' pines when you know it puts you in danger."

Lark gripped her napkin and her dark eyes flashed. "Do you know how much I love those trees? They're a part of my life! I will do anything to keep them the way they are!" She leaned forward. "They were a haven to me all these years! I won't allow them to be destroyed!"

"You are passionate about the pines, aren't you?"

Lark laughed and nodded. She sipped her lemonade, then patted her mouth with the white linen napkin. No one could begin to understand how she felt about the trees, least of all John.

He leaned forward, his eyes on Lark. "What of the money Clay Havlick would make if he lumbered the pines?"

"There are more important things in life than money!" she snapped.

"You mean health and happiness, I suppose."

She frowned. "Don't make light of it."

"You can have health and happiness and still have money."

"I know that, but there are other ways to get money. Cutting the pines would be terrible for everyone. Even you, John."

He shook his head. "The pines are nothing to me." He didn't add that they only meant money in his pocket.

"Don't you know God created the earth for our enjoyment?"

"I suppose I do," he said uncertainly.

"Have you ever seen a luna moth all dressed in green and looking like a royal princess? God created it; money can't buy it or produce it. Have you ever heard the golden notes of an oriole, an orange and black beauty? God created the oriole; money can't buy it or produce it. And the trees themselves! What beauties! Once most of the state was covered with trees. Do you realize the plant and animal life destroyed because of the lumbermen cutting the trees? These last trees must never be cut. I believe and the Havlicks believe God wants them left for others to enjoy."

John moved restlessly. If he wasn't careful he'd start to believe Lark. His mother talked that way. But he wouldn't let himself think about the heartbroken mother he'd left behind after the terrible fight with his father. "There's danger in the forest too, Lark."

"Do you mean the rattlesnakes this time of year? They can be dangerous, that's true. When it's this hot out you can't trust them to always rattle before they strike."

"Some people are like that," said John grimly.

"I know."

They talked a while longer and to John's surprise his respect for Lark grew. He'd have to guard against letting his emotions get the upper hand. He couldn't afford to get emotionally involved with Lark Baritt or it would ruin everything.

Outdoors John stopped Lark with a hand on her arm. "May I see you again, Lark?"

She stiffened. Had she heard correctly? "I'm sure you're joking, John. You know my background."

He frowned. "What do you mean by that?"

"You're a fine lawyer and probably had a good upbringing. I was raised at the asylum." Lark couldn't get used to calling it a "home." She looked down at her hands. "I'm not . . . not . . . good enough to associate with you."

A muscle jumped in John's cheek. How could she think that? She was modest and her standards high—two things the women he'd associated with didn't have. "Lark, I will take you to supper tomorrow night and every night after that!"

Lark laughed shakily. "We'll settle for tomorrow night, then. After that . . . well, we'll see."

John nodded. "Then I'll see you in the office tomorrow morning." He settled his white straw hat in place as he looked down the street. "I understand the asylum has a new matron."

"Yes." Lark laughed softly. "Mercy Kettering, a fine woman. Already the children have learned to respect her."

"I look forward to meeting her." John tipped his hat and walked away.

Lark walked slowly back to the asylum to speak to Zoe before she went home. Zoe wanted to talk to her about Tris Havlick and what she could do to make him interested in her even if she was only an orphan. Lark's mind was full of thoughts of her supper with John Epson. She frowned slightly. Why would he want to take her to supper and spend time with her? She stopped at the end of the brick walk in front of the asylum as she tried to think of a reason.

Her red hair flipping about her slender shoulders, Zoe ran down the sidewalk to meet Lark. "Thank goodness you're finally here! I'm so excited I'm ready to burst."

"What is it? Did Tris declare his undying love?" asked Lark with a laugh.

"It's not about Tris," said Zoe, fluttering a paper. "You got a telegram!"

Lark shivered and clutched Zoe's hand. "A telegram? Where is it? What does it say?"

CHAPTER 10

♦ Lark's hands shook as she opened the telegram. The collar of her shirtwaist seemed to bite into her soft flesh. For a minute her eyes wouldn't focus on the words. Finally she read, "Matt Baritt died of the fever December 18, 1889." Lark swayed and the telegram fluttered to the porch floor beside Zoe's feet.

"What's wrong, Lark?" asked Zoe anxiously.

Lark lifted her skirts and ran away from the asylum like a mad woman. Tears streamed down her ashen cheeks as she sped down the street and across the bridge toward the white pines, her haven.

Zoe picked up the telegram and read it. Tears burned her eyes. "I must find Clay. He'll know what to do," she whispered brokenly.

With her skirts held high, Zoe ran to the restaurant where she knew Clay usually took Veda. They were just walking to his buggy. "Clay!" called Zoe urgently as she ran to him, panting for breath.

He turned with a worried frown. Two men walked past and looked at them strangely.

"What's wrong?" asked Veda impatiently. She'd waited

several days for time with Clay and she was annoyed at Zoe's interruption.

Zoe pulled Clay aside and showed him the telegram. "Lark ran away crying," whispered Zoe.

"I'll find her," Clay said softly. He folded the telegram and pushed it into his suit coat pocket and turned to Veda. "An emergency has come up. I'll drop you at your home and see you tomorrow night."

Veda's face hardened. She wanted to shout her anger, but she knew she couldn't without upsetting Clay. "I hope it's nothing serious."

"It's nothing for you to be concerned about," said Clay as he handed her into his buggy. He turned back to Zoe. "You're a good friend. Run on back to the asylum and don't worry."

"Thank you, Clay." Zoe rubbed away her tears, tried to smile, and walked slowly away toward the asylum. A white cat ambled out of the corner store and rubbed against her ankles.

The buggy swayed as Clay stepped in. Absently he gathered the reins in his hands. Veda tucked her hand through Clay's arm and rested her head against his shoulder. Inside she was seething with anger. She'd planned to talk Clay into eloping tonight. "Will you tell me what happened?" she murmured, nestling close to him.

"Nothing that concerns you," Clay said, his voice even and unemotional as he drove toward her house. He couldn't bring himself to discuss Lark's business with Veda.

Veda's eyes blazed with anger as she sat up straight and folded her hands in her lap over her handbag. She had spent a fortune on the green silk dress she was wearing and the new green and black hat and Clay hadn't noticed. She dare not let him see how angry she was, though! "Everything that concerns you, concerns me," she said gently. "Is it your family?"

"No." Clay stopped the team outside Veda's door.

"Did something happen to the Wagon Works?"

"No." Actually, several men had gotten drunk on the job

again. He'd reported the illegal whiskey to the sheriff, but he hadn't been able to learn anything about it.

"Oh, Clay! Please tell me what's wrong or I'll imagine all kinds of terrible things." Veda stuck her lip out in a slight pout, something that always worked with her father.

"It's Lark," said Clay reluctantly as he helped Veda from the buggy.

Veda jerked away from Clay and her eyes flashed. "Lark Baritt! You cut our time together short because of that *orphan?*"

Clay jumped back in the buggy, tipped his hat, and drove away. He would have to deal with Veda's anger later. Right now he had to help Lark.

Veda stormed into the house, slamming the front door after her. She flung her handbag on a table outside the parlor door and ran to her father's study. She flung open the door, then stopped with a shocked cry.

Flushing with guilt, Willie jumped away from embracing Silent Waters. He'd thought it was safe for her to be in the house because Veda had gone out with Clay, Agnes was locked in her room, and the hired help was out for the evening. A warm breeze blew in through the open French doors. The tick of the mantle clock over the stone fireplace sounded loud in the quietness of the room.

Silent Waters looked hungrily at Veda, her eyes traveling slowly from Veda's head down to her beautifully clad feet. Oh, she was a beauty! What mother wouldn't be proud of her?

"Papa?" whispered Veda as she looked wide-eyed and helpless at him, then at the Patawatomi woman. It had never occurred to Veda that her father would be unfaithful to her mother.

"Why are you back, Veda?" asked Willie sharply. He desperately wished he'd turned Silent Waters away when she'd come knocking on his study door, but he hadn't been able to meet with her as regularly as he'd planned. Just seeing her at the door had left him as helpless as a lovesick boy.

"Clay went to help Lark Baritt!" Veda spit out the name as she balled her fists at her sides.

"Lark Baritt," muttered Silent Waters.

"Leave us, Silent Waters," said Willie briskly.

Silent Waters shook her head as she stepped toward Veda. "Laughing Eyes," she said softly and reached out to touch Veda's smooth cheek.

With a startled cry, Veda jumped back. "Don't touch me!" She shivered at the thought of an Indian touching her. Everyone knew they weren't like other humans.

Silent Waters stumbled back as if she'd been struck. Her own daughter wouldn't allow her to touch her! Tears filled her eyes and she turned helplessly to Willie. "What have you done to my child?"

Willie slapped Silent Waters across the cheek and the sound rang through the room. "Get out of here now!"

Silent Waters squared her shoulders. Her red calico dress fit snugly across her breasts down to her slender waist, then flared over her hips to fall in graceful folds at her moccasin covered feet. A rolled red scarf tied around her forehead held back her shiny, thick black hair. "If you force me to leave, I will take my daughter, my Laughing Eyes, with me."

Willie shook his head. He'd never been in such a tight spot. He saw the disgust for Indians on Veda's face. If she learned this Indian was her mother, what would she do? But he saw the determination on Silent Waters' face. This time she wouldn't be denied. Willie took Silent Waters' hands in his. He could feel the calluses on her hands and could see the look of love in her eyes. A pulse throbbed at her throat. Even though her body was rigid with anger, just touching her sent a wave of passion through him. "I'll take care of it," he said softly. "I promise you." He kissed her fingers, but she still didn't relax. "If you want to please me, leave us now. I'll talk to you later."

Veda pressed her hand to her racing heart. "Papa! How can you have anything to do with her?"

Willie turned to Veda with a frown and said sharply, "Don't

say anything against Silent Waters, Veda, or you'll have to reckon with me."

"Papa!" cried Veda in shock. He had never spoken to her in that tone before. First Clay cut short his time with her to run to that Lark Baritt and now this from her father who always sympathized with her. Her world was crumbling apart.

Willie pulled Silent Waters close and whispered against her smooth hair, "Come back tomorrow night."

Silent Waters trembled in his arms. How she longed to stay with her man and her daughter! "I will be back," she said softly.

Willie kissed her and didn't want to let her go. He walked with her to the French doors that opened into the garden and she slipped out. He watched until she was out of sight behind the barn, then he closed the door and with an unsteady hand lit the kerosene lamp on his desk. The flame burned high and he turned it down to keep the globe from blackening. Slowly he turned to face Veda.

"Papa, how could you hold . . . *her* and kiss . . . *her?*"

Willie ran his trembling fingers through his already mussed graying red hair. Could he tell Veda her real mother was an Indian full of love for her? How could he make her understand Indians are people, too, after all the years Agnes had taught her to despise them? "Sit down, Veda." He reached for her arm, but she pulled away. "Sit down!" he snapped as he pointed to the brown leather sofa.

Shocked again at his tone, Veda perched on the edge of the sofa, her hands on the smooth leather. Usually the smell of Papa's leather sofa soothed her, but tonight it turned her stomach. Why was he being mean to her? And why had he kissed that squaw?

Willie sat in the massive leather chair facing Veda. He tried to collect his thoughts, but his mind whirled with things to say to Veda and later to Silent Waters. "A man must make choices in his life, Veda," he said weakly. "Once I lived with Silent Waters. I loved her and she made me happy. But I knew I couldn't marry her. I needed a proper wife to help me make a name for myself. So, I married Agnes Groff." He gripped the arms of the chair. "Sometimes these things are necessary."

"Does Momma know about Silent Waters?"

Willie tipped his head to acknowledge that she did.

Veda's stomach knotted painfully. "Is that why she locks her bedroom door against you?"

Willie didn't want to go into that. "I want to talk about you and me and Silent Waters—not Agnes."

"I don't want to hear about Silent Waters!" Veda wanted to press her hands over her ears the way she had when she was a child when something unpleasant was about to be said. Her green silk dress suddenly felt hot and looked ugly to her.

Willie shook his head, then sighed tiredly. "Veda, I'd give anything if I didn't have to hurt you, but I must. It's time you knew the truth."

"Papa, don't . . . don't . . ." Veda saw the anguish on his face, but she hardened her heart toward him. He deserved her anger. "I don't want to hear anything about that Indian!"

"She is not *that Indian!* She is your mother."

Veda crumpled against the arm of the sofa. Had she heard correctly? "My mother is upstairs in bed."

"No. Agnes raised you." Willie ran a finger around his collar. "But she's not your mother."

The strength drained from Veda's body. "Do you mean the Indian woman is my mother?" she whispered hoarsely.

Willie nodded slightly.

"Is that why she called me Laughing Eyes?"

"Yes. It's your Indian name."

"I won't listen," she whispered, covering her ears and shaking her head.

He waited until she dropped her hands back in her lap. "You have to know the truth," he said crisply. He took a deep breath and blurted out the story of her birth and why he'd taken her from Silent Waters. "She didn't want to let you go, but I had to have you with me because I loved you so much. She already had my only son. I couldn't give you up too."

Veda gasped. "Red Beaver? He's my brother?"

"Yes."

Veda shook her head and moaned. She was part Indian! How could she survive the shame? She wanted to do something or say something that would hurt Papa as badly as she'd been hurt. "Clay Havlick will never marry me when he learns the truth."

"He won't learn the truth."

"But he might!"

"He's your chance for wealth and power," snapped Willie. "Don't ruin it."

Veda thought about it and finally nodded. "What if he does find out?"

Willie ran a finger around the snug collar of his shirt. "Then you'll have to talk him into eloping with you within the next few days before he can find out."

"I don't think I can."

"Don't lose your self-confidence, Veda."

"But Papa, I am no longer . . . whole."

Willie frowned. "What do you mean by that?"

"An Indian is not really human. You told me that."

Willie's face turned as red as his hair. "Agnes told you that and I was forced to agree even when I didn't. I know Indians are as human as white people even though others don't agree. Someday the rest of the folks in the United States will know it too." Willie pushed up off the chair and sat beside Veda on the sofa. "Now, what's this about young Havlick going to help Lark Baritt?"

Clay caught up with Lark at the edge of the Havlick property. She was running wildly and crying hysterically. Her hair had pulled loose from the bun at the nape of her neck and flowed around her shoulders and down her back. Dust covered the bottom of her skirt and her shoes. He jumped from the buggy and gripped her arm. Tears poured down her face as he turned her toward him.

"He's dead," she whimpered, looking through her tears into Clay's worried face.

"I'm so sorry, Lark."

"Dead before I could get to know him."

Clay wiped her tears away with his white handkerchief.

"I have no one," Lark whispered.

Clay pulled her close and held her tightly. He felt the flutter of her heart and the tension in her body. Wind blew her skirts around his legs and the intimacy of it sent a shudder through him. "You've made it through worse things, Lark. You can make it through this."

Lark shook her head and her forehead rubbed against the rough fabric of his jacket.

"God is with you, Lark. He never leaves you. He is your comfort and your strength."

She let the words sink into her heart until she was able to lift her head. She realized she was clinging to him and he was holding her. Flushing, she stepped away from him and tried to stop the wild thudding of her heart. She glanced up at the sky, surprised to find it already dark. "I must get home."

"I'll take you." Clay wanted to help her in the buggy, but she slipped past him and climbed in alone.

"Where's Veda?" asked Lark sharply.

Clay slapped the reins on the horses and they stepped forward. "I had supper with her, then took her home."

"Don't see her again." The words burst out before Lark knew she was going to say them.

Clay's jaw tightened. He turned off the road to cut across to the cabin. "Pa says Red Beaver is Willie Thorne's son with Silent Waters. Veda isn't, he said."

With trembling hands Lark pushed her hair back. She couldn't look at Clay. "The Thornes and Silent Waters know the truth."

"Don't you ever give up?"

"No."

The next morning Lark walked slowly through the pines with Sears beside her. She rested the cudgel on her shoulder as she walked. She tried not to think about all she'd missed by not meeting her father, but thoughts crept in anyway. The smell of pine seemed almost overwhelming. The heat pressed in on her and she wished she'd worn her old calico dress instead of her breeches. The buckskin kept her from getting too many scratches and gave her legs more protection in case a rattlesnake struck, but the leather was hot.

She walked through the briars while bees buzzed around her. Just as Lark caught a flash of movement to her right Sears growled low in his throat. Red Beaver had warned her Silent Waters wouldn't give up trying to harm her. Was it Silent Waters or was someone else after her? Maybe it was a deer or even a bear.

She scanned the area around the spot where she thought she'd seen movement. But she saw only tree trunks and underbrush. Her heart lodged in her throat.

Suddenly Silent Waters stepped onto the trail in the exact spot where the bear cub had stood weeks ago. Fear pricked Lark's skin and she stopped in the same spot where she'd stopped between the sow and her cub. Sears growled and Lark silenced him with a reassuring pat on the head.

Her eyes wild, Silent Waters brandished an old hatchet above her head. She'd found the hatchet in the shed the night before when she'd sneaked back to Red Beaver's farm. She'd hidden in the barn so Red Beaver couldn't lecture her again on her treatment of Lark. Silent Waters took a step toward Lark, then stopped. Her dress was torn in spots and pine needles clung to her long black hair. "You have hurt Laughing Eyes."

Lark gasped. "Veda Thorne? But how?"

"You are trying to steal her man!"

"I'm not!" Lark rubbed her arm over her revolver to reassure her it was still there.

"I hate the Havlicks, but Laughing Eyes wants Clay Havlick. You will not steal him from her."

"I'm not trying to steal him! Listen to me, Silent Waters."

"I will kill you. That will be my gift to Laughing Eyes. Then maybe she will love me as a daughter should love her mother."

"No! It's not me you should harm. I did nothing to you. And the Havlicks did nothing to you. It's Willie Thorne who hurt you. He cheated you of your daughter."

Silent Waters trembled and almost dropped the hatchet. "Laughing Eyes hates me. I am Patawatomi. Willie's white wife taught Laughing Eyes to hate Patawatomi."

"She could be taught differently. Look at Hannah Havlick. She was taught the same way, but she loves Red Beaver. She looked into his heart and saw a man like other men. She vows he is the man for her."

"I will kill you."

"It won't make your daughter love you."

Silent Waters tipped back her head and wailed. The sound spread across the swamp and lifted to the pines where the great boughs muffled it. Killing Lark would have to make Laughing Eyes love her! Nothing else would.

Lark gripped her cudgel. Should she try to strike Silent Waters with it? Lark knew she couldn't pull her revolver and fire quickly enough to disarm Silent Waters. The woman's great anguish kept Lark from doing anything.

Suddenly Silent Waters lifted the hatchet high and sprang forward with a loud yell.

Taking careful aim for the hatchet, Lark threw the cudgel sideways. It spun through the air, struck the hatchet, and drove it from Silent Waters' hand. The hatchet flipped back into the swamp. Sears growled and raced toward Silent Waters. She turned and lunged for the hatchet, caught her foot in a tangle of creeping thorny vines, and fell headfirst into the quagmire.

"No!" cried Lark, leaping forward to help Silent Waters.

Sears stopped at the very edge of the mire, growling menacingly.

Silent Waters struggled to stand, but her feet and legs sank into the muck. Wildly she looked for the hatchet, saw it, and grabbed it. The extra movement pulled her in to her waist.

"Grab my hand," cried Lark as she reached out to Silent Waters.

Silent Waters drew back her arm and hurled the hatchet at Lark.

Lark saw the feeble effort and easily dodged the hatchet. It landed in the mass of wild roses behind her. "Silent Waters, just fall forward and grab my hand," cried Lark. "The mire will support you for a while. Give me your hand and I'll pull you out!"

"I will sink," said Silent Waters in a defeated voice. "I will not put my hand out to you."

"If you fall forward toward me and stretch out your hand, I can pull you free. Please, let me help you. You don't have to die!" Lark's eyes burned with tears as she stretched out to try to reach Silent Waters.

"This has happened to me. It is my time to go," said Silent Waters tonelessly.

"I can't reach you and I can't get help fast enough." Lark dropped to her knees in anguish and Sears sank down beside her. "Dear God, please help us!"

"Don't call on your god for me," said Silent Waters as she sank lower.

"I don't want you to die without knowing God. Red Beaver has told you of God's love, of Jesus giving himself for you."

"I will not die. My spirit will walk these pines forever."

Lark groaned. "Your spirit will be doomed to hell for all eternity without God. You must know that."

Silent Waters didn't answer.

Great tears welled up in Lark's eyes and ran down her hot face. Sears licked her face, but she pushed him away. She picked up her cudgel and leaned heavily on it. She didn't want to stay to watch Silent Waters die, but she couldn't leave her alone.

Without a cry, a sob, or a sigh, Silent Waters sank below the muck and mire until not even a strand of hair was visible.

Lark covered her face and sobbed. Finally she walked back

to the cabin and weakly struck the bell twice. In minutes Tris and Hannah rode across in the wagon.

"What happened?" asked Tris in concern.

"Are you hurt?" asked Hannah, rubbing Lark's arm.

Lark told them Silent Waters had tried to kill her and had fallen in the swamp instead and was dead. She didn't tell them Veda Thorne was Silent Waters' daughter. "She wouldn't let me help her. She wouldn't hold out her hand to me."

"Oh, Lark! Don't blame yourself. It wasn't your fault," said Tris.

"I must go and tell Red Beaver," said Hannah.

Tris caught her arm. "You can't. Pa won't allow it."

Hannah pulled free. "I'm going, Tris. I love him."

Tris looked at her a long time and finally nodded. "Take the wagon," he said softly.

Hannah hugged him, then leaped in and shouted to the horses. The wagon bumped and swayed across the field.

Tris turned to Lark. "Are you all right?"

"No. It was awful." Lark sank to the bench with Sears at her feet.

Hannah found Red Beaver slopping the hogs. She threw her arms around him and told him what had happened. She didn't mind the sour smell of slop or the dirt on Red Beaver's hands as he held her tight.

"Did she hurt Lark?"

"No."

"I'm thankful for that."

Hannah stroked his cheek. "Your mother is gone and I'm sorry."

"I tried to help her."

"I'm sure you did."

"She didn't want anything to do with God."

"Don't torture yourself, Red Beaver." Hannah stood on tiptoe and kissed him. "Let's get married."

"What about your family?"

"They'll be upset of course, but I don't care! I want you. I'll make my family understand."

Red Beaver shook his head. He wanted to marry Hannah no matter what, but he couldn't have the Havlicks angry at her. Hannah couldn't live without her family. "They'll never accept me."

"Then it's their loss. I love you, Red Beaver."

He kissed her as if he'd never let her go. "And I love you. But that's not always enough."

Red Beaver rode to town on his gray gelding and stopped at Willie Thorne's tavern. It was noon and the front door was locked, but Red Beaver went around back and knocked.

Willie flung open the door, then whistled in surprise. "What brings you here?"

"My mother is dead. She tried to kill Lark Baritt and now she's dead. It's time you called off your revenge on the Havlicks."

Willie sagged against the door frame, the color drained from his face. "Silent Waters," he whispered. He was to see her tonight and tell her he'd settled the problem with Veda. He was going to tell her that soon her daughter would be able to speak to her, even get to know her and love her.

"Are you all right?" asked Red Beaver in concern.

"No. No, I'm not. I loved your mother."

Red Beaver didn't respond. He couldn't understand the kind of love that destroys lives.

"I want to see her. I want to hold her one last time before she's put in the ground," said Willie.

Red Beaver shook his head. "She is buried deep in the swamp. No one can see her ever again."

"I must tell Veda her mother is dead."

"Veda?"

Willie rubbed an unsteady hand across his face. "Veda is your sister. I took her to live with me and my wife as our own child."

Red Beaver shook his head as if to clear his brain. "I was seven when Silent Waters gave birth to Laughing Eyes. But she told me the baby died. I never knew you took her to your white wife."

Willie nodded.

"I ran to the woods and wept because my sister died." Red Beaver remembered the pain he'd felt at seven. Anger at his father rushed through him, then he refused to keep it. "Your hatred for the Havlicks brought all this agony on us, but it won't destroy me. I refuse to let it destroy me or the ones I love!" Red Beaver turned on his heel and strode to his horse.

Willie walked slowly inside the tavern, sank down on a ladder back chair, and buried his face in his hands.

Later Willie pulled himself together enough to go home. He found Veda sitting on the white bench in the flower garden, the cat on her lap.

Veda jumped up. "Papa, what is it? You look terrible."

Willie sank to the bench and pulled Veda back down beside him. "It's terrible news."

"Clay learned the truth and won't marry me!"

"No." Willie shuddered. "Silent Waters is dead."

Veda sighed in relief. "Now I won't have to think about having an Indian mother."

Willie jumped up and jerked Veda to her feet. "You will always be part Indian even if you choose to ignore it."

Veda trembled at his anger. "Nobody will have to know."

Willie raised his hand to strike Veda, then let it fall at his side. "The Havlicks will pay for this. Silent Waters died trying to help me get the pines. She will not have died in vain!"

Veda breathed easier. Papa was himself again.

Willie laughed wickedly. "After you and young Havlick are married I'll tell the whole Havlick family you are part Patawatomi. Then I'll tell the whole town! Those Havlicks will lose their high standing in the community as well as their precious pines."

CHAPTER 11

♦ Lark froze on the path in the pines. Sears stood beside her and Silent Waters crouched several yards away, a hatchet in her hand. More sunlight than usual shone through the boughs. The pine smell filled the air and took Lark's breath away. No animals made a sound.

Silent Waters lifted the hatchet high and sunlight glinted off its head. In a ringing voice Silent Waters cried, "My gift to Laughing Eyes is to kill you, Lark Baritt!"

"No!" Frantically Lark grabbed for her revolver, but the holster was empty. She gripped the thing in her hand, then looked to find both hands were empty. Where was her cudgel? She stared in fear at the wild look in Silent Waters' eyes. "Leave me alone. Please leave me alone." Lark sobbed.

Silent Waters threw the hatchet. It arched through the air and before Lark could duck, it struck her forehead and sliced through her head, splitting her skull. Lark screamed and grabbed her forehead.

She screamed again and sat straight up in her bunk, sweat soaking her nightdress and sheets. Moonlight streamed through the window and she sank back to her pillow, shivering uncontrollably. It had been a dream but it seemed so real she could feel the pain in her head. "A nightmare," she whispered. It was the same nightmare she'd had every night since Silent Waters died. Lark moaned. When would the nightmares end? When could she sleep again?

Lark pushed herself up and sat on the edge of the bunk with her damp face in her hands. A cricket sang in the corner. Sears whined and scratched at the door. Weakly Lark stood, her cotton nightdress sticking to her sweat-soaked body. What had happened to her good life? The cabin no longer seemed to be the haven it had been.

"I'm all right, Sears," said Lark as she opened the door. A hot breeze dried her skin as she stroked Sears. "It was just another nightmare." Since Silent Waters died Lark had let Sears sleep just outside her door instead of tying him at his dog house. "I'm all right."

Sears licked her cheek and the back of her hand. She hugged him, her head still pounding with pain.

Slowly she closed the door and heard Sears settle on the other side. She walked to the table and lit the lamp. The smell of sulfur and kerosene made her wrinkle her nose. She sank to a chair and clasped her hands together on the table. "I can't go on like this," she whispered and the whisper seemed loud in the silent cabin. Even the crickets had stopped singing.

She touched her Bible, then pushed it away. She didn't want to read God's Word now. It would tell her to forgive and forget, let go, but she would not forgive or forget that Anna Pike had kept her father from her. She would not forgive or forget that Willie Thorne was to blame for what she'd suffered and continued to suffer because of Silent Waters. It was Willie's fault that Veda was going to marry Clay and lumber the pines.

Lark doubled her fists and clenched her jaw. Anna Pike was gone, but Willie Thorne was still in Blue Creek within easy reach. "I'll get him if it's the last thing I do!" she shouted. The log walls muffled her shout, but the words continued to ring in her head.

From the corner of the shed behind the Thorne house Red Beaver watched Veda sit on the white bench in the flower garden and call to her cat. Red Beaver's heart raced and tears pricked his eyes. He could see Veda's resemblance to Silent Waters. Why hadn't he seen it before? If she'd worn her hair down with a rolled band around her head, he would've noticed immediately. But she'd always looked too much like a wealthy white woman. He knew her white gauze dress was very expensive.

Taking a deep breath, Red Beaver walked around the shed and through the flower garden. He'd changed from his work clothes to a nice pair of dark pants and a blue plaid shirt. He stopped beside a large patch of marigolds and waited for Veda to notice him. She looked sad and his heart went out to her. Was she grieving over the death of their mother? It had been a week since Silent Waters died.

Veda felt eyes on her and she glanced up from her cat, then stared in shock at Red Beaver. He seemed to be memorizing her.

"They said you died," Red Beaver whispered. "I was only seven and I mourned for a long time."

"What are you doing here?" Veda asked hoarsely, her hand at her throat.

"I was seven. Every day for weeks I went to the woods where no one could see me, and I cried. I couldn't let anyone know I wasn't man enough not to cry. I loved you, Laughing Eyes."

"No," whispered Veda.

"I did," said Red Beaver softly.

Veda bowed her head and swayed. Finally she lifted her eyes. "I was taught to look down on my own flesh and blood. That was a cruel thing to teach a child."

"Very cruel." Red Beaver knelt at the bench and looked into her face. "We can begin again."

"No."

"We are still blood."

"Don't say that!"

"No one can take that from us."

"They already have," Veda said woodenly.

"You have been wronged, Laughing Eyes." He reached out to take her hands.

"Don't!" Veda held her hand palm up against his touch. The cat jumped to the ground and ambled away. "Don't. Don't call me that."

"It is your name."

"My name is Veda Thorne. *Veda Thorne!*"

Red Beaver never took his eyes off her ashen face.

"I am Willie Thorne's daughter."

"Yes," said Red Beaver.

Veda bit her lip and laced her fingers together.

"And I am Willie Thorne's son."

Veda pressed her hand to her throat.

"Our mother hinted to me that you are helping our father steal the white pines from Clay Havlick. Is that true?"

A shiver ran down Veda's spine. Looking into Red Beaver's dark eyes made it impossible for her to lie. She just didn't answer him.

"How can you destroy the pines?"

"I didn't say I was."

"Look deep in your heart and see what is right, then no matter how hard it is, do it." Red Beaver reached again for Veda's hand, but she pulled away from him.

"Don't touch me!"

Red Beaver forced back the pain the words caused him. "You have been hurt, but you can choose your own path now. You can take your life and make it into something worthwhile."

Veda took a deep, steadying breath. "I will marry Clay Havlick." She moistened her lips with the tip of her tongue. A bee buzzed around a rose bush. Butterflies flitted around the row of blue bachelor buttons. "No one can stop me."

"What if Clay learns the truth?"

Veda scowled. "Get out of here!"

"I will go if I must, but I'll be praying for you, Laughing Eyes. God loves you just as you are—part white, part Patawatomi."

"No!" Veda clamped her hands over her ears and shook her head hard.

Red Beaver gently pulled her hands from her head and held them tightly. He smelled the clean smell of her skin and saw the rise and fall of her breast. "If you ever need me, my sister, I'll help you."

"Let me go," Veda whispered hoarsely, but she couldn't find the strength to pull free.

"You know where I live. You are welcome in my home any time."

Veda's heart turned over. His words and his touch burned her. "Let go of my hands."

"Please listen to me!"

"If you don't leave, I'll call for help."

Red Beaver tucked her hands back on her lap and stood before her. "I am your brother."

"No!" Veda shook her head hard.

"Nothing you can do or say will change that."

Veda stared up at him, her heart a block of ice in her breast. "Go," she whispered.

Red Beaver's eyes filled with tears. "You are my sister, Laughing Eyes."

"Go!"

He turned and walked away, his shoulders bent and his steps slow.

Veda sat for a long time without moving, her eyes on the path Red Beaver had taken.

Wednesday morning Clay left Flame at the livery, then walked to the Wagon Works. At the sight of the finished wagons parked outside the building in an empty lot he stopped dead in his tracks. The wagons they'd painted yesterday had splashes of black paint over the green. "Who did this?" His voice rang through the early morning and startled birds pecking in the grass. He ran to the first wagon and touched the black paint. It came off on his fingers. Who had splashed the black paint on the freshly finished wagon boxes? Anger raged inside him. He grabbed a rag from inside the shop and rubbed the paint from his fingers. August was almost over. The men had been drinking on the job, and that had cost precious time. Then several missing tools had caused further delay. Now this! If he couldn't fill the contract, he couldn't make the first large payment due at the bank. If the bank wouldn't give him more time he could easily lose the pines. Somehow he had to stop whoever was making trouble for him.

"I'll hire three more guards," he said sharply. The added expense frustrated him. Already he'd hired Dag as guard because he'd been willing and even eager to do it. Dag patrolled the area at night, slept until noon, then worked from noon until six in the shop. Clay had talked to the sheriff twice already and had gotten nowhere. The sheriff promised to look into it, but he hadn't learned anything.

His head buzzing with plans, Clay opened the doors of the two buildings and let the fresh air fill the hot interior. He glanced around at the parts of wagons laying where the men had worked on them. Today they would've been ready to assemble a few more wagons.

Clay paced across the front of the shop as he waited for his workers to arrive. He pulled off his tan straw hat and jabbed his fingers through his dark hair. Maybe he should've stayed in buggy making with Pa. Maybe he wasn't cut out to make his own fortune like Pa and Great-grandpa Clay had done.

Clay rammed his hat back on and squared his shoulders. He would not give up without a fight! Pa hadn't and neither had Great-grandpa Clay. Jig had told the stories often to Clay until he knew them by heart.

Maybe Pa would help make the bank payment. Clay shook

his head. Pa had plenty of assets, but often cash money was hard to come by. And he would not ask Pa to borrow money to help him!

At six when the sun was already turning warm, all the men came to work at once. Clay watched as they spotted the defaced wagons. All of them were outraged and wanted to know who'd done such a terrible thing. Clay knew they'd have to rub the excess black paint off, let the rest dry, then repaint the wagons. It would take valuable time.

"Somebody's out to get you, Boss," Leander said as he wrapped his fingers around the suspenders of his bib overalls.

"You got enemies?" asked Polaski as he scratched his head, then rammed his cap on.

Willie Thorne popped immediately into Clay's mind, but he rejected the idea that Willie was responsible for his troubles. Maybe Willie was so angry about him marrying Veda that he wanted to make Clay call it off. "It won't work," muttered Clay. He waited until the men quieted and shouted, "Men, gather round! I have something to say before you get to work." He stood before them, his feet apart and his hands resting lightly on his lean hips. "Men, it's obvious that someone is trying to sabotage the Wagon Works. I suspect it could be one of you or several of you." He saw their uneasy looks. Some of the men whispered among themselves. Some shifted their weight uneasily. "I'm not saying it is." Clay narrowed his dark eyes. "We have contracts to meet and we are going to meet those contracts on time, if not early! All these things that have happened are small things, but they've delayed production. Now, in the event that the culprit is here among you, be it known that when you are caught, you shall be prosecuted, and I'll see you sent to prison."

Clay looked around the crowd, sizing them up. Many of them met his eyes, but others stared at the floor. A couple of rough looking men glanced at the wagons.

"From what I've witnessed you're all hard workers. Meeting the contracts means your jobs, your livelihood. If we do not meet our contracts, we're all finished. Your jobs are on the line, so report any suspicious activity to me immediately. All these incidents are over and done with—they're behind us. Now, let's get to work. And keep your eyes and ears open!"

Just before noon Clay called Malda, Knegrave, and Von Tol to him. The three men looked nervous as they followed him outdoors to stand in the shade of a great oak. Clay cleared his throat. "Men, I need your help. I know I can trust the three of you."

They shrugged and looked pleased.

"I want you three to take turns guarding the Wagon Works."

"Dag's doing that already," said Von Tol with a nod of his blond head.

"I know," said Clay. "But things are still happening. It's too big a job for one man." Clay studied the men carefully. He'd known them most of his life. Two were his age and one was about ten years older. "I want this to be kept a secret between the four of us. I don't want to say a word against Dag, but things do keep happening."

"It's mighty strange how he's the one that keeps findin' the cases of whiskey," said Malda.

"He is my guard," said Clay, but he felt the same way. On the sly he'd look into Dag Bjoerling. Clay frowned slightly. He liked Dag and hated to think he'd do anything underhanded.

"You want us to keep our eyes and ears open?" asked Van Tol with a wide grin.

Clay nodded. "I want you three to work as guards. Split the time into three shifts and don't let anyone know you're guards for me. Let them all think you're still laborers." Clay assigned them the shifts and sent Malda home to sleep so he could be on guard all night. "Do your best to stay out of Dag's sight," said Clay as Malda walked away.

Later in the day Clay rode Flame to his forest to get away from the Wagon Works and have time to be alone. He leaned dejectedly against a giant pine looking down on the river. The oppressive heat burned through his blue shirt and gray pants.

How could he marry Veda in two weeks when he was so far behind in production? He lifted his head and looked at his great inheritance. Sometimes he wondered if it really was an inheritance or a giant weight on his shoulders. The pines were worth a fortune, yet he wasn't gaining any money from them. Was he wrong not to lumber them, even a part of them so he could be out of debt and out from under the pressure of meeting his deadline?

The morning sun burning through her yellow sunbonnet, Lark rubbed her hand over the smooth black buggy, then touched the green, machine-buffed leather. She wasn't in the mood to buy a horse and buggy, but she felt she had to have the freedom owning her own afforded her.

"It's a fine buggy," said Free as he watched Lark.

"I can see that," said Lark. Never in her life had she considered buying her own horse and buggy, but she had the money and didn't want to depend always on the Havlicks to loan her one.

"All the gear wood is made from the very best, carefully selected second growth Michigan hickory. The reaches are ironed full length with Norway iron." Free patted the wheel nearest him. "I use only the highest grade second growth hickory in the wheels too. Notice how the round edge of the steel projects over the felloes to protect the wood from wear."

"I do want it," said Lark. "For my sake I'm glad your customer couldn't take it after all."

Free smiled. He knew he could've sold the buggy to five different people, but he was glad to see Lark get it. He'd sold it to her for $65 even though he could've gotten $75 from Jake Spelling.

Lark touched the brass plate engraved with *Havlick Buggy.* She'd be proud to own such a buggy.

Free walked Lark to the pen where he had the bay mare. "Look her over and see if she's what you want," said Free.

Lark held out her hand and the mare walked to her. "What's her name?"

"Evie named her Star because of the white mark on her face."

"Star. I like that."

"She's trained to ride or pull a buggy. I have a spare saddle I can throw in too. It belonged to Grace, but she didn't want it after she got married and moved away." Grace was Free's married daughter. She and her husband had just had twins and Evie and Jennet had gone to Grand Rapids to be with them for a while.

Several minutes later Lark drove to town in her own buggy pulled by her own horse. She tried to feel excitement, but she couldn't. Since she'd learned her father was dead, the only emotion she'd been able to feel was anger at Matron. It seethed inside her. Matron had stolen her father from her just as she'd stolen the money he'd sent.

Lark drove the buggy around back of the Home, unhitched Star, and turned her into the pen. Lark slapped dust off the yellow gingham dress she'd bought last week from Sally and straightened her matching sunbonnet.

"You look like you lost your best friend," said John Epson as he walked up. He'd waited for Lark so he could have a few minutes of her time before she started to work.

Lark turned with a slight smile and he tipped his white straw hat to her. "Hi."

"You've turned down supper with me for several days." John took her hand in his and smiled into her eyes. His job was getting harder and harder because he'd come to care for Lark. When the time came to kill her, he didn't know if he would be able to do it. But Willie Thorne had insisted he get her away from the pines one way or another. John squeezed Lark's hand. "Today is the day you'll share dinner with me, won't you?"

"I can't, John." Lark liked the attention John had been paying her lately, but she couldn't find the strength to respond. She tugged on her hand and he reluctantly released it. "Maybe tomorrow."

John frowned as he rubbed his well-trimmed beard. "You've been saying that for over a week."

"I know." Lark couldn't imagine why he'd want to bother with her.

"I won't take no for an answer for tomorrow, Lark." John walked beside her through the back door of the Home.

Smells of roast beef and freshly baked bread filled the air. The cook and student helpers were already making dinner. All the windows in the Home were open to stir the hot air. Usually the temperature dropped at nights and cooled down the house, but the past two nights the temperature had stayed too high. Today Lark had dressed in the coolest clothing she had, and had even left off her bustle. She'd heard several women say the bustle would soon be a thing of the past. She hoped so, but wondered if that was true.

"You seem a long way off, Lark," said John as he opened the office door for her.

"I was thinking about bustles," Lark said. It was easier to think on that than on the harsh reality of life—on what Matron had done to her and on the death of her father.

John laughed. "I don't think I want to discuss bustles."

Lark flushed as she sat at her desk. She tried to keep her mind on the bookwork for the Home, but had to go over the same work several times. During Clay's bookkeeping her mind wandered and she pulled it back and started all over again.

Just before noon John stood up and brushed his hands together. "Well, that's that. I've finalized the adoption papers for Maggie and Linda. Their new parents should be here tomorrow to get them."

Lark frowned. "I didn't know they were going to be adopted."

"That's because you're living in a fog, Lark."

"I know." Lark sighed heavily. Maybe it was better to live in a fog where she had a cushion against pain. In the back of her mind she remembered God was her strength and help, but immediately she turned away from that thought.

John walked around her desk and sat on the edge of it beside her. "I want to help you, Lark."

"There's nothing you can do."

"Tell me what's wrong? Is your guard job too much for you?"

"No. It's nothing I can talk about, John."

He saw the dark circles under her eyes. "I care about you, Lark. Come back here where you can get your sleep. Ask Clay Havlick to hire someone else as guard. I happen to know someone who needs a job."

Lark shook her head. "I'll never come back here to live."

"Have it your way." John touched her cheek, then walked out the door.

Zoe slipped in, her eyes sparkling with unshed tears. She'd left Carrie in charge of the babies. "Lark, could I talk to you?"

Lark nodded absently.

Zoe pulled John's chair up near Lark's desk. Hot wind blew in the window and a coating of dust covered the furniture even though they'd dusted already this morning. "It's Tristan."

Lark didn't want to listen, but she nodded again.

"We went to the Sunday school picnic a while back and he hasn't asked me out again. I don't know what I'm gonna do!"

"I don't either."

"Please help me, Lark."

"Zoe, I can't even help myself."

Zoe jumped up and put the chair back in place. "I won't bother you, Lark. I'm sorry. I was only thinking of myself. Oh, but I love Tris! Why won't he love me back?"

Helplessly Lark shook her head. Right now she felt like there was no such thing as love.

Tears slipped down Zoe's cheeks as she walked around the

desk and hugged Lark. "I'm sorry I bothered you with my problem when you're feeling so terrible. Don't forget God is with you."

Lark's throat closed over and she couldn't answer. She absently watched Zoe leave the room, then turned toward the curtains fluttering at the windows. Laughter and the ring of an ax floated in from outdoors. Was God with her as angry as she was?

Just then a gray haired, blue eyed man walked into the office. He held a white wide brim straw hat against his broad chest. "Lark Baritt?" he asked.

She nodded.

"I understand you've been looking for me."

She frowned, searching her mind to try to remember who she'd needed to see. No one came to mind. She looked the man over and noticed his expensive dark suit and gold tie pin. "I'm sorry, but I don't know who you are, sir."

The man smiled as he stepped closer. "Matt Baritt."

"He died last year," Lark said in a wooden voice.

The man shook his head. "Not so!" he said and thumped his chest. "*I'm* Matt Baritt. And I'm very much alive."

The room spun and Lark gasped as she gripped her desk to keep from falling off her chair. What a terrible, terrible joke! "Why are you doing this to me? My father is dead."

Matt Baritt walked to the desk and bent down toward Lark. "I'm not dead. I am your father."

"No." Lark shook her head.

"I left you here twenty-two years ago with a box with a photo, two letters from Meriel, your mother, a little white dress and bonnet, and an envelope with $80 in it. Your mother died just after you were born and I couldn't take care of you and had no one else to turn to."

"I don't believe you," whispered Lark.

"I wrote and sent money regularly. Anna Pike knows I did." Matt rubbed a hand over his clean-shaven jaw. "I didn't think you wanted me to come for you. Then recently I started hearing from every lumberman I knew asking if I'd contacted you. They said you were looking for me."

Helplessly Lark shook her head. She wanted to stand, but she had no strength in her legs. "This is a dream."

Matt touched Lark's hand. "I am real. So are you."

"But I got a telegram saying you were dead."

"I don't understand that. Maybe someone was playing a cruel joke." Matt pulled out his wallet and handed her his identification. "I am Matt Baritt, your father."

Lark trembled as she took the paper. She studied it and held it to her heart. Who had sent the telegram? She couldn't think of anyone who would be that mean. Was it Anna Pike? Lark forced thoughts of Anna Pike from her mind as she looked at the man standing across the desk from her. "Why didn't you come to get me years ago? Why didn't you at least come to see me?"

Matt flushed. "I tried."

"Why didn't you try harder?"

Matt fingered his hat brim. "I was afraid."

Lark dropped his identification paper on the desk between them. "Afraid? What could you possibly be afraid of?"

"You," said Matt softly.

Lark was quiet a long time. "Me?"

"I thought you hated me for leaving you here. When Anna Pike said you refused to answer my letters, I was afraid you'd refuse to see me if I did come. In fact, she implied you would."

For a while Lark couldn't speak. Anger at Anna Pike raged inside her until she thought she'd explode. "I never even knew about you until a few weeks ago. Matron lied to you all those years. She took the money you sent and kept it for herself, and she never told me about the letters."

Groaning, Matt rubbed an unsteady hand across his eyes. "Oh! I never thought she was lying."

"Didn't you even suspect? Did you even check it out?"

Matt shook his head. "I should have. Please forgive me." He walked around the desk and stopped just inches from her.

"Yes. You should've."

Matt brushed a tear from his eye. "I've been without you for twenty-two years. Please don't send me away now. You're my daughter! I love you. I want to get to know you."

A sob rose in Lark's throat and escaped before she could stop it. She brushed at her tears, but couldn't wipe them away.

"Lark," said Matt softly. He caught her hand and rubbed the back of it. "We named you Lark after our favorite bird." His voice broke. "We wanted you so badly! Your mother fought to stay alive, but she was too weak. She kissed you, handed you to me, and died." Matt lifted Lark to her feet. He held her hand against his cheek and closed his eyes. "I tried hard to tend you, but I couldn't. Life was hard. There was no one to help me."

Lark trembled as she listened to her father. Did he really mean what he said? How hard it was to believe she had a father and he actually loved her and wanted her!

They stood in silence, studying each other. Children's shouts and laughter drifted through the open windows. Smells of dinner filled the room.

"Are you really Matt Baritt, my father?" whispered Lark.

Matt nodded.

"I don't know what to call you."

Matt shrugged and grinned. "Pop? Dad? Pa? Father? I don't know. Anything. What do you want to call me?"

"I don't know." Lark wiped her eyes with her hanky, then stuffed it inside her cuff.

"We'll wait and see. Right now I think we should go have dinner. I already asked your matron Mercy Kettering if you could have the rest of the day off. So, you're free if you want to be."

"I'll show you all around. Did you know I'm the guard for the Havlicks' white pines?"

"The guard? You're just a little girl!"

"But I can use a cudgel and a revolver. And I have a big Dalmatian at my side while I walk the trail."

"I'm impressed."

Lark smiled.

"I've heard of the white pines the Havlicks have saved. Everyone has, I think. I would like to see them."

"I'll take you around the trail," said Lark. She told him some of the adventures she'd had and he scowled and shook his head. She felt like she was talking double speed as she tried to share her entire life with Matt Baritt in a few minutes.

At the restaurant they both ordered perch, then laughed. Since neither of them liked coffee, they drank lemonade.

"Where do you live, Lark?"

She told him about the cabin. "How about you?"

"I travel around a lot, but I have a house on Mackinac Island." Matt leaned forward and his blue eyes twinkled. "I'd like you to go back with me. I could hire someone to take care of my business and we could have time together."

Lark's stomach knotted. Live away from Blue Creek?

"Does that frighten you, Lark?"

"A little. I've never been anywhere but here."

"We could travel. See the world! Have you wanted to see London or Paris or New York City?"

Lark balled her napkin. "I have wanted to see Grand Rapids. Or Detroit."

"Then we'll go!"

"Oh, my." Lark had thought she'd only experience distant places through the books she read.

Just then someone walked into the restaurant. It was very late for dinner customers. Lark glanced up to see Clay and Veda. He looked as if he hadn't slept well in a long time and her face was pale. Matt noticed Lark studying them.

"Who are they?" asked Matt softly.

Lark told him. "Her father wants Clay's white pines." Lark had already told Matt all about the Havlicks, Jig, and their years of friendship. "Jig asked me to keep them from marrying each other."

"That's a mighty big order," said Matt, shaking his head.

"I know." Lark glanced at Clay again. "He looks so tired and unhappy."

Matt shot a look at Lark. "Do you love him?"

Lark gasped. "Of course not! I just don't want him hurt by Veda or Willie Thorne."

"I see."

Lark flushed and looked down at the crumpled white linen napkin beside her plate.

Clay sighed tiredly as he looked across the table at Veda. He'd agreed to pick her up for dinner, but had forgotten until he'd gone back to work and found her there. He'd talked to her about his busy schedule, but she hadn't wanted to listen. "I know you don't want to postpone the wedding, but I don't have time to get married this month."

Veda's eyes flashed. Was he trying to get out of being married because he'd heard she was part Patawatomi? "It doesn't take long to get married, Clay."

"It's not fair to either of us to try to begin a marriage while I have to work twelve to fifteen hours a day."

"I don't mind a bit. I just want to be with you."

"We don't even have a house."

"I know one that just went on sale. It's not too far from your Wagon Works."

"I can't afford a house right now."

"Papa will pay for it."

"No!" Clay shook his head hard. "I won't be obligated to Willie Thorne for anything!"

Veda forced back the stream of angry words on the tip of her tongue. "I suppose I understand, Clay, so I won't suggest it again." She reached for his hand. "But please don't call off the wedding just because you don't have time for it. We could take a couple of hours anytime and get married. Tomorrow even! I just can't live without you!"

Clay's pulse leaped and he smiled. It felt good to be loved that much. "I don't want to live without you either, Veda, but I want to be fair to you. We shouldn't start off our married life this way."

"I can handle it if you can."

Clay squeezed her hand. "I'll give it some thought."

"I'll speak to Pastor James tomorrow and tell him we'll get married in a couple of days."

Clay's stomach knotted. Things were moving too fast for him.

"I'll make a good home for you, Clay. We'll have children and a house full of love." An icy band tightened around Veda's heart. Their children would be part Patawatomi. How would Clay survive that? Veda bit her bottom lip. How would she?

Clay glanced across the restaurant and caught sight of Lark and Matt. Clay stiffened. Lark was going out entirely too much lately. First with John Epson and now with a man old enough to be her father.

Veda followed Clay's gaze and jerked her hand free. "If you're going to look at her all afternoon, then let's leave!"

Clay flushed. "I only wondered who she is with. I feel responsible for her." Suddenly he longed to take back the promise he'd made Jig on the day he'd passed on.

Across the room Lark smiled at Matt, then glanced over at Clay. He looked upset again. Just what were they talking about?

"I'd like to meet that young man," said Matt, pushing back his chair. "Introduce us, Lark."

Hesitantly Lark stood up, her mouth suddenly bone dry.

CHAPTER

12

♦ Lark saw the anger in Veda's eyes as she and Matt stopped at the table. "I hope we're not intruding," said Lark stiffly. She suddenly remembered she wasn't wearing a bustle. Veda was wearing an organdy dress with a white background and lavender flowers with tiny green leaves. A small gold locket hung to her breast. Lark forced back a flush of embarrassment over her appearance and said, "My father wanted to meet you."

Clay jumped up in surprise. He didn't notice the stares of the four other occupants of the restaurant. "But I thought your father had died."

"Obviously not," said Veda crisply as she gripped the linen napkin.

"It was a mistake," said Lark. She introduced them, feeling awkward even though she handled the introductions the way she'd learned and taught in deportment.

Matt smiled at Veda and shook hands with Clay. "It's a pleasure to meet Free Havlick's son," said Matt.

"Do you know my pa?" asked Clay.

"Only by reputation as a lumberman."

"Are you a lumberman?" asked Clay, trying to size the man up.

Before Matt could answer Lark said, "He is a naturalist and had a book published on plant and insect life."

"How interesting," said Clay, wondering about Matt Baritt's expensive summer suit, starched white shirt, and polished manners.

Veda moved restlessly. She wanted to excuse herself, but she didn't want to upset Clay. She had convinced him to marry her soon and she couldn't take a chance on him changing his mind.

Seeing Veda's agitation, Lark felt her anger against Veda and Willie Thorne rise dangerously. She had to get away before she said something she'd regret later. She gently tugged Matt's arm. "We must be going."

Matt was aware of Lark's tension and wondered about it. "It was nice to meet you both," said Matt, tipping his head.

"You too," said Clay while Veda managed a small smile.

"I'd be interested in seeing your Wagon Works," Matt said.

"You're welcome any time," said Clay.

As Lark left the restaurant, Matt was close beside her. The street was empty except for a small black dog dodging around the wheel of a parked wagon. Lark heard the shout of a boy somewhere behind the bank. The heat pressed against her as she lifted her bonnet in place and tied the strings under her chin.

"Why are you so upset, Lark?" asked Matt in a low voice as they slowly walked toward Lark's buggy.

"I'll tell you later," said Lark in a tight voice. She waited until they were driving out of town, then told Matt about Willie Thorne, Silent Waters, her death, and the nightmares.

Matt shook his head and clicked his tongue. He waited until Lark stopped at the side of the corduroy so they could hear as they talked. "What kind of man is Willie Thorne?"

"A terrible one."

"Why don't Clay's parents stop him from marrying Veda?"

"Well, I haven't discussed it with them. I'm certain they are against it. I imagine they've even forbidden it. But he's very stubborn. That I know. Clay is about as stubborn as a person can be."

Matt thought for a minute, then said, "I think I'll see what I can do."

Lark looked closely at this stranger who was her father. Just what did he mean? She wanted to ask, but was afraid of the answer.

Clay rode Flame out of his yard, stopped, and glanced across the field toward Lark's cabin. He'd seen Lark recently with John Epson taking a leisurely stroll around town. In Clay's opinion Epson was entirely too cozy with Lark. Clay frowned. Just what kind of man was Epson? Why was he interested in Lark Baritt? She was out walking the trail in the pines or he would've ridden to the cabin to talk to her and demand some answers.

An eagle flew high in the sky. A rooster crowed on the top rail of the fence as Clay nudged Flame forward.

In town Clay left Flame at the livery and walked toward the Wagon Works. A few men stood outside the boarding house talking. Two dogs snarled at each other in front of the bank. The smell of smoke hung in the air. He frowned and his stomach tightened. The smell was unfamiliar and it grew stronger with each step he took.

Suddenly Clay broke into a run. He pulled off his straw hat to keep it from flying off his head. Sweat stung his skin and dampened his blue work shirt. He saw Dag looking at the finished wagons. "What happened?" called Clay in alarm.

Dag turned, shaking his head. His work pants and shirt were wrinkled and his blond hair mussed. "It's awful," he said. "Somebody tried to burn the wagons."

Clay could see scratched places on several wagons. He ran from wagon to wagon. It looked as if someone had splashed kerosene on the wagons and set them on fire. They had burned only a while, then had gone out. But each wagon was left with deep scars. They were not fit to sell. Clay knotted his fists and shook his head helplessly. "How could this happen? Did you see anything? Did anyone?"

Dag shrugged and spread his hands wide. "I could only guard part of the night because I got sick and couldn't walk. But Malda was hanging around here, so I asked him if he could guard the rest of the night and I'd pay him from my own pocket. He agreed."

Clay glanced around. "Where's Malda now?"

Dag knew Malda was tied up and unconscious in the wagon bed in front of them, but he said, "I figure he went on home. I got here only a few minutes ago and didn't see him anywhere. But I wanted to tell you why I couldn't stand guard last night. I didn't want you to hear it from Malda." Dag rammed his fingers through his blond hair, leaving it mussed even more. "I take all the blame for this, Clay. I should've stayed instead of asking Malda to guard for me! I should've worked even as sick as I was."

Just then Malda groaned and hoisted himself up to the side of the wagon. "Help me," he said gruffly.

"Malda!" cried Clay.

"Help me."

With Dag beside him, Clay climbed into the wagon bed where he found Malda's hands and feet tied and a lump on the back of his head.

"Are you hurt?" asked Dag as he hunkered down beside Malda.

"Did you see who did this?" Clay asked as he untied Malda.

Malda shook his head, then groaned in pain. "I didn't hear or see a thing. Dag here asked me to take over for him, and I agreed." Malda looked at Clay trying to send a silent message. "I said I'd be glad to since I couldn't sleep no how."

Clay's frustration mounted as Malda described how someone had hit him on the back of the head during the early morning hours.

"When I came to the wagons were burning and I thought I was going to burn up with them." Malda shivered. "The flames burned bright for a while, then died down. The smell was terrible. I'm surprised it didn't bring folks out here. I don't know if I passed out again or fell asleep."

Clay patted Malda's shoulder. "I'm glad you're alive to tell about it."

"Me too," said Malda.

"Dag, take him to the doc, then see that he gets home.

They walked away and Clay leaned weakly against the wagon. He had to stop whoever was trying to ruin him. With the finished wagons scarred it was impossible to meet his contract. "Dear God, I need your help bad," muttered Clay.

"Having a bit of trouble here, I see," said Matt Baritt as he stopped beside Clay.

Clay jumped to attention, flushing that Matt had seen him almost in tears. "Sorry, I didn't hear you walk up."

His straw hat pushed to the back of his gray head, Matt frowned thoughtfully as he walked up and down the row of wagons. "Lark said you'd been having problems. I'd say it's mighty serious." Matt smiled at Clay. "I hope you don't mind that she talked to me about you."

Clay shrugged. It was too late to mind.

"I have a suggestion I'd like to make," said Matt, studying Clay carefully. "How about if we get together this afternoon to talk?"

Clay hesitated and finally agreed. He'd promised to meet Veda at Pastor James's office just after work, but he could take time for Lark's father.

"Some place private. How about your pines? Lark showed them to me yesterday."

"That'll be fine."

"I'll borrow Lark's buggy. We can ride together and talk," said Matt.

About two in the afternoon Matt stood in the pines near the stream with Clay beside him. Sears lapped water from the stream. Squirrels chattered high in the pine boughs and frogs croaked along the edge of the stream. Matt was in his shirt sleeves. He'd left his suit coat folded on the buggy seat.

"I can see you're in a hard place right now, Clay," said Matt.

Clay nodded. He hated to admit it, but it was true.

"Here's what I can do for you." Matt pushed his straw hat to the back of his head. "You have a payment due at your bank soon and no way to pay it."

Clay flushed. "That's right."

"I'll loan you the money to pay the bank off completely, and enough to hire more men so you can meet your contracts."

Clay felt as if his brain had stopped working as he stared in shock at Matt. "Why would you do that?"

"To tell you the truth it's because of Lark." Matt watched carefully for Clay's reaction.

"Lark? What does she have to do with this?"

"She told me about Willie Thorne and his daughter. They want the pines."

Fire flashed from Clay's eyes. "Well, they don't. Lark is wrong about that. But even if it were true, they can't get the pines."

"They can if the bank forecloses on you. The pines will belong to the bank and Thorne can buy them."

Clay's stomach knotted. "I don't want to think about it."

"You have to. It's a possibility."

Clay groaned and rubbed an unsteady hand over his face. The smell of pine was strong around him. He could hear small animals scurrying under the pine needles.

Matt reached down and patted Sears on the side. He didn't speak for a while. "I will loan you the money as I said. It would keep the pines out of Thorne's hands. I'll be willing to sign a contract with you, giving you extra time to pay, and with a statement that I will never have the pines lumbered in the event you can't pay me and the pines become mine."

"What's the catch?"

Matt folded his arms across his chest. "There is a catch."

"I thought so."

"You can't marry Veda Thorne until you have filled your contracts and given me the first installment of the loan."

Clay frowned. "That's a strange request. Is that it?"

"Yes."

"But why that?"

"Because I believe Lark. I think Veda is after the pines."

"She's not."

"Then you're safe, aren't you? Waiting to be married until December won't hurt anyone. If you're really in love, you'll still be in love in December."

"You're right." Clay trembled at the thought of facing Veda with the change of plans.

"And another thing," said Matt.

"What?"

"You can't tell anyone I'm holding your note. Not even Lark."

"She's my bookkeeper. She'll know."

"Change bookkeepers. You can tell her she's working too hard. She does work too hard. Besides, I want time with her so we can get to know each other." Matt pulled off his hat and ran his hand around the inside band. "And I'd like you to find another guard for the pines. It's too dangerous for Lark."

"I know it is, but she desperately wants the job. It won't be easy to take it from her."

"Do it anyway."

Clay tugged at his collar. Could he do it? Lark's tears made it impossible for him to refuse her anything she wanted. "I don't know if I can."

"Do your best and I'll do what I can." Matt looked deep into the forest, then up at the sweep of giant boughs. "I'm glad you saved these trees. I want my grandchildren to enjoy them someday."

Clay frowned. "Grandchildren? Is Lark planning to get married?"

"Of course."

"I didn't know." Clay thought of Lark with John Epson. "I hope she marries the right man."

"I'm sure she will. She has a good head on her shoulders." Matt slapped Clay on the back. "Let's get back to town and finalize our deal. I have to send a telegram. By Monday afternoon you'll have the money to pay the bank. Send out word today to bring more men to work. And if I were you, I'd hire trained guards. Take the men off who are doing it now and put on men who are trained to keep a place free of saboteurs."

"I'll do that," said Clay. He held his hand out to Matt. They shook hands and smiled at each other. Clay hadn't expected his day to take such a strange turn. "I feel like a big load has been lifted off my shoulders."

"I'm glad I could help." Matt's nerve tightened. What would Lark do if she ever learned of the deal he'd struck with young Havlick? Matt shrugged. What else could he have done? Saving Clay and the pines were important to Lark; therefore, they were important to him.

Clay tied Sears back up, then ran to the buggy. The flowers seemed brighter and smelled better. Clay patted Star's neck. He knew he could even face Veda about postponing the wedding.

Friday afternoon Lark stood at the window in her office and looked out at the children playing in the yard. Zoe had the babies on a large quilt and they seemed glad to be outdoors too.

John walked in quietly and smiled as he watched Lark watch the children. He stepped up behind her and slipped his arms around her waist. "You look happy today," he whispered in her ear.

She gasped and tried to pull away. "Don't, John!"

He turned her in his arms and smiled into her eyes. "Have you ever been kissed by a man with a beard?"

Lark gasped and her pulse leaped. She'd never been kissed by anyone. She wanted to pull away, but felt too weak to move.

"Why are you doing this?"

He could say it was part of his plan to get her away from her job at the pines, or that he was trying his best to get her to trust him so totally she'd do anything he asked of her. Either was true. Instead with a low chuckle he said, "You're a desirable woman and I'm a man."

"Please let me go."

"I will." John stroked her cheek, causing her heart to flutter. "You're very special. I care for you more than you'll ever know."

"I . . . I didn't know," she whispered. She'd dreamed of this, and now after she'd given up all hope, it was happening.

John cupped Lark's face in his hands and gently kissed her lips.

His mouth felt strange against hers. She hesitantly returned his kiss and found she liked the feel of his lips on hers and his beard brushing her face. What did the kiss mean? Breathlessly she pulled back from him. "Please let me go, John," she whispered.

He tightened his hold on her. "I have a better idea."

"What?"

"Marry me and I'll never have to let you go."

Lark gasped. "You can't want to marry me."

"Why not?"

"I'm plain as a post!"

"Who said so?"

"Everyone! The looking glass!"

John laughed softly. "There's more to a woman than her looks. You are not as plain as a post. You're beautiful. And you have an inner strength that I admire."

Lark's head spun. Her pulse raced. Being held close to John made her have feelings she'd never had before. But could she marry him? Last year she'd have agreed without hesitation, but today she couldn't say yes so quickly. Maybe she wouldn't say yes at all. "I don't know what to say."

"Don't say anything. Think about what I said and we'll talk about it again over supper."

"I'm having supper with my father."

John stiffened. "Your father?"

"Yes." Lark pulled away from John and he let her go. "You don't know, do you? He came yesterday! He's not dead after all! Someone played a cruel joke on me."

"Are you sure?"

"What do you mean?"

"Maybe the man who claims to be Matt Baritt is an imposter. Maybe he's after something."

"From me? I don't have anything."

John shrugged. "Just be careful. Don't trust him."

Lark fingered the high collar of her green shirtwaist. She already trusted Matt. But maybe she should check him out further.

John sank back against his desk and crossed his arms. "I'd like to meet him. Could I join the two of you for supper?"

Lark thought for a minute, smiled, and nodded. "Yes. I'd like that. I want the two of you to meet. I think you'll like him, John, and he's sure to like you."

John doubted that, but didn't say so.

"We're having supper at my cabin about six," said Lark. "Does that suit you?"

"I'll be there." John stepped close to Lark, cupped her face in his hands, and kissed her again. "Think about what I said. I want you to be my wife."

Lark blushed. His wife! "I will think about it."

Clay walked around the Thornes' house with Veda's hand in his. Giant oaks shaded the yard, protecting them from the terrible heat. "Are you sure your pa won't be coming home?" asked Clay as they sat on the white bench in the flower garden.

"He said he'd be gone until late." Veda lifted Clay's hand to her lips. "Now, tell me why you didn't want to meet with Pastor James tonight."

Clay kissed Veda lightly while he searched for just the right words to say. "You won't want to hear."

Veda tensed. A bee buzzed past, but she ignored it. "Tell me anyway."

Clay held Veda's hands up against his chest. "We must wait until the end of December to get married."

Veda jerked her hands free. What had happened to her careful planning? "I don't want to wait that long!"

"That's sweet of you and it makes me feel good, but I've been having problems at the Wagon Works and I can't get married sooner."

Veda burst into tears. "You really don't love me, do you?"

"Don't say that!" Clay tried to pull her close, but she pushed him away. "Please try to understand," he begged. "All of my time and energy must go into filling the contracts. I must have workers from dawn until dark."

"What will I do with my time?"

"I don't know. What do other expectant brides do?"

Veda searched for something to say. "Get their homes ready."

"Then do that. I'll check into the house you were talking about. There might be a way I can get it."

"Do you mean it?"

"I'll see about it." Clay didn't know if he could, but he liked the idea of getting a home ready so they could move right in when they got married.

Veda snuggled close to Clay. "I'll like living with you."

Clay lifted her face and kissed her.

They talked about the house and what they both wanted in a home.

"I know what I want to buy you for a wedding gift," said Veda with a smile.

Clay hadn't thought that far ahead. "What?"

"A ring filled with diamonds just like Momma bought Papa." Veda's stomach knotted and she had to force her mind away from her parents and her personal problems.

Clay shook his head. "I don't want anything that expensive."

"But you're worth it!"

"I don't think I'd wear a ring."

"To business meetings and church you would."

"Maybe so."

"What will you give me, Clay?"

"What do you want?" Right now he thought he'd give her the moon if she asked for it.

"A month long honeymoon."

"I can't do that."

Veda laughed. "Oh, all right! I know you're busy with your business." She looked impishly at him as if thinking hard about another gift. "I know what you can do." She paused and smiled sweetly. "You could give me the white pines."

Clay pulled back, his body suddenly stiff. "The pines?"

Veda saw the startled look on his face and she knew she had to retreat. She managed to laugh. "I was teasing, silly! I don't want the pines. I would like an emerald brooch, I think."

Clay looked closely at Veda. Had she been even a little serious in asking for the pines? What if Jig had been right? Abruptly Clay pushed the terrible thought aside. "Then I'll get you an emerald brooch." He pulled her close and kissed her.

After supper Lark stacked the dirty plates. She would wash them later. She followed Matt and John outdoors to the bench. The tension between the two men filled the yard just as it had filled the cabin. Lark frowned as she sat down while they stood looking into the forest. Sears ran to Lark and she rubbed his neck. Maybe Sears felt the tension too.

John turned to Lark. "I'd like to come out early in the morning and walk the trail with you."

"I don't know if you should, John. There's a lot of danger out there this time of year with the terrible heat and all."

"You can do it, so can I." John sat beside her. "I want to see just what you do when you guard the pines. I want to have the experience with you."

Matt frowned. What was John up to?

Lark glanced at Matt, then back at John. "I leave here before five. Can you be here that early?"

John nodded. "Oh, wait! I have to go out of town until Tuesday, but I can make it Wednesday morning. Then we'll drive to work together."

"Sounds fine to me," said Lark. She couldn't look at Matt. She could sense he didn't approve. She already knew he didn't approve of her guard's job because of the danger.

John squeezed Lark's hand. "I'll see you sometime Tuesday. Take care of yourself while I'm gone."

Lark smiled. "I will. Be sure to wear heavy britches and boots when you come to walk the pines. The snakes are pretty bad this time of year."

"I will." John stood and shook hands with Matt. "I must be going. I'll talk to you soon. Probably Tuesday."

"I'm sure," said Matt.

John smiled at Lark as he took her hands in his. "Thank you for a wonderful supper and a very pleasant evening."

"I'm glad you came," Lark said, suddenly feeling light headed. If Matt hadn't been there, John would've kissed her. Her lips tingled at the thought.

Lark stood beside Matt as John stepped into his buggy and drove away. The rattle of the harness and the creak of the buggy faded finally. A whippoorwill called and another answered. "He asked me to marry him," Lark said softly without looking at Matt.

Matt sucked in his breath. "Uh-mmm. What was your answer?"

"I told him I'd think about it."

Matt wanted to tell her to drop Epson like a poison rattler. But he had a feeling Lark would take Epson even more seriously if he told her not to. "I'm sure you'll do the right thing," Matt said. Silently he prayed that she would do just that. "Did he give you a time limit to answer him?"

"No. Why?"

"I just think it would be good for you to take several days. This is a serious step."

"I agree."

"He might want an answer Wednesday morning."

"He might."

"Will you give it to him?"

"I don't know. If I've decided I will." Lark finally looked at Matt. "Would you like another glass of lemonade?" She still wasn't ready to trust him completely enough to tell him her whole heart.

Saturday afternoon Matt found Clay standing near a finished wagon at the Wagon Works. Sounds of men's voices, sawing, and hammering came from inside the buildings. Matt shook hands with Clay and smiled.

"I've hired ten more men," said Clay, rubbing back his damp hair. "And my brother Tris is scouting around for more."

"Good." Matt cleared his throat. "Did you know John Epson proposed marriage to Lark?"

"What?" cried Clay. "No, I didn't know that. I hope she turned him down."

"She's thinking on it," said Matt. Being a father was a little more complicated than he had thought. "Have you heard anything against him?"

"Not that I can think of."

"What do *you* have against him?"

Clay rubbed his hand down the side of his face. Too many sudden changes were taking place and he didn't like it. "Nothing I can put my finger on."

"I don't want to see Lark hurt," said Matt.

"I don't either."

"When will you tell her you no longer need her services?"

"Maybe tomorrow."

"Make sure it's not too late. I don't want her to know anything about our deal. It's between us."

"I understand," said Clay, but he wondered if he really did.

He watched Matt walk away, then Clay leaned against a wagon. Would he wake up and find he'd been dreaming a way out of his problems? It was too good to be true.

Clay's stomach was tied in knots when he met Matt outside the bank Monday morning. What if Matt had changed his mind and the deal was off? What if he still lost the Wagon Works and the pines? He'd planned to see Lark over the weekend to relieve her of her jobs, but when he wasn't at the Wagon Works Veda had kept him busy.

"Were you able to hire the rest of the men you need?" asked Matt after they shook hands outside the open door of the bank.

Clay nodded. "My brother Tris went to Grand Rapids and brought them back with him last night. They're all at work now. My lumber order came in this morning by train, so I'm all set." It all still seemed too good to be true.

Matt cleared his throat. "Not quite," he said, his eyes on Clay.

"What do you mean?" Clay's heart fell to his feet like a rock. He was in too far to have Matt back out now.

"I have one other thing to ask."

A shiver ran down Clay's spine even though the day was oppressive with heat. "What?"

Matt brushed a fly off the sleeve of his gray suit. Could he go through with his plans? This was harder than any business deal he'd ever made. He shrugged. "It's nothing you can't handle."

Clay stiffened even more. "Maybe you'd better tell me." Matt rested his hand on Clay's arm and urged him away from the doorway to the corner of the building. A horse and buggy drove past on the sawdust covered street kicking up a cloud of dust. Already Clay was having trouble breathing, he was so anxious about what Matt might say.

"First," Matt began, "let me tell you what I did shortly after I arrived here and met my daughter."

Sweat popped out on Clay's wide forehead. His suit coat suddenly felt hotter than long handled underwear. He had a premonition he wasn't going to like what Matt would say next.

"I listened to what Lark said about the Thornes. And I heard a few other rumors, so I hired a gardener to work undercover at Thorne's house."

"What?" cried Clay. It was even worse than he'd thought.

"I wanted to check for myself to see if Lark was right about Thorne and his daughter."

"You spied on them? You had no right to do that!"

Matt sighed heavily. "My daughter is involved and that gives me every right." Matt looked squarely at Clay. "My man heard Veda and Willie Thorne talking together in the flower garden. She said she couldn't convince you to elope or to sign over the pines to her."

"No," Clay groaned. He leaned heavily against the building, not trusting his legs to support him. "I don't believe it. There must be a mistake. Veda wouldn't do that—plot against me. Willie might, but not Veda. She loves me. She's told me many times." Clay felt as if his heart might break.

Matt reached out and gently touched Clay's shoulder. He understood Clay's disappointment and pain. He shook his head slowly. "I'm sorry, Clay. I'm very sorry, but you must know the truth even if it hurts you." He took a deep breath. "Thorne told Veda she had to do both. He told her to work harder to get you to elope with her *and* get you to sign over the pines to her. He said she should seduce you if she could find no other way."

Helplessly Clay shook his head. "No. No, I don't believe it."

"It's true, Clay. Thorne said you are an honorable man, that if Veda could get you in a 'compromising position'—as a last resort—you would marry her no matter what the consequences may be. My man overheard him say all of that. I'll let you talk to him to hear it for yourself."

Clay's face flushed with heat, then all the color drained away, leaving him white and trembling.

Matt waited until Clay had thought through what he'd just heard. The dusty town around them seemed to pause too. After several minutes, Matt said, "I told you Epson asked Lark to marry him. I know she doesn't love him and I doubt he loves her. There's something else going on there. I'm not sure what, but I know I don't like it whatever it is."

Clay frowned. Where was all this leading?

"Lark loves you, Clay."

Helplessly Clay shook his head. How could that be?

Matt tapped Clay's shoulder with his finger. "But since she knew you were going to marry Veda, she's considering marrying Epson."

Clay groaned and rubbed his hand over his face. Lark couldn't possibly love Epson. She'd never given him a hint of a special feeling for the man. Surely he'd know—he'd promised Jig he'd look after her. Had he been too distracted to notice or to listen?

Matt cleared his throat. What he needed to say next would be the most difficult part. He had no idea how Clay would react. He wanted to keep quiet, but it was too important not to say it. He forced out the words, his heart in his dry throat.

"Clay, I want *you* to marry Lark."

"What?" Clay jumped away from the wall of the bank, his back straight and his shoulders square. This was too much. "Me marry Lark? You can't mean it!"

Matt waited until two women walked past and out of ear shot. "Yes, I do. You won't have any problem sweeping her off her feet."

Sweep her off her feet? He wouldn't know how to begin. He wasn't Tris!

"She loves you. I'm sure of it. I think, if you would let yourself think about it, you'd know it's true."

"I can't listen to any more of this," said Clay, but he didn't move.

Matt rubbed his hands up and down his sleeves. This was almost as hard on him as on Clay, but he had to finish it.

"Marry her within the week and I'll tear up the loan papers. The money *and* the pines will be yours and Lark's together—free and clear."

"I can't believe this," said Clay hoarsely.

"It's my deal with you," said Matt.

"You're going to pay me to marry your daughter."

"It's not like that at all. We're both businessmen. I am offering you a business deal. If it weren't best for Lark, I wouldn't suggest it."

Clay ran his fingers through his dark hair, then smoothed it back in place. "How do you know she'll marry *me?*"

"I know. I've seen the way she looks at you. I hear the sound in her voice when she speaks your name. When we're together she talks mostly about you. It's as though she thinks about you all the time."

Clay blushed. He'd never thought about Lark loving him.

Matt took a deep breath. What would happen to him if Lark ever learned of this plan? She would be wildly angry. She might reject him. But for her sake he had to take the chance.

"You can convince her to marry you. Just ask her. If she hesitates, tell her you need her to marry you to get Veda Thorne out of your life. That'll work for sure. Lark will do anything to help you. And she doesn't want you to marry Veda."

Clay's heart jerked strangely. After a long thoughtful moment he nodded. "All right. I'll do it."

"This week?"

"Yes, this week. I'll ask Lark to marry me." The words sounded strange to his ears. Had he really said them?

Matt held out his hand. "Let's shake on it."

Clay looked at Matt's hand, then finally reached out to him. They shook hands, then Clay followed Matt into the bank.

CHAPTER 13

♦ Outside the bank after the business transaction Clay held his hand out to Matt. "Thank you. I hope I can do all that you asked of me."

Matt clasped Clay's hand. "You will. You're a man of your word."

Clay nodded. He was that.

Matt fell into step beside Clay. "I'd like to meet your family," he said.

"All but Tris are still in Grand Rapids with my sister. She and her husband had twins."

"Twins! That's wonderful. I'm sure you're all proud."

Clay hadn't given it much thought since he was so busy.

"Do you want children when you marry, Clay?"

"I suppose so."

"Maybe you and Lark will have twins."

Clay bit back a cry of shock. He hadn't thought that far ahead. Maybe it was time he considered just what he was getting into. He would be expected to be a true husband to Lark. A blush crept up his neck and over his face.

"I didn't mean to embarrass you," said Matt as they crossed the quiet street. "I'm looking forward to grandchildren, especially since I had to miss seeing my own child grow up." His voice broke and he brushed a tear from his eye.

"I'm sorry," said Clay. He knew his parents valued time with their children. Would he be that kind of parent? The idea was so new to him he couldn't begin to think of an answer.

Matt patted Clay's shoulder as they walked down the board sidewalk past the last store, then turned toward the Wagon Works. Several children ran down the middle of the road, shouting and laughing. Matt glanced at the children, then at Clay. "Have you spoken to Veda yet?"

Clay shook his head. "I was too angry. I want to face her when I'm in control." When he learned the truth, he'd wanted to rush to her house and throttle her until she admitted the truth.

"That's wise. She'll take the broken engagement hard and so will her father."

"Do you think they'll cause more trouble for me?"

"Yes, they will. You can count on it." Matt pulled off his straw hat, rubbed his handkerchief around the inside band, and settled it back in place. "If Thorne is snake enough to use his own daughter to try to get the pines, he'll try something else. Maybe violence."

Clay shook his head. "I have wondered if he's behind the treachery at the shop."

"I thought the same thing, but you can't do anything until you can prove it. Did you hire the guards?"

"Yes, men from Big Pine who've worked as guards at the lumber mills."

"What did you tell the men you were using?"

"I told them that I'd made other arrangements for security, but they could continue working as laborers. They all agreed to stay on." Clay narrowed his eyes thoughtfully. "Dag wanted to continue as a guard. In fact he was very determined. He said he felt a personal interest in seeing that the wagons are safe. But he gave in when I said he couldn't." Clay explained who Dag was, the suspicions he'd had, and the feelers he'd put out to check up on him. "He is a hard worker and very skilled. So far I haven't learned anything about him that's bad."

"I'll ask around about him, too, and see if I can come up with something."

"Thanks, Matt, but it's not necessary. You've helped me more than you should—more than I can ever repay. You've done enough."

Matt shrugged. Helping Clay really wasn't his aim. He wanted to take care of Lark, to help her. He'd missed all those years with her. He wasn't going to be denied any longer. "Have you seen Lark yet?"

"No. I must deal with Veda first." Anger rose inside Clay at the thought of Veda. How could he have let her trick him so easily? He'd been taught never to strike a woman, but he wanted to double his fist and punch her across the state, and then send Willie after her.

Just as they reached the Wagon Works, Veda stepped out of her buggy parked along the street and walked toward Clay. She wore a cream colored skirt with a large bustle and a cream and rose shirtwaist with wide puffed sleeves. Under the small flowered hat, her face was set with determination. Matt tipped his hat and quickly said goodbye. He stood off aways under a tree to see what happened.

Clay glanced toward the shop where the men were hard at work. No one seemed to notice Veda. He felt anger burning just under the surface of his calm facade as Veda stopped just inches from him. He smelled the clean scent of her lilac soap and saw a flash of anger in her dark brown eyes.

"Why have you been avoiding me, Clay Havlick?" she asked sharply.

Clay struggled to keep his anger in check as he gripped Veda's arm and led her back toward her buggy. "I'm very busy, Veda. I'll call on you this evening."

"No!" Veda jerked free and faced him squarely. Papa had said she had to make this look very good. "I don't want to see you this evening or any evening again! I am calling *off* the engagement." Her eyes flashed and she raised her chin in a pose of self-righteous indignation.

Clay stared at her in shock. He had planned to break the engagement. Now he was speechless. "I don't understand," he said weakly.

"You don't care one whit for me! I don't want to see you again as long as I live!"

Clay felt at a loss. Finally he said, "It is for the best. You'll find someone else to marry and so will I."

Veda looked as if she'd been struck. Papa had expected Clay to beg her to marry him even though he didn't have time. What had happened? "I will never marry," she said, trying to keep her voice from trembling. She stepped up into her buggy and without another word, drove away.

His head spinning, Clay watched her go. Had Matt lied to him about Veda? Clay saw Matt standing under an oak several yards away and strode to him. "Veda just broke our engagement."

Matt whistled in surprise. "What game is she playing this time?"

"Is it a game? How do I know I can trust you, Matt Baritt?"

Matt shrugged. "I guess you'll have to look in your heart and see."

Abruptly Clay turned away. He couldn't trust his own heart any longer.

"You have a Scripture to hang on to," Matt said softly. "The sons of God are led by the Spirit of God."

Clay remembered Jig telling him that same thing many times. He'd gotten so tangled up in his business and then with Veda that he hadn't taken time to pray or listen to God. It was past time to get back to spending time reading his Bible and praying. Jig had always told him he had an inheritance greater than the white pines—the promises in God's Word. All of God's blessings belonged to him, but first he had to know them. Then he had to claim them as his own.

"Is something wrong, Clay?" asked Matt.

Clay turned to face Matt. "Yes, it is! You just reminded me to let God's spirit lead me. I haven't been doing that lately, but I mean to do just that from now on!"

Matt smiled. "Good for you, Clay Havlick. Keep in mind you gave your word to marry Lark *this week*."

Clay nodded even though he didn't feel good about what lay ahead. He had given his word and he would keep it. He couldn't back out now and lose his business and his pines.

Just before leaving for the cabin, Lark ran to Matron Kettering's office. It felt closed in and stuffy and there was a strong smell of peppermint.

"Zoe said you wanted to see me immediately."

Mercy stood stiffly beside her desk. Her cheeks were flushed bright red and the fire of battle flashed in her blue eyes. "I just learned that the tavern on Main Street is opening at this very moment! We must march right down there and close it!"

"I thought the mayor refused to give Willie Thorne a business permit."

"I did too! But he's opening and we can't let the townspeople down by letting it stay open." Mercy picked up the tambourine that lay on the corner of her desk. She shook it hard and the jangle filled the room. "I've asked for others in the League to meet us outside the bank."

"I wish Jennet Havlick was here," Lark said, "but she's still in Grand Rapids. She'd want to march on the tavern." A shiver ran down Lark's spine. She'd never done such a brash thing in all her life. Could she push the doors open and walk right in and declare boldly that drinking was of the devil and that the men should get home to their loving families?

"Get your Bible," Mercy said as she tied her dark bonnet on over her light brown hair.

"It's at my cabin."

"Then take one of these." Mercy pointed to four huge

Bibles piled on a shelf behind her desk. "You can never have too many Bibles." Mercy struck her tambourine against her palm again and the jangles rang inside Lark's head.

Several minutes later Lark stood outside Willie Thorne's tavern with four other women. A dark green sign with shiny black lettering that read THORNE'S TAVERN hung above the swinging doors. Noisy piano music drifted into the street. So did a woman's squeal. Lark glanced at the others. The group didn't seem to be very big considering how many belonged to the Temperance League. Maybe some of the members found it hard to march on the tavern. Or maybe the women were too busy with their families.

Lark could see men stopping on the street outside the hardware and feed store to stare at them. A dog barked in the distance and a horse neighed.

Mercy held the big black Bible against her breast and the tambourine out from her hip; she lifted her chin and called, "Ready, ladies?" Mercy slapped her hip with the tambourine and marched through the door of the tavern singing "Onward Christian Soldiers." The other women marched in rhythm with her, their voices blending proudly with hers. Lark followed close behind, her voice a mere croak.

Inside, the tavern was dimly lit and smelled of beer and sweat. Several men at the bar turned at the singing. They shook their heads and swore. Other men sat at small round tables while girls in scanty red dresses walked from the bar to the tables serving the customers.

Angrily Willie Thorne pushed back his chair and strode toward the women. "Ladies," he shouted over the singing and tambourine, "you have no right in my establishment! Leave immediately or I'll call the sheriff." He saw Lark Baritt and three women he'd seen on the sidewalks with a woman he knew was matron of the orphan asylum.

Mercy stopped singing and, ignoring Willie, shouted, "You men! How can you waste your hard earned money on strong drink? Get home to your families. You are sinning against God and against your own bodies. Leave this den of iniquity now before you lose your everlasting souls!"

Lark tried to keep singing, but her throat closed over and no sound came out. Her cheeks burned with embarrassment. Then she looked at Willie and fresh anger rose inside her. She stepped toward him and shook her finger right in his face. "You have harmed enough people already, Willie Thorne. I was there when Silent Waters died. It was a terrible death and I shall never forget it. *And* it was all because of you and your greed. Leave this place and this town. You're not wanted here!"

Willie Thorne shrank back at the mention of Silent Waters and the horrible way she'd died. He turned to a large bearded man at a nearby table. "Get them out of here," Willie said hoarsely.

"We'll leave," Mercy shouted as Willie stalked toward his chair. Her voice was loud for such a small woman. "But if you don't close your doors and stop selling this evil liquor, we'll be back. And we'll come back again and again until you leave our good town."

"Sure, sure," said the bearded man. He gripped Mercy's arm and gestured toward the door. He towered over her and easily could have picked her up and carried her out. "You get out of here right now and stop making trouble."

Lark moistened her dry lips. The room was small and crowded. It had grown quiet. A cloud of embarrassment hung in the air as the customers and serving girls waited for the interruption to be over. Lark saw a blond haired man duck his head and turn away as if he was embarrassed for her to see him.

"Let go of me, sir," cried Mercy, trying to break free as the bearded man dragged her toward the door. The other three women rushed out of the tavern, leaving Mercy and Lark behind. Struggling to stay on her feet, Mercy looked all around the room. "I've seen you all and I will recognize you again. When I see you on the street or in church, I'll tell everyone who can hear that you were in here, in this evil place, drinking and carousing."

Lark walked toward the door with as much dignity as she could summon. She paused in the door for one last look and saw the blond man deep in conversation with Willie Thorne.

Outside the tavern Mercy smoothed down her skirts and tied her bonnet back in place. With her chin held high, she said, "They haven't seen the last of us!"

As the other women hurried away, Lark wondered if they'd ever follow Mercy into the tavern again. She knew it would be very hard for her to do.

"I know that young blond who sat in there," said Mercy as they walked toward the Home. "He was in the Home in Grand Rapids a few years ago when I taught there." She frowned thoughtfully. "His name escapes me right now, but I'll think of it."

Lark dabbed perspiration from her face with her small white hanky. She wondered what Matt would think of her latest exploit. Facing rattlesnakes, bears, and tree robbers seemed much easier than marching into a tavern with the Temperance League.

"I have it! His name is Dag. Dag Gotland! Yes, now I remember." Mercy nodded and smiled. "He was fourteen when I taught him arithmetic. I hate to see him take to drinking."

Lark listened numbly as Mercy talked about her days in Grand Rapids. The sun seemed hotter than the day before and Lark wondered when the hot spell would end. She longed to be back in her cabin in the forest.

When they reached the Home and she had listened to Mercy's promise to invade Willie's tavern again if he kept it open, she said goodbye to Mercy, grateful the experience was over. She was against drinking but she wasn't sure their march had done any good. She hitched Star to her buggy and wearily climbed in. "Let's go home, Star."

About to flick the reins, she heard, "Did you forget about our date for supper?"

Matt walked toward the buggy, his hat pushed to the back of his head. He was shaking his finger at Lark.

Lark laughed, feeling better at once. "I sure did. Sorry."

Matt frowned. "What's wrong? It's not like you to forget things."

He climbed into the buggy, then Lark told him about the visit to the tavern. She finished the story with, "It was awful."

Matt laughed. "I'd like to get to know your Mercy Kettering. She might be little, but she sounds mighty."

Lark laughed. "I happen to know she's walking among those maples over there." Lark pointed to the clump of trees between the Home and the house south of them. "You get acquainted with her while I go home and collapse. I'm tired all the way to the bone."

Matt squeezed Lark's hand. He'd decided to tell her about the loan he'd made to Clay and the rest of the agreement, but now he had a way out. It was probably best she didn't know anything anyway just like he'd first planned. "You go on home and I'll see you tomorrow," he said.

"Tomorrow? That would be nice. Just how long do you plan to stay around here?"

"As long as I'm welcome."

Tears pricked Lark's eyes. "I hope I don't get used to having you around only to have you leave."

"I promise that won't happen." Matt stepped from the buggy, then stood beside it and looked up at Lark. "I saw a house for sale in town. It's over near the Wagon Works. I was thinking about buying it. What do you think?"

"The one with lots of windows and at least six bedrooms? I love that house!"

"Then I'll buy it."

"Just like that? Do you have enough money to do that kind of thing?"

Matt nodded. "I have more than enough."

"Do writers make that kind of money?"

"No, but lumbermen do."

Lark stared at Matt in surprise. She didn't know much at all about this man who was her father. "Are you a lumberman?"

"Yes. I started out much the way Free Havlick did. Grant Bigalow and I went into partnership and we made a great deal of money in the Upper Peninsula. I invested my money and built up a nice nest egg for myself." He shrugged. "Some would call it a fortune."

"I didn't know," said Lark weakly.

"I want to share it with you."

Lark pressed her hand to her throat. What would it be like to have a fortune? She'd thought she had one when Jig left her $1500. She knew Matt was talking about a great deal more than that.

"I'm going to buy that house for you, Lark, and you can move in right away."

Lark gasped. "You can't do that!"

"I can if I want." Matt laughed. "I want to give you everything!"

"I wanted a father the past twenty-two years."

Matt's face fell. "I know. Fear wrecks lives, Lark. My fear kept us apart. I vow I will never again let fear keep me from doing what I want for my daughter. I will buy that house and I will furnish it just the way you want. You plan on moving in right away."

"What about my cabin?"

"Bring it with you!"

Lark began to laugh and Matt joined in.

With Sears beside her, Lark filled her canteen at the well just after dawn. "This heat has to let up, Sears. I can't take it much longer." Lark hooked her canteen to her belt beside the revolver and holster, picked up her cudgel, and headed into the pines. Her feet were hot inside her heavy boots and the leggings she wore made her legs itch. She was wearing her old blue calico dress instead of her leather pants and jacket because of the heat.

A rabbit hopped into sight, then streaked away, but Sears ignored it. A deer drank at the stream. Nearby a raccoon sat watching. Lark flung her cudgel high in the air, then caught it deftly. She remembered the first time she'd done that. She'd almost broken her fingers as she tried to catch it. Now she barely felt the sting in her palm.

At the quagmire, mosquitoes buzzed over the top of it. Green and blue dragonflies flitted here and there. Several black crows teased an owl on a branch. The owl snapped angrily, but the crows kept cawing. She loved the early morning time in the forest.

As Lark pushed through the briars she heard the frightening whir of rattles and froze. Usually when it was this hot even the rattlesnakes didn't give a warning. She checked in front of her and saw a snake coiled and ready to strike. Sears stood without moving a muscle. Finally the snake crawled away through the pine needles.

"Close one, Sears," Lark said, her voice trembling slightly. Sears licked her hand and she felt better. Side by side they walked past the huge tree root. So many memories of dangerous encounters were connected with it, she had difficulty just passing by. She looked down on the quiet river. No one was on it yet. Men were still looking in the swamps for logs, so they'd be out and around later.

Sweat soaked Lark as she walked to the spot where she would cut across the pines and turn back to the cabin. She stopped and listened. She thought she'd heard the ring of an ax, but the only sounds she could hear were the normal sounds of animals and insects. It must've been her imagination.

Sears pressed his nose tight into Lark's hand. The short hairs on the back of her neck stood on end. Someone was nearby, she was sure of it. She brushed her arm across her revolver and gripped her cudgel tighter. The loud musical rattle of a sandhill crane startled her and she almost cried out.

Her senses alert, she walked fast to the cabin. Who had

been watching her in the pines? Had Matt hired someone to protect her because he knew of the terrible dangers?

Standing at the well, Lark studied the pines. Had someone followed her? She glanced at Sears. He was watching the pines also. Prickles of fear ran over her skin, but no one stepped out. Finally Sears ran to his bowl and lapped water. With a relieved sigh Lark struck the bell to signal the hired man at the Havlicks' that all was well. Clay would already be at the Wagon Works and Tris had left last night for Grand Rapids to be with the family.

Just as she was trying to relax Sears looked up and growled low in his throat. Lark stiffened.

"Lark Baritt, it's me. Dag Bjoerling. I came to see you."

Lark frowned, but didn't pull her revolver. Clay had told her Jig's grandson was working for him, but so far she hadn't met him. "Come on out from behind that tree," she called.

Dag stepped around a pine smiling hesitantly. He wore heavy boots, work pants, and a blue chambray shirt. He had a cap on his blond head. A revolver was stuck in his belt and he carried a long walking stick whittled from a sapling.

Lark recognized him as the blond man at the tavern who Mercy had said was Dag Gotland from Grand Rapids. He could not be Dag Bjoerling from Sweden as he'd said he was. Had Clay learned this man was an imposter? If he didn't know, she'd have to warn him. "What can I do for you?" she asked.

"Give me a ride back to town. I was trying to find Red Beaver's place and got lost."

Lark didn't believe that, but she didn't let it show. "I must change my clothes before I can go to town. You could go to the Havlicks to see if Clay has left yet."

Just then Sears lifted his head and whined. Lark frowned. Was someone else nearby, someone that Sears knew? Lark turned to Dag and whispered, "Someone's lurking about. When I shout, draw your gun and be ready to fire."

The color drained from Dag's face. He didn't want anyone hurt or killed. He pulled his gun and pointed it at Lark.

"What're you doing?" she cried.

"Drop the gun and the club. If your dog makes a move toward me, I'll shoot him dead." Dag knew he wouldn't shoot the dog, but he had to make Lark think he would.

Trembling, Lark dropped the revolver and cudgel on the ground. "What do you want?"

Just then John Epson walked from behind the cabin, his hat in his hand, his face red.

"John! I'm so glad to see you!" Lark cried, taking a step toward him.

"Stay!" snapped Dag. She froze, looking from John to Dag.

"Listen to him, Lark," said John, wiping his face with a large white handkerchief.

"John?" whispered Lark, trembling, suddenly too weak to stand. "What is it? Why are you here?"

"We have men ready to cut the trees," said John.

Lark stumbled back and sank down on the bench. Sears sank at her feet and laid his head on her heavy boots. "Cut the trees? You, John?"

He shook his head. "I'm only here to see that you don't stop them."

"You won't get away with it."

"We will," said John.

"What about me? What will you do with me?" Lark knew they couldn't let her go.

John flushed. He didn't want to think about that.

Dag held the revolver out to John. "Keep her here while I check on the men. We have a whole crew working. It won't take them long."

Lark groaned. While Dag and John talked she glanced down at Sears and whispered, "Fetch my cudgel, Sears. Fetch."

Sears padded to the cudgel and carried it to Lark. Her heart hammered so loud she thought the two men could hear it. She took the cudgel from Sears and stood it close to her, covering it with her skirts.

Dag glanced at Lark, then ran into the pines. Lark knew

they would begin at the easiest place above the river to lumber the pines. The sawers would cut a tree, others would chop off the limbs and branches, then they'd roll the huge trunk down the hill to the river and float it to Blue Creek. They'd put a log mark on each end of the log and no one would ever know it came from Havlicks' pines.

"Why are you doing this, John?" asked Lark.

He frowned at her, then down at the revolver. "Do you know how much money each pine is worth? It's more than most people make in a year! I had a chance to share the money and I took it."

"Is that why you paid attention to me?"

"Yes. I tried my best to get you interested in something besides the pines. I tried to get you away from here to keep you out of this. But you wouldn't listen. I'm sorry, Lark. I like and respect you. You deserve better than you're going to get."

"Just let me go, John. You know they'll kill me." Lark couldn't move without giving away the cudgel at her side. "Willie Thorne is behind all of this, isn't he?"

John laughed gruffly. "Willie Thorne? You've got it all wrong, Lark. It's Matt Baritt. This is how he made his fortune."

Lark cried out in searing agony. "You're lying!"

"Don't believe me if you don't want to. But I speak the truth." John's eye twitched. He rubbed his well-trimmed beard.

Suddenly Lark flung the cudgel, sending it spinning sideways. It struck Epson's elbow and the revolver flew from his hand. He cried in pain as he grabbed his arm. Lark leaped for the revolver, scooping it up before John could move.

"You won't shoot me," said John, his eyes hard. "I know you well, Lark Baritt."

"I'll shoot if I must," she said harshly.

John stared hard into her eyes, then bolted for the woods. Lark took aim, but couldn't fire. John was right. She could not shoot him. She caught up her cudgel and sprang toward the bell. She struck it twice with her cudgel, then leaped after John with Sears at her heels. She could hear John crashing through the underbrush ahead of her. If he didn't stay on the trail, he wouldn't last long among the swamps and rattlesnakes. Did he know enough about the woods to be on guard? He was in good shape and he was a fast runner. That would help him.

She thought of the men in the woods. If they heard the bell they'd run off before anyone could reach them and capture them. If they hadn't, she'd make John tell her exactly where they were working.

Lark ran carefully, watching for every danger. The terrible heat pressed against her, making it hard to keep going.

Up ahead John's dirt covered face was streaked with sweat as he hesitated at a bog. If he didn't go through it, Lark would catch him. If he did go through it, he might lose his shoes in the muck. His heart raced as he looked back. He couldn't see Lark but he could hear her coming after him.

He heard the sickening whirring of a rattlesnake. Fear stung his fingertips as he caught sight of the huge coil. He sprang back just as the snake struck, missing him by a hair's breadth. He leaped forward through the bog. He sank ankle deep in the mud but miraculously his shoes stayed on his feet. Reaching the needle-covered ground on the other side, he thought he was safe for the moment.

There was a sudden searing pain in his leg. He cried out, stumbled, and sprawled to the ground. He saw the snake, but he was too paralyzed with fear to move. Without a sound the snake struck again, sinking its fangs in John's face between his beard and his eye. He screamed and clawed at his face. The snake struck again in his arm and he screamed again.

Lark leaped forward, caught up the snake with her cudgel and flung it away. Sears growled deep in his throat as he crouched near John. "Oh, John!" Lark cried as she knelt beside him. Tears burned her eyes as she caught his hand and held it tightly.

John's eyes filled with tears. "This is it for me, Lark," he said hoarsely.

"I'm sorry." Tears slipped down her ashen cheeks. "God loves you and always has."

"You sound like Ma," whispered John, remembering even though he tried not to. "She always prayed for me."

"She prayed and God always answers prayer, John!"

"It's too late for me. I never thought it would end like this. Where did I go wrong?" His voice cracked. "I know where. I let greed take hold of me. I thought later, after I'd made myself rich, then I could straighten out my life. Maybe even repent. Now it's too late."

"Oh, John, don't give up!"

Great drops of sweat rolled down his face. A squirrel scolded nearby, then the raspy buzz of insects covered the chatter.

"It's too late for me. It's funny. I always thought I had plenty of time. I'll have to pay for my sins just like Ma always said. It's too late to call on Jesus."

"No, it's not! It's never too late to pray," said Lark with a sob.

"I'll die and spend all eternity suffering in hell." John moaned and his eyes glazed over from the pain.

"John, can you hear me? Ask Jesus to forgive your sins and become your Savior. He loves you, John! Think of your mother's prayers." Lark leaned down to John. "You must not die without God! He loves you! Call on him now before it's too late! Confess your sins, John. Ask him to forgive you. Claim his promises. Please don't wait another minute!"

"I can't pray," he whispered brokenly.

"You can! You must! God loves you and you know it. You've known it since you were a little boy at your mother's knee."

John's heart seemed to melt as he thought of the times he'd prayed with his mother. Life had been so simple then. But it suddenly seemed simple again. He could call on God! "Dear Jesus, forgive my sins," he whispered. "Forgive me for wasting my life. I accept you as my Savior. Forgive me for hurting Lark." John couldn't move his head, but his eyes sought Lark's and held them. "Forgive me, Lark," he whispered. "Please forgive me."

Lark bit her lip as tears streamed down her cheeks. "I forgive you." John stiffened. Then his body relaxed. His head rolled against her knees.

She stayed beside him on her knees for a long time. "Thank you, Heavenly Father, for hearing John. I do forgive what he did to me."

Finally Lark stood and Sears leaped to her side. She'd have to send someone to get John's body to give it a proper burial. Then she remembered that John had said her father was behind all the trouble, that he was the one stealing the pines. She clutched her throat and cried out in pain. She had found her father only to learn he was a thief. She looked up at the pines towering over her. Why couldn't everyone look at the trees the way she did? They were things of beauty, not just a source of money to line the pockets of the greedy.

With an anguished moan she looked down at John. Had he told her the truth about her father? Why hadn't she asked John before he died? He would've told her the truth. She bit her lip. She'd have to find out herself.

CHAPTER 14

♦ Her cudgel in her hand, Lark walked slowly back to the cabin. She heard no sounds of lumbering, but that didn't mean the tree robbers weren't at work somewhere. Her legs felt so heavy she could barely walk. She thought about John and groaned at the terrible pain he'd been in. Thankfully he'd accepted Jesus as his Savior before he'd died. As she reached the cabin, Matt rode up on a horse he'd hired at the livery. His tail waving, Scars ran to Matt.

Lark knotted her fists at her sides as anger raged inside her. Tangles of hair hung around her damp face and neck. Her dress was torn and dirty and an angry red scratch ran from the back of her left hand up her arm.

"Lark, what's wrong?" asked Matt in alarm as he stopped near her. He saw her anger and couldn't understand it. "You didn't get to the Home on time and I was worried about you."

"John Epson is dead!"

"Dead?"

Her voice rising at every word, Lark told Matt what had happened and what John had said. When she finished she was shouting, "How dare you come here and make me love you, then cheat and steal?"

Matt shook his head. "Lark, as God is my witness I am not after the trees or money from them. John was not working for me. Can't you see it was a lie?"

Lark raked back her hair and held it at her neck. "How do I know what's true?"

Matt helplessly spread his hands. "I don't know what to say. I love you, Lark, and I wouldn't do anything to hurt you."

Lark saw the truth in his eyes, but still she held back from him. "How can you love me? You don't even know me!"

"I love you anyway. You are my child."

Lark soaked in the words, almost daring to believe them.

"Willie Thorne is very deceitful. I learned that John Epson worked for him in the past." Matt didn't tell her that he'd had a detective check into John's background because of his association with her. "He was probably working for Thorne on this deal."

"Can I believe you?" asked Lark in a low, tired voice.

"Yes, you can." Matt took her hands and held them tightly. Because of the terrible heat he was in his shirt sleeves and lightweight gray pants. "You can ask about me anywhere in the Upper Peninsula and get a good report on me. Send telegrams around if it'll make you feel better."

Lark's anger slowly slipped away. She desperately wanted to believe Matt. "Do you really think John was working for Thorne?"

"Yes. I do."

Just then Clay rode up to the cabin and jumped off Flame before she'd stopped. Clay ran to Lark and gripped her arms. He saw the torn dress and the tangled hair, then the scratch on her arm. "Are you all right? Did anyone harm you?"

"John Epson was going to kill her," said Matt.

"What?" cried Clay as he fiercely pulled Lark close and held her tight. "I knew I shouldn't have let you stay as guard!"

Matt walked to the bench and called Sears to him. He smiled as he watched Lark and Clay. He had figured it right.

They did love each other. Maybe they didn't know it yet, but soon they would.

Lark clung to Clay. She never wanted to let him go. She smelled his sweat and dust and felt the thump of his heart. "Did you find the thieves? Did they get any pines?" she asked.

"They had one down, so my men are finishing it to float it to the mill."

"Didn't you catch anyone? Not even Dag?"

Clay held Lark from him enough to look into her face. "Dag was there?"

"Yes." Lark told what she'd learned from Mercy.

"He didn't come to work today. He sent word he was sick." Clay shook his head helplessly. "You will not stay as guard, Lark. It was never safe, but the danger is even worse now. You're coming home with me."

Lark shook her head. "I can't do that. I'm staying here!"

Clay suddenly realized this was the perfect time for his plan. "I won't let you! Do you know how much I'd worry about you?" That was very true. "I want you to marry me, Lark. I can keep you safe."

Lark's eyes widened in shock. "Marry you?"

Clay pulled her close again and touched his lips to hers. Just the touch of her lips sent waves of feelings through him that surprised him.

Lark felt his lips on hers and before she could stop herself, she returned his kiss with a passion she hadn't realized she could feel. She felt as if she'd waited her whole life for Clay's kiss. Wave after wave of passion swept over her until she was weak with a longing she'd never known existed. She loved Clay Havlick! When had that happened?

Finally Clay lifted his head. His heart thundered inside him. "Marry me now, today."

"Isn't this a strange time to be thinking of that?" Lark was sure he couldn't mean what he had said.

"What better time? I can't let you out of my sight for fear someone will try again to harm you."

Lark suddenly felt too weak to stand. She clung tighter to Clay.

"Will you marry me, Lark? Right now?"

"I will," Lark whispered in a daze. Suddenly she remembered Veda Thorne. "What about Veda?"

"We are no longer engaged. It's you I want to marry." The words rang true in Clay's heart and he was surprised. Maybe his admiration for Lark would someday turn into love.

"Oh, Clay!" Lark's eyes blazed with love. "We'll be happy together. I love you!" The words burst from her, but she didn't care. She did love him.

Clay pulled her close and kissed her again so he wouldn't have to say the words and tell her a lie. He liked the feel of her soft, but strong body. He knew his family would welcome her with open arms. He kissed her again. Maybe they would be happy together.

Two hours later Lark stood before Pastor James with Clay on one side of her and Matt and Zoe on the other. She wore a white organdy dress she'd bought from Sally and held a bouquet of pink and crimson gladiolus. Lark's face glowed with a happiness she'd never felt before in her life. She smiled at Clay as Pastor James read the marriage ceremony. Clay looked handsome in his light gray suit and white shirt with a black tie.

At the close of the ceremony Clay kissed Lark lightly on the lips, but he still felt it down to his toes. Lark blushed, then turned to hug Matt and Zoe.

Outside the church Matt said, "Clay, I'm giving you and Lark a house as a wedding gift. It's the big white frame and red brick near the Wagon Works. It is already furnished, but if you want to change anything, do it and I'll pay for that."

Lark's head spun. She couldn't imagine having a father with money.

"Here's the key." Matt handed Clay a skeleton key. "I had Mrs. Larsen from the boarding house take food there for you." He looked lovingly at Lark. "Zoe had three of the girls from the Home pack your things in the cabin and take them over. And I moved Sears and his house to your new home. I even took over your horse and buggy."

"You've thought of everything, haven't you?" asked Clay sharply.

Matt smiled, but he shot Clay a warning look. "I tried to. Now, I'm taking Zoe back to the Home and I'm spending the evening with Mercy."

"Have a wonderful life, Lark." Zoe hugged Lark tightly and whispered against her ear, "Wouldn't it be perfect if I married Tris?"

Lark laughed softly as she nodded. Today everything seemed perfect.

Clay took Lark's arm and led her to the buggy. Several boys were playing in the field beside the church barn. "I hope you never regret marrying me," Clay said as he handed her in.

"I won't," she said. "How could I? I love you."

Clay flushed with guilt as he kissed her lightly, then drove toward the very house Veda had wanted. He didn't tell Lark that.

Lark sat as close to Clay as she could as they stopped in the driveway. "I've admired this house a long time," she said. "When the Masters moved out, I'd dream it belonged to me. But I never thought about sharing it with my husband." She chuckled softly. "I never thought I'd have one."

Clay let her talk as they looked around. The wide yard was groomed nicely and brightly colored flowers were in full bloom. Star stood in the pen beside the big red barn and Lark's buggy was parked outside the shed where they'd put it later. Sears barked and whined as he tugged on the rope tied to his dog house. The house was two stories high with a black roof and dormers upstairs. The front was brick and the other three sides were wooden siding painted white.

"Isn't it grand, Clay?" Lark jumped to the ground and looked all around. She ran to Sears and patted his head. Someone had filled his container with water and had even given him a bone to gnaw on. "This is our new home, Sears. We'll be happy here."

Clay laughed as he watched Lark dash from one thing to the next. He liked to see her so happy and full of excitement after being so frightened earlier. "We'd better go inside," he said, feeling a little hesitant.

"You're right." Lark ran to the door and waited while Clay unlocked it. This morning she had thought she was going to die. How different her day had turned out!

They stepped into the wide hallway with doors opening to different rooms and another to an enclosed stairwell. The home lacked a personal touch, but it was beautiful and grand. It smelled of roses. Lark ran from room to room downstairs while Clay followed behind her, enjoying her reaction. He would never be so excited about a house. But she'd lived in the Home and then at the cabin. No wonder she was so excited about the house.

In the kitchen Lark found the basket of food. "I'll fix us something to eat. Are you hungry?"

Clay shrugged. Suddenly he was hungry. "I'll eat and then I must get back to work. I have a change of clothes in the buggy."

Lark unloaded the basket as she talked about the Wagon Works to Clay seated at the round oak table. "It sounds like you won't have any trouble meeting your contracts."

"I shouldn't unless something else happens. But with the new guards I hired, they should keep intruders away." Clay told her about another new contract to be filled by March. "And I'll be hiring a new bookkeeper."

"You don't have to do that! I'll be glad to do it."

"You're my wife now and you don't have to work."

Lark gasped. "I never thought of that. I can't imagine not working!"

"You'll have enough to do here to keep you occupied. And if you want to continue helping at the Home, you can."

Lark sank to a chair and stared at Clay. "My life has changed so much so quickly that I can't take it in. I don't know what I want to do." Suddenly she thought of Willie Thorne. "But I do know I want to run Willie Thorne out of town!"

Clay caught Lark's hand and gripped it tightly. "Please leave him alone. He's a dangerous man. I don't want you hurt."

Lark smiled lovingly at Clay. "You're sweet, Clay. But I can't stay locked in this house and never face anything."

Clay ran his finger beside the scratch on her hand and arm. "Put salve on this scratch before it gets infected."

"I will."

Clay pushed back his chair and stood. "I'd better change and get back to work. I won't be home until after dark."

"You be careful. I don't want anything to happen to you." Lark circled Clay's waist with her arms and laid her cheek against his chest. She heard the thud of his heart and felt the smooth cotton of his shirt. Life was suddenly so perfect that tears filled her eyes. She lifted her face and looked at Clay. "I love you," she whispered hoarsely.

Clay bent his head and kissed her just as he knew she expected of him. He wrapped his arms around her and kissed her again, then again. He had to leave, but he found he couldn't let her go. She had a strange effect on him that he couldn't understand. He'd never felt this way when he'd kissed Veda. But then she'd never responded with passion like Lark was doing. "I don't want to leave," he said against her mouth.

"Then stay." Lark's stomach fluttered at the thought of sharing intimate times with Clay. It wasn't anything she'd learned in deportment and she didn't know what was expected of her.

His green plaid shirt open at the neck, Willie Thorne angrily paced his study. Veda sat on the sofa, her hands locked in her lap, her light blue skirt hanging gracefully over her slim ankles.

Willie slammed his fist down hard on his desk making the

pencil cup rattle. "The men didn't get a single tree! Dag said Havlick's men came too quickly and they all ran before they were caught. I don't know what happened to John Epson, but Dag said he'd nose around."

Just then the door opened and without asking Willie's permission Agnes Thorne walked in. Her face was pale, but her gray hair was neatly combed and she wore a dark green traveling dress. "I am leaving, Willie. I decided last night. I suppose I owe you the courtesy of telling you."

Willie frowned. "Go back to your room, Agnes. I don't have time now for you."

As though she hadn't heard him, Agnes turned to Veda. "I want you to come with me. I love you. You are Silent Waters' daughter by birth, but I raised you and in my heart you belong to me. Will you come with me?"

Veda slowly stood and took Agnes's hand in hers. "I love you, too, Momma."

"Veda, I forbid you to leave this house," snapped Willie. "I won't live without you."

"You will," said Agnes sharply. "You don't need anyone or anything. You have your greed and your desire for revenge. You need nothing more."

Willie lifted his hand to strike Agnes, but Veda jumped between them and pushed Willie back.

"I have some things to settle first, Momma," said Veda softly as she squeezed Agnes's hand. "But you go ahead and I'll join you in a few days. Maybe we can go to Europe again."

"I'd like that," said Agnes. "We had fun there, didn't we?"

Willie sank to the edge of his desk. How could he tell Agnes and Veda there was no money left to do anything? Unless he could get his hands on the pines, they'd be broke before the middle of September. He'd sold liquor several places illegally, but that didn't bring in the kind of money he needed to save their home. "Agnes, please don't leave," he said tiredly. "I need both of you here with me."

Agnes shook her head. "You only needed Silent Waters and

Veda. Now Silent Waters is dead. I will not let that happen to Veda."

Willie trembled violently. "Don't even speak her name!"

"You can live with your son if you get lonely," said Agnes. "If he'll have you."

Veda's head throbbed as she listened to her parents fight. She had never heard her mother stand up to her father before. Veda was afraid he'd strike her if she didn't stop talking.

The sky darkened rapidly outside the open French doors and thunder boomed. Within minutes the temperature dropped and rain lashed against the house. Willie paced his study like a caged animal. He'd planned to meet with Dag just after dark. Lightning lit up the sky and Willie cringed. He didn't mind getting soaked to the skin or the noise of thunder, but lightning could kill and he hated being outdoors where he was in danger of being fried to a crisp.

"Finally the heat spell has broken," said Agnes with a loud sigh. "Veda, I'll wait until tomorrow to leave. Can you be ready by then?"

Veda glanced at her father and finally nodded.

"You're not going," said Willie.

"I will go, Papa. I am tired of trying to get Clay Havlick interested in me."

Agnes looked from Willie to Veda. "You don't know, do you? Gert told me only a few minutes ago that Clay Havlick married Lark Baritt this afternoon."

Willie shot from his desk and Veda cried out in astonishment. "You lie, woman!" bellowed Willie, shaking his fist at Agnes.

Agnes turned on her heels and left the study, slamming the door hard behind her.

Veda pressed her hands to her cheeks. "I can't believe he'd marry that orphan when he could've had me!"

"I knew I should've had her killed last month when I talked to Epson about it. But he swore he could handle her."

"I suppose there's nothing more we can do," said Veda,

suddenly very tired. She touched the pearl brooch at her high neckline and thought of how nice it would've been to be married to Clay.

Willie slammed his fist into his palm. "I'll kill her myself! It was her fault Silent Waters died."

Veda frowned. "Papa, you can't go around killing people."

Willie gripped Veda and shook her. "Don't tell me what I can't do!"

"Papa, you're hurting me!"

Abruptly Willie released her and paced the room again. If only the lightning would stop so he could go to the tavern!

Veda trembled as she sank to the sofa. She'd never seen her father in such a state. "Why can't we just go back to Grand Rapids again? We were happy there. There were three men there who wanted to marry me."

"But none had the wealth of the Havlicks!"

"I know, but they had money enough."

"I should burn down the pines. Yes! If I can't have them, I'll burn them. I could do it now tonight and everyone would think lightning struck and started the fire." He seemed to be talking to himself. "It's been so dry, they'd burn fast. What would the Havlicks do then? This is my best plan yet! Burn down the pines *and* the Wagon Works."

Veda saw the wild look in her father's eyes and her stomach knotted painfully. Would he really set fire to the pines?

"I'll go as soon as the lightning passes. I will burn the Wagon Works and the pines! It'll serve the Havlicks right."

Helplessly Veda shook her head. Nothing she could say would help now. She slipped from the room and ran to find Gert.

"I need your help," cried Veda as she stopped just inside the kitchen.

Gert stood near the windows with a cup of tea in her hands. She glanced nervously at her black cap and apron folded neatly on a chair, then carefully set down her cup. "What is it you want?"

Veda laced and unlaced her fingers. Her cheeks were bright red and her eyes full of worry. "I must speak to Clay and Lark. Momma told me they were married this afternoon. Where do they live? How can I reach them?"

"It wouldn't do for you to visit them now, I believe."

"This will not be a visit! I must speak to them! It's urgent."

Gert wanted to refuse, but she told Veda where Clay and Lark lived. "You won't be going out in this storm, will you? It's as dark as midnight."

Veda grabbed her rain gear from the back porch and ran to the barn for her buggy. She found Ray Moline doing the chores and ordered him to quickly harness the buggy. As she waited she glanced toward the garden bench and thought of Red Beaver's visit. Maybe Red Beaver could stop Papa from burning the Wagon Works and the pines.

"You be careful, Miss Veda," said Ray as he stopped the black mare near Veda. "This weather ain't fit for ducks."

Veda nodded absently as she climbed in the buggy and drove away. Lightning lit up the sky and thunder cracked. Rain blew in against her, soaking her to the skin. She drove the black mare over the bridge and along the corduroy toward Red Beaver's farm.

Without warning the mare reared and a buggy wheel rolled off the side of the log road into the steep ditch. The sudden lurch threw Veda from the buggy. She landed in the ditch. Muddy water soaked her clothes under her rain gear. Mud squished between her fingers. Before she could stand, the mare raced away, the buggy bucking along behind it.

Slowly Veda pushed herself up. Her hair hung in wet tangles around her shoulders and her skirts clung to her legs. Mud sucked at her small kid shoes. She struggled back on to the corduroy, took three steps, bumped against something, and almost fell. She looked down at the hump and saw it was a man. "That's what startled the mare!" she muttered. She bent down to the man and in the flash of lightning saw he was in his twenties and wore a tweed suit, wet and muddy. She touched his neck to see if he had a heart beat and heard him groan. She sighed in relief. "Can you stand?" she asked over the noise of the rain and thunder.

"I think so," he said with a thick Swedish accent.

Veda steadied the man until he stood upright. He swayed and she caught him, supporting him the best she could. "My brother's farm is nearby," she said. Calling Red Beaver her brother made her weak in the knees, and she had to force strength back into them to keep walking. "We'll go there."

In silence they struggled up the long lane that led to Red Beaver's farm. Lightning flashed again, striking a lone maple several feet away. The crack of the breaking tree trunk struck fear in Veda. She'd never been in such danger in her life.

"Run!" shouted the man as he tightened his hold on Veda. He stumbled and Veda steadied him, her heart thundering. With one mighty effort they ran to safety. The crashing branches barely missed them. The ground shook under their feet.

"God is good to us," said the man weakly.

His words pierced her heart.

Finally they reached Red Beaver's back door. Wind and rain whipping her skirts tight around her, Veda knocked hard on the door.

Hoping against hope that it was Hannah Havlick, Red Beaver flung the door wide, then cried, "Laughing Eyes!" He took the weight of the man from her and helped them both to chairs in the warm kitchen. He gave them towels to dry with, then poured hot coffee for them.

Red Beaver leaned toward the man. The ties of his blue rolled headband swung forward. "I am Red Beaver. Who are you?"

"Andree Bjoerling from Sweden. Nephew to Dag Bjoerling. Jig to his American friends."

Red Beaver nodded. "I knew Jig well."

Veda stared in alarm at the dark haired man. What would

Papa do when he learned of this? Dag Gotland's impersonation of Jig's grandson would be found out.

"I am looking for Lark Baritt and the Havlicks." His Swedish accent made it hard for Red Beaver and Veda to understand him.

Red Beaver told Andree how to find the Havlicks' farm and that Lark lived in a cabin in the pine forest. Veda realized he didn't know Clay and Lark were married and had a house in town, but she didn't speak up.

"I came to see where Uncle Dag lived all these years and to meet the friends he made."

"You can stay the night here and see them tomorrow." Red Beaver stood. "We must get you into dry clothing. You're welcome to change into my clothes. They might be loose on you, but they'll be dry."

"That sounds very good to me." Andree smiled as he slowly stood. He winced and looked down at his bloody pant leg. "I have hurt my leg."

"I'll tend it," Red Beaver said as he helped Andree into his bedroom.

When she was alone in the kitchen, Veda looked around. Silent Waters once worked here. She had laughed and cried in this room. Papa probably sat at this very table and ate with Silent Waters and Red Beaver. Tears smarted Veda's eyes. She blinked them quickly away as Red Beaver returned. She jumped up and reached for Red Beaver, then dropped her hands at her sides before she touched him. "Papa needs your help, Red Beaver! He is making crazy plans to burn Clay's pines and the Wagon Works."

"Then I must stop him." Red Beaver grabbed his hat and rain gear off a hook near the door. "Stay here and take care of Andree. I'll be back as soon as I can. Is Willie Thorne still at his house?"

Veda nodded. "He won't go out until the lightning stops." She told him about Clay and Lark getting married and all about what she and her father had planned to do.

"He should've stayed with my mother," Red Beaver said. "They were happy."

Veda couldn't imagine what life would be like if she'd been raised half Patawatomi.

"Get out of those wet clothes, Laughing Eyes. You'll find our mother's clothing in her bedroom."

Veda nodded. The thought of dressing in Silent Waters' clothes made her uncomfortable.

In the barn Red Beaver saddled his spotted gelding and swung easily into the saddle. He galloped quickly to town in spite of the storm. He stopped first at the house Veda had described as Clay and Lark's new home. A pale light burned in a back window and he ran to the back door, leaving his gelding in the yard. He knocked and Lark flung the door wide, expecting to see Clay.

"Red Beaver, come in out of the rain!" cried Lark, stepping aside. "Is something wrong?"

"Yes. Is Clay here?"

"No. He's at the shop. Why?" Lark's stomach knotted in fear. "Why, Red Beaver?"

Quickly he told her and she ran to get her rainwear.

"I'll find Clay. You go see Willie Thorne," said Lark.

Red Beaver nodded and ran back into the lashing rain storm.

Lark knew it would be quicker to go to the Wagon Works on foot instead of saddling Star. She knew Clay was working late because of taking so much time with her after their wedding. She smiled as she remembered his touch and his kisses. It had truly been a remarkable day.

By the time she reached the Wagon Works, she was soaked. The doors were closed, but a light shone weakly from a window near where Clay had his desk.

Lark inched open the door to keep the rain from blowing into the shop. She could see Clay and Matt deep in conversation farther down near a half-finished wagon. Their backs were to her and they didn't hear her enter. She eased the door shut and walked toward them. Thunder boomed and she jumped. As she walked quietly toward them, her heart swelled with pride and love. *My husband and my father,* she thought with joy. They were speaking in low tones. As she drew nearer, she could understand the words.

"I feel terrible for not telling Lark the truth," she heard Clay say.

Lark froze. The truth? What could he mean?

"Just leave it be, Clay," said Matt tiredly. "I thought of telling her, but changed my mind. She doesn't need to know. She'd misunderstand. There's already been enough pain in her life."

Clay shook his head. "It's not right for me to pretend I married her for love. What if she learns you gave me enough money to save my business and the white pines on the condition I'd marry her?"

Lark's body shook so hard she could hardly move.

"She'll never know the truth," said Matt. "I love her too much to let her learn that."

"She's a fine woman," said Clay. Thinking about his time with her this afternoon sent his pulse racing. "We can be happy."

Lark slowly crept back to the door and out into the storm. She leaned against the door, her head spinning and her heart broken. Clay didn't love her! He had married her for money!

She stood for a long time. Finally when her head had stopped spinning, she remembered why she'd come. For one wild minute she considered not telling Clay, but she couldn't let his business or his pines be destroyed.

Taking a deep breath, Lark opened the door. Her face burned and her throat almost closed over. "Clay! I have news!" she called, her voice cracking.

Clay ran to her. "Lark, what are you doing out in this weather?" He put an arm around her, but she slipped away from him in the pretense of greeting Matt.

"What's the news that brings you out, Lark?" asked Matt.

Lark told them quickly, staying as far from Clay as she could without being obvious.

"I'll put out extra guards tonight here and at the pines," said Clay. "And I'll go see Willie Thorne myself."

Lark gasped. "What if he tries to kill you?"

"I'll go with you," said Matt. "He won't kill us both."

Clay and Matt began to discuss a plan for confronting Willie and while they were deeply engrossed in conversation, Lark slipped away. Slowly she walked back to the house that moments before had been her heaven on earth.

"Oh, God, help me," she whispered as she stepped into the warm, dry house. Water streamed from her clothes and made a puddle on the highly polished wood floor. "I can't survive on my own. Please, Lord, show me what to do." She wanted to grab her clothes and run back to the safety of the asylum but it wouldn't be home any more. She crept to the bedroom she shared with Clay and slowly undressed. Her head buzzed as she slipped on her nightdress. She sank to the edge of the bed that was still mussed from this afternoon and buried her face in her icy hands. Her joy was gone and her heart was broken.

CHAPTER 15

♦ Rain dripping from his raincoat and pants and his hat in his hand, Red Beaver stood in the middle of Willie Thorne's study. A lamp on Willie's large oak desk cast a weak glow over the room, revealing only part of the stone fireplace and the sofa. Rain lashed at the French doors and windows. Red Beaver ignored the puddle of water spreading around his feet as he squarely faced Willie. "You must stop your vendetta, Willie Thorne."

"Go back to your farm, Red Beaver. Leave my house."

"You have already caused my mother's death."

Willie winced.

"Do you want to die? Do you want to destroy Laughing Eyes too?" Red Beaver's voice was strong and deliberate.

Willie scowled as he raked his fingers through his graying red hair. "What about you, Red Beaver? What will I do to you?"

"I have Jesus as my helper," said Red Beaver. "Laughing Eyes doesn't. Nor do you. I can survive."

Willie wanted Red Beaver to leave so he could get on with his business. He felt the bulk of his gun in the shoulder holster under his jacket. He'd pick up kerosene and matches on the back porch. He'd already told his men to do any damage they could at the Wagon Works. "You go on back home, Red Beaver. There's no need to talk about this."

"Laughing Eyes is at my home," said Red Beaver. "I didn't want you to worry about her."

"She can take care of herself." Willie nodded, his head too full of his plans to consider Veda's whereabouts or her safety.

Red Beaver caught Willie's hand in his and gripped it firmly. "I have never stopped loving you, my father."

The words and the action penetrated Willie's thoughts and his eyes filled with tears. "I've missed you all these years, Red Beaver."

"I wanted you with us, Father."

"I'm sorry there wasn't room in my life for you." Willie looked at the strong young man before him and pride stirred in him. "Silent Waters raised you well."

Red Beaver didn't tell him that Jig had been the biggest influence in his life.

A rap at the French doors drew their attention. In the light from the lightning they could see Matt standing there. He had learned the location of Willie's study from the gardener he'd hired to spy on Willie's family.

"He won't want to see us," said Clay, hunched against the pouring rain. "Get ready for a fight."

Willie opened the door and stared in surprise at Clay and Matt.

Clay pushed inside and Willie was too weak to hold him back.

"Red Beaver," said Clay, nodding his head.

"Hello," said Red Beaver.

Matt pulled off his hat and rain poured from it. "We came to talk sense into you, Thorne. We know about your plans to burn Clay's place and his trees. You can't do it."

Willie grabbed for his gun, but before he could draw it Clay jerked his arm behind his back.

"Let me go!" shouted Willie.

Red Beaver pulled the gun from Willie's shoulder holster and emptied the shells into his hand. "No more killing, Father."

Willie strained away from Clay as he looked pleadingly at Red Beaver. "Help me get away, Red Beaver. You're my son."

"I won't help you destroy others," said Red Beaver with a shake of his head that made the ties of his rolled scarf dance around his head.

"You're going to the sheriff with us," said Clay.

"You have nothing against me," snapped Willie.

"There are men who'll testify against you," said Matt as he clamped on his hat. "We'll start with the men you hired to sabotage Clay's Wagon Works. Then we'll hear from the men you hired to lumber the pines. And young Dag, too. They'll all tell what they know. You don't have enough money to keep them quiet."

A muscle jumped in Willie's jaw. He didn't have enough money to buy silence from even one of them, much less all of them.

Angrily Clay gripped Willie tighter. "You sent John Epson out to destroy Lark, but he destroyed himself instead. Bit by a rattlesnake. You're lucky Lark didn't die."

"You've lost, Thorne." Matt jabbed Willie in the chest with his finger. "Earlier today I checked on your finances."

Willie cringed.

Matt crossed his arms over his chest as he eyed Willie. "I learned you're flat broke."

"Shut your mouth!" snapped Willie, swearing savagely. Clay stopped him with a sharp jerk on his arm.

"Why didn't you come to me, Father?" asked Red Beaver. "I would've helped you."

Suddenly Willie lunged, taking Clay by surprise. Willie spun around and grabbed Clay by the throat, sinking his strong fingers into Clay's neck. "The Havlicks did me in! You're a dead man, Clay Havlick!"

Clay gasped for air and struggled to break Willie's death grip.

Red Beaver caught Willie's wrists and squeezed. Willie screamed and released Clay.

Gasping for air, Clay sank back against the desk with Matt hovering over him to see if he was all right.

Willie kicked and swore, but Red Beaver held him tightly. Finally the fight drained from him and Willie sank weakly against Red Beaver.

Clay and Matt hung back, silently watching Willie and Red Beaver.

"Agnes and Veda have nothing," whimpered Willie. "I don't know what they'll do."

"They'll survive," said Red Beaver softly. "I'll do what I can to help them."

"Agnes won't accept help from you," said Willie. He knew how she felt about Indians. "She can go to live with her cousin in Detroit. But Veda . . ." Helplessly Willie shook his head.

"She's a fighter," said Red Beaver. "She'll survive."

Before Clay's eyes Willie Thorne turned into a whimpering old man. "Let's get him to the sheriff," said Clay gruffly.

The rain stopped just as Clay reached home. He smiled as he thought of the warm embrace waiting for him. How had he survived without a loving wife all these years? He opened the back door and found a lamp glowing brightly on a small table, towels, and the dry clothes he'd worn earlier in the day. He chuckled. Life was good!

He blew out the lamp and opened the door into the kitchen where he saw Lark at the stove. She wore a flowered print shirtwaist and a green skirt that brushed the floor when she walked. Her taffy brown hair hung in a long tail down her slender back.

"I made something for you to eat," she said tonelessly. She wanted to burst into tears and demand to know why he'd married her, but she didn't.

Clay waited for her to run to him with open arms, but she didn't move from the stove. Slowly he walked to her, but didn't touch her. "Willie Thorne's in jail."

"Good. That should be the end of most of your troubles." Lark tried to smile, tried to act as if her heart wasn't broken, but she couldn't manage it.

Clay saw the haunted look in her eyes, but thought it was because she'd feared for his life. He pulled her close and held her tightly to him. "It's good to be back home with you." He kissed her and waited for her to explode with passion in his arms, but she didn't. He looked into her face. "Is something wrong?"

"The food's getting cold." Lark pulled away from him and carried a bowl of stew to the table. She sliced thick slices of fresh bread and set them beside the butter. She wanted to scream at him that she knew he'd married her for Matt's money, but she couldn't force out the ugly words.

"It smells good," said Clay as he sat down. "Aren't you having any?"

Lark shook her head. She couldn't swallow a bite.

As Clay ate he told Lark about the evening and about Jig's nephew at Red Beaver's. "I want to meet him. He wants to meet us too. Jig told him all about us in the letter he left for you to send."

"What about Dag?"

"We couldn't find him. Maybe he left town when he heard Epson had died before he could kill you."

Lark trembled. "Life is cruel," she said hoarsely.

"At times," said Clay. But this wasn't one of them. He smiled across the table at Lark.

In October Lark sat in the buggy beside Hannah as they drove to Red Beaver's farm. A pleasant breeze ruffled Lark's gray bonnet and skirt. Overhead a flock of geese was flying south for the winter.

"You're quiet again today, Lark," said Hannah as she folded

her hands over her handbag. "Are you sorry you agreed to go with me to see Red Beaver?"

"Not at all! I'm glad I can help the two of you have time together." Lark couldn't say that it was hard for her to be at the Havlicks and see the white pines. Just seeing the pines sent a stab of pain through her heart. Clay loved the pines more than he could ever love her. But then he didn't profess to love her. He hadn't told her once that he did, not even in their most passionate moments. Abruptly Lark pushed thoughts of Clay aside and forced her mind back on Hannah. "It's a shame the family is still against Red Beaver."

"He's Willie Thorne's son and he's half Indian." Hannah looked toward Red Beaver's house as they stopped in his yard. "But I don't care about either. I love him! And he loves me."

Tears burned Lark's eyes. How she wanted that kind of love between her and Clay!

Red Beaver ran from the big red barn, his face glowing with happiness at seeing Hannah. He liked the black skirt and white and blue plaid shirtwaist she wore. Sunlight glinted on his shoulder length black hair, setting the red highlights blazing. He wondered how Hannah's dark brown hair would look hanging down straight with a rolled scarf around her forehead. But no matter what she wore or how she looked, he loved her. "Hello, Lark. Hannah." He lifted Hannah down and held her fiercely.

Hannah clung to him. She found it harder and harder to leave him at the end of her visits. She liked the smell of his skin and the feel of his red plaid, soft flannel shirt.

"Would you like a cold drink from the well, Lark?" asked Red Beaver to be polite. He wanted to take Hannah for a walk away from his hired hand and even away from Lark.

"No, thank you." Lark stepped from the buggy with Red Beaver's help. "Have you heard from your sister?"

"Yes. She is living in Detroit with Agnes Thorne. Laughing Eyes says she can't accept being part Patawatomi, so she and

Mrs. Thorne agreed not to tell anyone. She does write to me once a month."

"Veda doesn't know what she's missing by being away from you," said Hannah, snuggling against Red Beaver.

"Maybe someday she will appreciate her heritage," said Red Beaver.

Lark excused herself, walked away from them, and stood at the pen beside the barn to watch the donkeys. Evie had wanted to come with them to see the donkeys as well as Red Beaver, but she'd had to go to school in town. Evie and Miles went to school with the plan to stay with her and Clay during the snowy days of winter. Lark wondered if she could hide her pain from them. She had been able to hide it so far from Jennet and Free.

On their return from Grand Rapids, Jennet and Free had given Lark a big party welcoming her into the family. Clay had sent them a telegram, telling them of the marriage the day after the wedding. A week later they'd returned, happy for Clay and Lark. Jennet had been full of excitement over the twins and had told Clay and Lark she expected the same from them. Lark had flushed with embarrassment, but Clay had laughed and agreed. Lark knew Matt wanted them to have a houseful of children so he could enjoy them all. Lark found it very hard to talk to or forgive Matt. He had betrayed her.

Just then Clay rode into the yard and jumped off Flame before she stopped. Clay's blue jacket flapped as he ran across the yard to Lark. His hat was gone and his dark hair was mussed a little. "Lark, I knew I'd find you here! What do you think you're doing?" he cried as he gripped her arm.

Lark pulled free, her face white. "Don't yell at me, Clay Havlick!"

"You know Ma and Pa won't allow Hannah to see Red Beaver."

"Hannah is a grown woman and can see anyone she wants."

"I won't allow my wife to go against what the family wants."

Lark's brown eyes blazed. "I am your wife, but I'm also a free person. I have rights!"

"You've been listening too much to those speakers at the Temperance League talking on women's rights. I won't have it!"

"It's but a few months until 1891, Clay Havlick. You can't keep women in the Dark Ages forever."

Clay frowned and shook his head. "I don't know what's come over you, Lark. It seems if I say 'black,' you say 'white.'"

It was true. She jumped on everything he said. The anger and hurt were eating away on the inside of her. She couldn't really blame him for not loving her. She was as plain as a post and she'd been raised in the asylum. He would've never married her if it hadn't been for Matt Baritt paying him to do it. Tears smarted Lark's eyes. Sometimes she found herself hating Matt as much as she'd learned to love him.

Clay glanced around the neatly kept farm yard. "Where are Red Beaver and Hannah?"

"I don't know."

Clay gasped. "You mean they're off by themselves somewhere?"

Lark knotted her fists at her sides and her breast rose and fell. "Yes, Clay, they are. Don't you trust them at all? Maybe they should have a hurried wedding yet this afternoon so they can really be together. You're for hurried weddings, aren't you?"

"Ours was different," snapped Clay. He couldn't understand the anger that he felt just under the surface of everything she said. He could see by the set of her jaw that he wasn't getting anywhere with her. "I'm taking Hannah home. Get the buggy and go on home."

Lark shook her head. "I came with Hannah so she could see Red Beaver. I won't leave her to be taken home like a naughty child!"

A muscle jumped in Clay's cheek. "I won't have Ma and Pa upset!"

"They should understand true love. They are in love, aren't they?"

"Of course."

"Married people should be." Lark turned away and stared across the cornfield that Red Beaver would be picking soon. Would Clay ever learn to love her? Probably not.

Helplessly Clay moved from one foot to the other. Finally he said, "You tell Hannah I don't approve of what she's doing."

Lark spun around. "What does it matter if you approve or not? Who are you to judge what Hannah does?"

Clay's anger flared, then he saw the pain behind Lark's anger and his died down. He touched Lark's soft cheek. "I wish things were the same as the day we were married. You were tender and loving, but for some reason you turned into a sandbur."

"Does it matter? You have what you want—your business and your white pines."

Before Clay could say another word Hannah and Red Beaver walked into sight. They were arm in arm and both looked as if they'd just been kissed.

At the sight of Clay, Hannah stopped and frowned, but didn't move away from Red Beaver. "Hello, Clay. I hope you didn't come to play the big brother and try to send me home."

"You should go home," said Clay.

Red Beaver stepped toward Clay. "What must I do to get your family's approval? Cut my hair like a white man's? Change my name to a white man's name?"

"Don't, Red Beaver," said Hannah, catching his hand in hers.

Clay moved uneasily. He didn't know why his family wouldn't put aside their prejudice and accept Red Beaver.

"I do have a white man's name, but you wouldn't like it." Red Beaver squared his shoulders and looked at Clay. "My white man's name is William Thorne. But your family couldn't accept that either."

Lark bit her lower lip. She couldn't stand to hear Red Beaver called William Thorne. It would bring back too many bad memories.

Hannah hugged Red Beaver and smiled into his face. "I love you if you're called Red Beaver or William Thorne. I love *you,* not your name."

Clay saw the love on their faces and envied them. He glanced at Lark just as she looked at him, a look of great longing. Their eyes locked and Clay couldn't move. What was she trying to tell him? What was it she wanted from him that he hadn't already given her?

Lark longed to have Clay pull her close and declare his love, something he'd never once done. Abruptly she turned away. A turkey gobbled nearby and a donkey brayed. Lark watched a fly buzz around a donkey's long ears. Finally she had herself in control enough to turn and face the others. "We can go now if you're ready, Hannah," she said.

"I'm as ready as I'll ever be," said Hannah, looking tearfully at Red Beaver. "I wish you'd give in and marry me even if my family doesn't agree."

"You need your family, my Hannah," said Red Beaver softly. "They're important to you. It would break your heart to be without them."

Hannah sighed. "I know. I'll go home and talk to them again." She turned to Clay. "If you'd talk to Ma and Pa, they might see things differently. You could convince them to let me marry Red Beaver."

"I can't," said Clay.

Hannah turned to Lark. "You could."

"Red Beaver could buy you, I suppose," said Lark bitterly. "He could offer his farm in exchange for you."

Clay shot a startled look at Lark. Had she somehow learned about his deal with Matt Baritt?

Red Beaver shook his head with a laugh. "I could never get her in exchange for my farm. She is priceless. No amount of money could ever buy her."

"Thank you," said Hannah.

"But if I could *give* my farm to get her, I would do it. I would trade everything if I could have her."

"I would trade everything if I could have you," said Hannah softly.

Lark's eyes filled with hot tears. Clay would never give up anything of his for her.

Clay saw Lark's tears and cocked his brow questioningly.

With a muffled goodbye Lark ran to the buggy and climbed in. She blinked away her tears as she picked up the reins in her gloved hands.

Several minutes later Lark dropped Hannah off at her house. She would not look toward the pines and think of life as it had been.

"Will you come in a while, Lark?" asked Hannah as she stepped to the ground.

"I can't today," said Lark. "I'm going to the Home to take care of some bookwork."

"Thanks for going with me today."

"I'll come again tomorrow if you want."

"Clay will get angry at you again."

Lark shrugged.

Hannah laughed softly. "Tomorrow then, about the same time? I told Red Beaver I'd be there even if I had to go alone."

"You'll never have to go alone," said Lark.

Several minutes later Lark stopped outside the Home just as a man with a baby dismounted, left his horse near Lark's buggy, and walked to her.

"You work here?" he asked gruffly.

Lark nodded. The man was poorly dressed and had a day's growth of whiskers. "May I help you?"

"I'm Chase Henry and I got to leave my baby girl here. Her

ma died and I can't find no one to tend her while I work. I'll only leave her a few months while I look for somebody to help me."

Lark's heart stopped inside her and she felt as if she'd heard the words herself when she was a tiny baby. "Are you sure you can't find someone?"

"I tried, lady." Chase Henry brushed a hand across his rough face.

"How will she survive without you?" cried Lark.

"I heard tell this is a good home. I can get to visit her regular like. I'll send money when I can." Chase thrust the bundle into Lark's arms. "Take her. Her name's Ruth after her ma."

Lark looked into the infant's tiny pink face. Fuzzy light brown hair peeked out from the small white bonnet. "How can you leave her?" whispered Lark around the hard lump in her throat.

"I can't," said Chase with a break in his voice. "But if I don't, she'll die. I got to work to keep her fed and clothed. But if I work, she won't get no care. I can't leave her, but I got to or she'll die."

A tear ran down Lark's face. "Let me take her to my home. I'll love her and care for her." Lark explained to Chase Henry who she was and how she came to be at the Home. After careful thought he agreed to give Lark legal custody of Ruth until he could come for her. They drove to Lark's home and Chase wrote out the paper giving Lark custody of Ruth. He left a small bundle of clothes and a paper with family information. Lark wrote her name and address and he tucked the paper carefully into his pocket.

"Let me hold my little Ruth one last time before I have to go." Chase lifted Ruth from Lark's arms and held her tight against his chest. He kissed her cheeks and rubbed his face against her soft hair. "I love you, Ruthie. I'm your pa. Your pa will always love you."

Tears spilled down Lark's cheeks as she watched Chase

with Ruth. Finally he pushed Ruth back into Lark's arms and ran from the house to his horse. Had it been that hard for Matt to leave her at the asylum twenty-two years ago?

Ruth squirmed and gave a tiny cry. Lark's heart jumped and she smiled. She found a baby bottle, heated some cow's milk, and filled the bottle. She changed Ruth's diaper, then wrapped her again in a soft pink blanket and sat in a chair at the kitchen table while Ruth sucked the bottle.

"Ruthie, I will take good care of you," whispered Lark. "I'll never lock you in a dark cellar with rats or make you stand in the hallway while others call you bad names." Lark's voice cracked and she swallowed hard. "I will love you and everyday I will tell you how much your pa loves you. I'll teach you about God and about nature." Lark's voice trailed off. Would she teach Ruth to walk the pines without falling prey to the dangers? She knew Clay had hired Jig's nephew Andree Bjoerling as guard, but she still had the freedom to walk the pines if she wanted. So far she hadn't set foot in the pines since the day John died.

Just then Matt knocked on the kitchen door and walked in with his hat in his hand. He wore a dark suit and a starched white shirt. He stopped short when he saw Lark with a baby.

Lark quickly wiped her eyes with the corner of the baby's blanket.

"And who is this?" asked Matt as he dropped his hat on a chair and looked down at Ruth.

Lark told him the story and Matt whistled softly. "I couldn't leave her in the Home," she explained. "I just couldn't! I didn't want her to suffer like I did."

Matt sat down slowly as if he'd suddenly turned into an old man. "I've tried to make it up to you, Lark. But I can't no matter what I do."

Lark held Ruth to her shoulder to burp as she looked at Matt. "I understand now that you couldn't keep me with you. A man alone can't tend a baby. I saw how hard it was for Chase

Henry to leave Ruth behind, but he did it so she could live. I understand now that is what you did for me."

Matt stroked Ruth's head. "Your hair was this soft. You were this tiny. I was afraid I'd break you."

Lark touched Matt's hand. "You do love me, don't you?"

"Yes. I've been telling you that for weeks now."

"I started to believe it, then I didn't think it was true. I didn't think I was important enough or good enough or pretty enough."

"Oh, Lark," whispered Matt. "You are!"

"I don't feel like it." Lark settled Ruth in the crook of her arm and held the bottle for her to suck.

"Lark, God loves you just the way you are."

"Sometimes it doesn't feel like it," said Lark barely above a whisper.

"God knew you while you were yet in the womb. You are fearfully and wonderfully made. He knows your name and he knows the number of hairs on your head."

"I guess I forgot," whispered Lark. Those were the same words Jig had said to her many times. Silently she asked God to forgive her for forgetting such an important thing. Forgetting is as bad as telling God he is a liar.

"Since you're good enough for God, why aren't you good enough for me or for anyone else who wants to love you?" asked Matt.

Lark gasped. "I never thought of it like that." Once again she held Ruth on her shoulder to burp her. "If I am that worthwhile, why did you have to . . . to pay Clay to marry me?"

Matt gasped. "How did you find out?"

"I just did."

Matt stabbed his fingers through his gray hair. "I was so afraid the two of you wouldn't get together even though you were right for each other."

"How can I love him when I know he was paid to marry me?"

Matt searched for something to say. "I wanted you to have everything you wanted. You wanted Clay Havlick."

Lark flushed to the roots of her taffy brown hair. "I don't want him if he doesn't want me."

"He seems happy to me."

"Would he ever give up the pines for me?"

Matt lifted his brows. "That's a tough one."

"No. It's not tough at all." Lark held the bottle to Ruth's mouth. "If he had to choose, he'd choose the pines."

"You could be right, Lark. If I were you I'd do something about it."

"What?"

"The Bible teaches sowing and reaping. You sow love and you'll reap love."

Lark considered that and finally nodded.

"The white pines are Clay's inheritance. But you both have an even greater inheritance from God—his promises. Sowing and reaping is only part of your inheritance. Take it and turn it into a great wealth. Sow love, then reap love."

Lark held Ruth tight against her shoulder as the truth of God's Word leaped inside her. She smiled at Matt. "Thank you. Thank you, Papa."

Tears glistened in Matt's blue eyes as he bent over Lark and kissed her cheek. "You finally gave me a name. Thank you! I've waited twenty-two years to hear it."

"I've waited twenty-two years to say it."

After Matt left, Lark fixed Ruth a bed in a wicker clothing basket that she set on the kitchen table. "You'll have a real bed soon, little Ruth." Lark kissed Ruth, then started supper for Clay.

For the first time in weeks Lark hummed as she stoked the fire to keep it hot enough to cook the beef roast in the oven. Two hours later as she dished up the potatoes, gravy, green beans, beets, and corn, Clay came home.

He heard Lark humming and he smiled with pleasure. "You

sound happy," he said as he washed at the wash stand just inside the back door.

"I am. And I have a surprise for you." Lark waited until he hung up the towel, then she slipped her arms around him and kissed him.

Clay stiffened. She hadn't kissed him voluntarily since their wedding day. He wrapped his arms around her and kissed her as if he'd never let her go.

Suddenly Ruth cried a loud lusty cry.

Clay jumped and stared at the basket on the table. "What was that?"

"A baby," said Lark with a laugh. "Come see!" She took Clay's hand and pulled him to the table. She moved the tiny pink blanket so he could get a good view of Ruth. "Her name is Ruth and she's going to live with us instead of at the Home."

Clay stared at the baby a long time. Finally he looked at Lark. "So, is that why I rated such a nice kiss when I walked in?"

"No! I wanted to kiss you."

"Why today and not yesterday or the day before?"

"Let's eat first and then I'll tell you."

Later while Clay ate his dessert of sponge cake covered with sliced peaches and a dollop of whipped cream, Lark told him about overhearing his conversation with Matt that long ago day.

"I had thought you'd married me because you loved me," she said. "It hurt to learn the truth."

"I'm sorry," said Clay as he reached for her hand. "I didn't mean to hurt you. I wanted to make sure you were safe from harm and I thought if you were with me, you would be."

"Being safe is nice, but being loved is better."

"You're right, of course."

Clay squeezed Lark's hand. Their eyes locked and they sat for a long time in the stillness of the room.

During a beautiful Indian summer day Lark drove to the white pines near the cabin. She lifted Ruth from the basket and carried her to the edge of the forest. The pine smell engulfed Lark and she closed her eyes and breathed deeply. She heard the rustle of small animals running through the pine needles and heard the caw of a crow and the screech of a blue jay.

"Ruth, these are our white pines. We've saved them for future generations to enjoy. They've been standing since only Indians lived here. When you're a grandmother, they will be standing here still."

Lark walked along the stream where she'd once walked with Jig. In her mind's eye she could see him with his old muzzleloader, wearing his deerskin pants and shirt, with moccasins on his feet. It made her feel sad to know Ruth would never know Jig and listen to his stories of the wilderness or hear him teach about God.

Just then Clay rode up on Flame and left her tied to the buggy. Quietly he strode to the pines, then stopped to watch Lark with the baby. Lark's blue serge dress with a pink baby blanket over her shoulder was a bright spot of color in the browns and grays and greens of the woods. He watched as Lark looked down at Ruth and talked to her. He could hear the murmur of her voice, but couldn't hear her words. A rush of emotion rolled over him, startling him in its intensity. This woman standing before him was his wife! She would be the mother of his children. He loved her!

"Lark!" said Clay.

She turned to him and joy shone in her face. "Clay! I thought you'd be at work."

"I was, but I missed you so much I wanted to see you. You'd said you were bringing Ruth here today, so I came here to find you." Clay ran the last few steps, then wrapped his arms around Lark and Ruth. They felt good in his arms. How blessed he was to have them! "Someday we will bring our children to see the pines," he said softly.

"Someday," said Lark, smiling.

Clay lowered his head and kissed Lark gently. He said against her lips, "I love you, Lark Baritt Havlick."

The words warmed her heart. "You love me?" she asked in wonder.

"Yes! You're my life!"

"Oh, Clay, I love you." Tears pricked her eyes. "I will always love you."

"I would give up my pines for you."

"You would?" Lark looked deep into Clay's eyes and saw he meant what he said.

Clay kissed her lips, then nuzzled her cheek. "My darling, precious wife." He kissed her again, then lifted his head to look into her eyes. "Do you want me to give up the pines?"

"No." Lark shook her head. The love she saw in his eyes left her weak and trembling. "We want them for our children."

"We'll have lots of children and they will love these trees as much as we do," said Clay. He lifted Ruth from Lark's arm and stood with them under the sweeping boughs of the huge pines.

Afterword

♦

On December 10, 1891, Lark gave birth to twins. After much consideration, she and Clay named the two boys Justin Clay Havlick and Trent Freeman Havlick. Someday the pines would belong to them.

ABOUT THE AUTHOR

Hilda Stahl is a writer, teacher, and speaker who offers writers' seminars and lectures to both schools and organizations across the country.

Born in the Nebraska Sandhills, Hilda grew up telling stories to her five sisters and three brothers, but she never thought of becoming a writer. Instead she wanted to be a rancher and raise horses and cattle.

After her first three children were born, Hilda began to write. To date she has published 92 fiction titles and 450 short stories and articles. She is a member of the Society of Children's Book Writers and is listed in *Foremost Women of the Twentieth Century, International Authors and Writers' Who's Who,* and *The World's Who's Who.* In 1989 she won the Silver Angel Award for *Sadie Rose and the Daring Escape.*

Hilda has seven children and seven grandchildren and lives in Michigan with her husband, Norman.